ACCLAIM FOR CARRIE STUART PARKS

"I love Carrie Stuart Parks's skill in writing characters with hysterical humor, unwitting courage, and page-turning mystery. I hope my readers won't abandon me completely when they learn about her!"

—Terri Blackstock, *USA TODAY* bestselling author of the If I Run series

"Over the years, Carrie has mastered forensic ard her own brand of offbeat humor. As a novelist she c with another: Puzzle writing—scattering puzzlectional universe and then dropping them into pls, revelations, and side-pocket whimsy until th, never too soon, always on the brink of disaster."

—Fran bestselling author

"Compulsively readable, *Fragments o*r-coaster ride with a lovable protagonist and a suspenseful, tw that kept me breathlessly glued to the page. Parks is at the top of her game in this new suspense novel. Highly recommended!"

—Colleen Coble, *USA TODAY* bestselling author of the Lavender Tides series

"Carrie Stuart Parks has been a favorite author of mine since I read her first book. She's one of the few authors I'll give up sleep for! Without fail, she delivers stories that reel me in and keep me turning the pages until I'm done and craving more. *Fragments of Fear* is sure to make you a Carrie Stuart Parks addict as well!" #CSPaddictandproudofit

—Lynette Eason, bestselling, award-winning author

"*Fragments of Fear* is a romantic suspense roller coaster ride not to be missed. Parks has mastered the art of drawing in the reader and gripping our imaginations in a way that keeps us turning the pages."

—Kimberly Rose Johnson, award-winning author

"From the first page of *Fragments of Fear*, I fell in love with Evelyn McTavish, AKA Tavish, an unlikely, quirky heroine who's fighting to regain control of her life after she discovers her dead fiancé isn't who she thought he was. Carrie Stuart Parks has drawn a very human character with insecurities to which we can all relate. There's nothing like a string of dead bodies and being in a killer's crosshairs to teach a woman to stand on her own two feet and discover that she's worthy of a handsome lawman's love. Tavish's sidekick, a wooly canine named Marley, will surely steal readers' hearts. I hope to see much more of this crime-solving duo in the future."

—Kelly Irvin, bestselling author of *Over the Line*

"Carrie Stuart Parks' latest, *Fragments of Fear*, is a heart-stopping read of suspense and God's mercy and grace. Tavish is the type of character who grips you tight in her clutches and takes you along on a wild ride until you turn the last page. It's a stay-up-late-to-finish novel. Highest recommendation!"

—Robin Caroll, bestselling author of the Darkwater Inn series

"Parks does it again! *Fragments of Fear* is stay-up-all-night fun, with plenty of twists and turns and a heroine you'll love to root for. Highly recommended."

—Rick Acker, bestselling author

"From the moment this book arrived in my mailbox, I inhaled it. Carrie Stuart Parks has a knack for creating interesting plots, unique characters, and a setting that lives and breathes. *Fragments of Fear* is a fascinating story from the first chapter and will keep you up turning pages to see if Tavish and Sawyer will survive the criminals out to destroy them. Just right for lovers of romantic mysteries."

—Cara Putman, author of *Delayed Justice*

"The sinister tone of this fast-paced story line creates an almost unbearable tension that will keep readers glued to the page. Acclaimed author Parks draws on her career as a forensic artist to imbue her stories with a true-to-life accuracy that will fascinate readers of CSI-type fiction."

—*Library Journal* for *Formula of Deception*

"Parks has created an intriguing female sleuth with depth, courage, and grit. The well-developed characters are complemented by a unique setting."

—*Publishers Weekly*, starred review for *Portrait of Vengeance*

"Rich characters, a forensic artist's eye for detail, and plot twists—Carrie Stuart Parks hits all the right notes!"

—Mary Burton, *New York Times* bestselling author

FRAGMENTS OF FEAR

FRAGMENTS
OF FEAR

CARRIE STUART PARKS

THOMAS NELSON
Since 1798

Fragments of Fear

Copyright © 2019 by Carrie Stuart Parks

Published in Nashville, Tennessee, by Thomas Nelson. Thomas Nelson is a registered trademark of HarperCollins Christian Publishing, Inc.

Thomas Nelson titles may be purchased in bulk for educational, business, fund-raising, or sales promotional use. For information, please email SpecialMarkets@ThomasNelson.com.

Scripture quotations are taken from the King James Version and the *Holy Bible*, New Living Translation, copyright © 1996, 2004, 2015 by Tyndale House Foundation. Used by permission of Tyndale House Publishers, Inc., Carol Stream, Illinois 60188. All rights reserved.

Publisher's Note: This novel is a work of fiction. Names, characters, places, and incidents are either products of the author's imagination or used fictitiously. All characters are fictional, and any similarity to people living or dead is purely coincidental.

Library of Congress Cataloging-in-Publication Data

Names: Parks, Carrie Stuart, author.
Title: Fragments of fear / Carrie Stuart Parks.
Description: Nashville, Tennessee : Thomas Nelson, [2019]
Identifiers: LCCN 2018059609| ISBN 9780785226130 (softcover) | ISBN 9780785226161 (epub)
Subjects: | GSAFD: Christian fiction. | Suspense fiction.
Classification: LCC PS3616.A75535 F73 2019 | DDC 813/.6--dc23 LC record available at https://lccn.loc.gov/2018059609

Printed in the United States of America

19 20 21 22 23 LSC 6 5 4 3 2 1

To two women who know how to be deep, dear, lifelong friends: Kerry Kern Woods and Lorrie Jenicek.

Trust in the LORD with all your heart;
do not depend on your own understanding.

PROVERBS 3:5

CHAPTER I

Evelyn Yvonne McTavish—Tavish to her friends—clenched the red long-stemmed rose and stared at the glossy casket. The brief graveside service had ended with the Unitarian Universalist pastor reading from Kahlil Gibran's *The Prophet*. The pastor's last words echoed in Tavish's mind. "And when the earth shall claim your limbs, then shall you truly dance."

"What does that even mean?" Tavish whispered. The unseasonably warm Albuquerque sun beat down on her black wide-brimmed hat, giving her a pounding headache. Her dress was itchy black wool made worse by her sweat.

The few mourners drifted away to their cars lined up on the pavement behind her, each first tossing a rose from a spray onto the lowered coffin.

Her mother had put in an appearance at the funeral home but left before the graveside service. Mother's stolen art had been released by the police and was being returned today. The stolen paintings were clearly more important than her daughter's grief.

Tavish felt . . . hot. Hollow. Empty. Squeezed dry.

The funeral director, standing in the shade of a nearby tree, shifted and took a quick look at his watch.

Of course. She was delaying them from finishing their work. Fake grass covered the pile of raw, tawny-colored earth—earth that would soon cover her fiancé.

She tried to picture his face. Before. The funeral home said his remains were unviewable, but they didn't realize she'd been the one to find his body. That was the image burned into her brain. He'd told her where to meet him, a parking lot near the Rio Grande River. He was in his car—a rental, it turned out. The shotgun was beside him on the seat.

She snapped the rose's stem in half.

He would have left a note. If it was suicide, he would have left her a note. If he loved her like he'd promised, he would have found a way to tell her why.

The late-afternoon sunlight caught the facets of her engagement ring's diamond, sending a shimmering light pattern onto the coffin's dark wood. He'd proposed just a week ago. They planned to have a celebration dinner this very night. He would have formally met her mother—and just as formally asked her mother for her hand in marriage.

She tore her gaze from the yawning grave and glanced at her grandmother's headstone a short distance away. *Grandma, I wish you were here.*

She felt rather than heard someone come up behind her. She stiffened, expecting more bland condolences or maybe even a nudge toward her car.

"I can't believe it's true," a woman's voice murmured. "I came as fast as I could."

Tavish nodded. She couldn't believe it either. She'd walked around for the past week like a cyborg—when she could get out of bed. She hadn't bothered to contact her accounting company and let them know why she was absent. They called and she'd just let the answering machine pick up. They'd finally stopped calling. She didn't care to know why. What difference did that make? Her life was over. And she hated that company anyway. Though Tavish's heart had been in her art ever since her grandmother died, her mother insisted she work "a real job" and had given her the firm. Now her mother could take it back.

"Why? Why?" the woman asked.

Why indeed? Tavish wished the mourner would leave. She needed these last few moments alone with Andrew. Her love. Her loss. She'd mentally planned their wedding, honeymoon, first home. The baby they would make. Family Thanksgivings and Christmases together. Now only emptiness stretched before her.

"I had so much to say to him," the other woman whispered. "I . . . I . . ." She quietly sobbed.

Tavish pulled a clean handkerchief from her pocket and held it out. The woman took it.

He'd brought meaning into her life, which had lost direction since Grandma's death. Before he came along, she'd been a fat, ugly lump of clay. He'd thought her intelligent, beautiful, and a brilliant artist.

The weeping continued, followed by coughing and throat clearing. "This is so wrong."

Wrong? Nothing's been right for a long time.

"He never would have left me." The woman's voice steadied. "Never. Not now. We were to have been married—"

Her words shot through Tavish's thoughts. "Excuse me?" She turned.

The strikingly beautiful young woman stared at Tavish through brown, glittering eyes. A black shift stretched across her pregnant belly.

Tavish tore her gaze from the woman's midsection and took a half step backward. "Oh. It's . . . I'm . . . This is extremely awkward, but I think you're at the wrong funeral. This is . . . was Andrew James."

"Yes. Andrew James. He's dead, and it's all my fault." She stared at the lowered coffin, then shifted her gaze to Tavish. Her eyes narrowed. "Or maybe it's your fault."

Glancing around for the funeral director, Tavish hoped to catch his attention and have him escort this obviously deranged woman away. She spotted the man walking toward the hearse.

"I made him choose," the woman said. She was now glaring at Tavish. "But it *is* your fault."

Tavish wanted to put her hands over her ears. "Please go away—"

"I never would have done that . . . made him choose between us"—the woman shook her head—"if I'd known he'd kill himself."

Tavish's stomach churned. "He didn't kill himself! He was murdered, and it was set up to look like suicide. I . . . found him."

The woman's gaze sharpened. "Do the police believe it was murder?"

"Not yet, but—"

The woman opened a faux leather tote bag, grabbed a photograph, and thrust it at Tavish. Andrew grinned out at her, his arm around the woman. In the background, Tavish recognized the distinctive shape of the Spirit Lodge and Spa on the edge of town. She sucked in air through numb lips. "That d-doesn't prove anything."

The woman snatched the photograph back. "You don't have to believe me. Think about all the times Andrew was gone—"

"He was an investment counselor. He had to travel—"

"Yeah. Right. Investment counselors do most of their work on the phone." The woman jammed the photograph back into her purse. "Did you ever go with him on a business trip? Did you ever meet a single client?"

"No—"

"And where are his clients? His friends? Family? Why didn't anyone come to his funeral?"

"Um . . ."

"Did you ever even go to his home?"

"He . . . he said he had a roommate."

"Yeah. Me."

Tavish opened her mouth but no words came out. She felt like someone had just sucker-punched her in the stomach.

The woman's lips tightened. "Did you think a man as handsome as he was would ever fall for *you*?" She held up the handkerchief Tavish had given her. "Who has embroidered initials on their handkerchiefs? Who even carries handkerchiefs anymore? You're a plain, dumpy rich girl. That's all he wanted. Your money."

"He . . . he had money . . ."

"Is that what he told you? Ha! That ring on your finger is nothing more than cubic zirconia."

Tavish's head buzzed.

"Want more proof that he was engaged to me? That I knew him? Andrew loved IPA beer, wore his father's dog tags, and hated his work. Shall I describe his—"

"No!"

"I knew about you, but you didn't know about me. I told him he had to break up with you or I'd make sure this little bundle"— she rubbed her bulging stomach—"would be your next news flash. Andrew took the easy way out." She turned to leave, then turned back. "None of this had to happen if you and all your money hadn't come along. Now neither of us wins." She pivoted and stalked away.

Tavish turned toward the open grave, staring at it blindly. She could barely breathe.

The funeral director coughed softly.

She blinked, dropped the rose's broken stem, then crumpled the petals and let them drift through her fingers. Carefully she removed the engagement ring, lifted a corner of the fake grass, and shoved the ring into the dirt. She straightened, turned, and walked to her car, never looking back.

CHAPTER 2

ALBUQUERQUE, NEW MEXICO
THREE WEEKS LATER

Is this, ah, Evelyn McTavish, thirty-five, zero three, seventeen seventy-nine?" The man's voice was unpleasantly high-pitched.

Tavish checked the caller ID again. Happy Tails Shelter. "Yes, this is Evelyn McTavish, but I don't know what those numbers mean, and I don't donate to charity over the phone."

"That's how the registration came back. Your name, them numbers, this phone number, and the address of 965 Westwood Estates."

Tavish glanced at her watch. "What registration?"

The man gave an exasperated sigh. "Your dog registration. From the microchip."

"I don't own a dog. Please don't call me again." She disconnected the call.

The phone rang again. Happy Tails Shelter. "Look," she began.

"No, you look, lady, and I'll give it to ya straight. Either pay up and get the dog, or we're gonna kill it." The man's voice rose even higher. "We don't kid around. What's it gonna be?"

She made an effort to loosen her white-knuckled grip on her cell. "And I'm telling you for the second time, I don't have a dog! I've never had a dog. I've never even owned a goldfish—"

"Alls I know is the microchip on this mutt is registered to you. The shelter is overcrowded with dumped dogs, and this one bites, so we can't place her in another home. Come and get her or she's dead." *Click.*

The cell phone dropped from Tavish's shaking hand and onto her lap. Her stomach tightened and knotted and the room spun. She glanced at her fingernails, several of which were wrapped in Band-Aids. Finding one that was exposed, she bit down on the remains of the ragged nail. The sting made her eyes water, but slowly the anxiety attack passed.

"I'm okay," she whispered. "This will pass. Breathe in calm, breathe out fear. Om Mani Padme Hum." She thought the chant sounded like a sick cow, but this week's therapist wanted her to try it. The counselor before that gave her a journal to write in. And the string of psychiatrists her mother had set her up with after Grandma's death all gave her drugs.

Once her heartbeat returned to normal, she stood. "It's not my dog. Why should I care? I've never owned a dog. Dogs are great for books and movies, like *Turner and Hooch* or *Lassie*." What if it was just a puppy? A tiny fur ball that just needed a home? A baby Old Yeller? Or Hachikō waiting by the train station? A lump closed up her throat and her eyes blurred. They wouldn't kill a poor, defenseless puppy.

They will if I don't save it.

She snatched the phone, then dialed her mother's house. One of her mother's gardeners or staff workers could retrieve the dog and find a place to keep it until she could locate the owner.

The housekeeper picked up. "Hi." Tavish couldn't remember this one's name. She hadn't set foot inside her mother's house since her grandmother's death more than a year ago, even though the front door was just a hundred yards away. "This is Tavish . . . um, Evelyn . . . Helen's daughter. Is Maria there?"

"Maria?"

"Maria . . . um . . ." What was her last name? It started with an *M.* "The lady who cleans my house. She works for my mother."

"No."

"Okay then. I need you to send someone to the Happy Tails Shelter and retrieve a dog—"

"*Lo siento, pero no tengo coche, señorita.* No car."

"The gardener . . . *el gardener* . . . ?"

"No. *Nadie está aquí todavía.*"

"Okay. Um, *gracias.*" Tavish disconnected, grabbed a handful of tissues and her purse and keys, then raced to her car. She punched the name of the shelter into her cell, then *directions.* That horrible man hadn't said how long she had to fetch the poor dog. "You'd better not hurt that little puppy or . . . or I'll . . ." What? Draw his picture? Stab him with a pencil? Throw crumpled-up newsprint at his head? Not a lot of vengeful acts available to her in her new career as a fine artist. Nor in her old career as an accountant. Hard to physically injure someone with numbers.

She could always just sit on him. The revenge of a fat lady.

She shot out of the driveway, almost sideswiping a passing pickup. The driver hit his horn.

"I'm so sorry!" *Should I stop and apologize?*

The pickup turned the corner and drove off.

She bit a piece of cuticle off her thumb. Her horoscope said she'd have a surprise today. Who would have believed the surprise would be an unwanted puppy?

At the red light, she tugged on the crystal pendant around her neck. *Come on. Come on!* She'd get the canine thing straightened out. Maybe pay them to keep it for a few more days. Just long enough to get through her gallery opening. She'd place an ad in the newspaper. Find the owner . . . somehow. She glanced at her watch. The Albuquerque pet shelter was in the opposite direction from the gallery.

≥≤

Cars and trucks parked unevenly in the packed dirt of the parking lot of Happy Tails Shelter. Tavish stepped into the dry, early-May sunshine and winced at the cacophony of wails and barking coming from the low pink-stuccoed building.

Inside the crowded lobby, a family of six hugged a wildly joyful yellow lab. The dog brushed against her, leaving fur on her tailored jeans. She brushed it off and avoided getting near two outdoorsy couples patting a shaggy mutt. In the corner, an elderly man held a small terrier. Three staff members wearing khaki shirts with *Happy Tails* and a dog's rear end—apparently the logo—embroidered on the pocket held clipboards and were gesturing to the attached paper. Everyone was shouting over the din of barking.

A short man wearing the Happy Tails shirt made his way to her side. He sported a five-o'clock shadow, sunken cheeks, large nose, and receding chin. "Can I help you find a new fur baby?"

Fur baby? She recognized the voice on the phone. "You just called me. The dog with the microchip—"

"Oh yeah." His smile faded and eyes narrowed. "So you came to your senses and don't want your dog killed." He turned and strolled toward the kennel area, not waiting to see if she followed.

Tavish caught up with him. "I told you on the phone. It's not my dog. I mean, dogs are fine in theory, and they make fine literature and films, but—"

He opened a door. The overwhelming sound of frantic barking and more people talking slammed into her ears. "I don't have a dog." She raised her voice over the din. "I don't know why my name and address were connected to it." The odor of disinfectant cleaners and urine burned her nose. "It must be a mistake."

Chain-link dog runs lined either side of a hall, with several dogs of all sizes and breeds in each run. She made sure she walked down the middle. At the end of the hall, a door with a window marked No Admittance led to additional runs. He paused and pulled out a set of keys at the end of a chain. After unlocking the door, he passed through and stopped.

In the first run, a small black dog with a coat that looked like dreadlocks lay with its head between its paws, eyes watchful.

"Marley?" Tavish approached the kennel. "Marley?"

The Puli stood and stared at Tavish.

Tavish turned to the man. "I recognize the dog. But it's not mine. As I told you, I don't own a dog."

Marley launched herself at the gate, leaping against it, barking wildly. The leaps turned to spins, then to a race from one end of the run to the other, long cords flying. She looked like an animated black string mop.

The man snorted. "I don't care what you say. This is your dog, lady. Look at how she's acting."

The happy canine, now spinning in one place, continued to bark.

Tavish stepped back and brushed imaginary fur off her pressed jeans. "This is John Coyote's dog."

"Yeah, yeah, whatever. Can you show evidence of vaccination, including rabies?"

"How can I show you . . . ? Never mind." After pulling out her phone, she thumbed through the numbers until she came to John's. "I'll call Marley's owner."

"You do that."

The phone rang. And rang. And rang. "He's not home." Tavish disconnected. "How long can you keep her—"

"You don't get it, do you, lady? Either you walk out of here with your dog, or she's toast." He leaned against the dog run.

Marley leaped away and lifted her lips, exposing sharp canines. The happy yips deepened to a bark worthy of a Doberman.

He straightened and jerked his thumb at the canine. "See what I mean? She's vicious."

Maybe she just has good sense. "Not usually."

The man's expression didn't change. "Look, ya either own a dog and take care of 'em, or ya put 'em up for adoption, or ya put 'em to sleep." He leaned forward, his eyes narrowing to slits. "Ya don't turn 'em loose where they'll get hit by a car, or shot, or killed by other dogs, or chewed up by coyotes, or starve to death. Got it?"

She pulled at a hangnail on her left finger. "Mister . . . um . . . ?"

"Brown."

"Look, Mr. Brown, I know this dog because I'm an artist and was commissioned to draw her and her owner. Well, actually paint them, but—"

Brown headed toward the lobby. "I got work to do. Either purchase her shots and get her license, or leave and we'll take care of her."

"Marley's owner is John Coyote, a retired archaeologist." She raced to keep up with him. Marley's yelps grew frantic behind them. "He's probably consulting on an archaeological dig somewhere, and Marley got loose. You just need to keep her—"

Brown stopped so abruptly that Tavish crashed into him. "Seventy-eight bucks. And you take her with you."

She stepped back and sucked in air to keep a panic attack at bay. "As I can't convince you of the truth, bring me whatever paperwork I need to sign and let me take Marley out of here."

Brown gave a snarky grin. "I knew you'd finally admit to owning the mutt. And you might groom her occasionally."

"She's not a mutt. She's small for her breed, but she's a purebred Puli. They're an ancient Hungarian sheepdog. That's a corded coat. It's not matted."

Brown turned and headed to the lobby again. "Yeah, yeah."

The front office was still chaotic with prospective owners and pets. Brown grabbed a clipboard and shoved it into her hands. "Fill this out and sign at the bottom. Eighty-nine dollars."

"You said seventy-eight."

"You heard wrong."

He's lying. Stand your ground. Confront him. She looked down, resisted the urge to rip off a Band-Aid and bite a nail, and took the pen and clipboard. She didn't have a choice. There was no way she'd convince Mr. Brown that Marley wasn't her dog, and if she didn't pay up, Marley would die. She filled out her own name and address, then pulled out a black American Express credit card.

Brown shook his head. "Cash. Or check."

She returned the card and wrote a check for eighty-nine dollars. "The dog, please." She had to wait another twelve minutes before Marley appeared.

"Promise me you'll never let this dog end up like this again," Mr. Brown said.

"I promise Marley will never see you or this dog prison again. And I keep my promises."

Marley apparently forgot Tavish's earlier abandonment and greeted her with excited, high-pitched barks. Tavish gingerly took the end of the cheap blue nylon slip lead and led her to the car. She hadn't brought a towel or blanket for the canine to lie on. She opened the back door. Marley readily jumped in.

"Watch out for the artwork. They're in that bag on the floor—"

Marley leaped to the front seat, leaving dusty footprints all over the immaculate interior. "You need to get into the back seat."

The dog ignored her.

"Marley, I mean it."

A woman passing the car stared at Tavish and frowned.

Tavish glanced around. Several people were watching her. She slipped into the driver's seat and started the engine to engage the air-conditioning. "You were making a scene."

The dog wagged her tail.

Tavish checked her watch, then dialed the gallery.

The clerk answered. "Hogarth and Montgomery Art Gallery, Lambert speaking."

"Hi, Lambert, it's Tavish. I'm running late—"

"I should say you are." He sniffed. "Mrs. Hogarth will be *most* displeased. She wanted to hang those last two works an hour ago."

Marley stuck her nose in Tavish's hair, pawed at her hand, then licked her face just as Tavish opened her mouth. "Ack, akkk, ak!" She grabbed a tissue and scrubbed her tongue.

Lambert sniffed again. "Well, *you* may not care about your work, but we have a reputation—"

"She just stuck her tongue in my mouth." Okay, that didn't sound right. "I mean—"

"Miss McTavish, I don't care about your personal life. I will tell Mrs. Hogarth you are delayed."

One day I'm going to be famous for my art and I'll take great delight in snubbing you. To your face. Marley began to settle and curled up on the seat, nose jammed against the edge. "You're a huge encumbrance in my life."

The dog huffed once and started snoring.

"I saved your life, you know."

Marley's feet twitched as if she were chasing a cat.

"Lassie would have been grateful. Cujo would have been grateful." She adjusted the air-conditioning vent to blow on the dog. "I suppose you didn't get much sleep in the doggie slammer."

Tavish reached behind her and made sure the framed drawings were still upright on the floor. She tugged on her crystal. "So, Marley, here's my dilemma."

You're talking to a dog.

She cleared her throat. "I'm sure John's talked to you a lot, right?"

Marley opened one eye.

"I thought so. I have to deliver those two framed works, but Mrs. Hogarth would have a meltdown if I brought a dog into her gallery."

Marley closed her eyes, shifted, and snuggled deeper in the seat.

"Right. I'll try John again." She dialed. The phone rang ten times before she hung up and started the car. "I agree. His answering machine should have picked up." She rubbed the slight tingling between her shoulder blades. "John must be beside himself looking for you . . . or . . . maybe he's out of town and a dog sitter accidentally let you loose."

But he'd never mentioned what he did with his dog when he traveled.

She gave another tug on her crystal. "Well, my dreadlocked friend, since I'm already late, I might as well be even later and drop you off first. Even though, of course, John's home is way out of town."

She stared at the sleeping dog for a moment. "You didn't by any chance pick up fleas, did you?"

Marley sat up, barked once, then stared at her.

"Okay, no offense meant." She put the car into gear and pulled out into the street. "So here's the deal. My life is . . . complicated right now. I don't have time to locate your owner, but you have a doggie door in the backyard and I'll make sure you have water. If I don't see John today, I can return and check on you tomorrow."

She turned toward Interstate 40 and the Tijeras Canyon, heading east. "It's not that I don't like you or anything. It's just . . . I've never owned a dog. Don't get me wrong. I love books and movies about canines. It's just . . . well, at your home, you'll have dog stuff . . . like food, and toys, and . . . stuff. And besides, I'm not really very good company." She glanced at the Band-Aids on her fingers.

Marley rolled onto her back.

"Really, Marley, that's a most immodest angle. Anyway, John can settle up the eighty-nine-dollar bail. And I can ask him why he listed my name and address on the microchip embedded in you, especially since I hardly know the man. I mean, he was just a client, a patron."

Marley snorted in her sleep.

"Right. I forgot you were present when I came over."

Although she'd only been to John's home once, it was recently, and she remembered the way. John's home was tucked into the mountains, surrounded by ponderosa pines and sagebrush. After turning off the interstate, she tracked down a narrow road until she reached the end of his drive, passing few houses and even fewer signs of life. It was difficult to see his house through the planted trees and shrubs, and the wrought-iron gate ensured his privacy. She tugged her cell out of her jeans to try his number one last time, but she didn't have cell service.

Rolling down the window, she mentally reviewed his passcode. One-zero-six-three-four-zero-three-three-two. She was good at remembering numbers. She hoped he hadn't changed the code. The fresh scent of sage drifted through the open window. Marley sat up, looked around, and barked.

The gate was already open. The narrow paved driveway curved around to a separate garage a fair distance from the house, with a path leading to the Pueblo Revival–style home. She drove slightly past the house, then turned around and parked under a shade tree. Exiting the car, she slipped her cell into a rear pocket. Taking Marley's lead, she unloaded the dog, then paced to the garage and glanced through the window. John's late-model Toyota was parked in its usual spot.

High overhead, a pair of large black birds gave a grunting cry as they circled. Wind rustled through the pines and sent the dry grasses hissing. The *clack-clack-clack* of her heels on the pavers sounded abnormally loud as she approached the entrance. Marley pranced ahead, pulling at the leash.

The front door stood open several inches.

"John? Mr. Coyote? It's me, Tavish."

The wind answered with a chindi, a dust devil on the hillside.

"Mr. Coyote?" She nudged the door open.

John Coyote lay sprawled just inside the door on the hand-painted tile floor. Round burn marks the diameter of a cigarette dotted his face, and red bruises circled his wrists. His shirt was stained maroon, a knife extended from his chest, and a puddle of coppery-smelling blood formed a moat around his body.

His eyes stared upward at eternity.

CHAPTER 3

avish sped backward away from the body, stumbled on the uneven pavers, and landed hard on her backside. The cell in her pocket flew out, landing with a *crunch* on the stone.

"No, no, no, no!" She stayed on the ground and put her hand over her mouth to stop the mindless chant.

Marley approached her motionless owner, sniffed, and let out a forlorn howl.

"Oh, Marley . . ." Tavish stood and reached for the dog, then froze. John had been tortured and murdered. She spun, checking out the landscape.

Nothing moved. Even the wind had died down.

How long had he been lying there? She reluctantly reentered the house and approached the body, her legs trembling, and looked again at his face. She gagged. Flies had just discovered him. He hadn't been dead long. Outside, her phone was in pieces. Where was John's phone?

She couldn't leave Marley to mourn for her master while she

dialed the police. After picking up the twenty-five-pound dog, she carefully stepped around the body and found John's landline in the living room to her left. She placed the dog on the floor. "Sit. Now stay." Marley charged from the room, returning to her master.

In the living room, the sofa's cushions were ripped and strewn across the floor. A shattered lamp was underneath the broken coffee table. A chair lay on its side in the center of the room with a rope still attached. Bookshelves that had held a few ancient Native American artifacts were bare, the contents now a pile of rubble on the floor. Photos of various archaeological dig sites were shattered and tossed aside. An empty wall safe stood open in the corner of the room.

Tavish bit down on a fingernail, then lifted the handset. No dial tone. She pulled on the phone cord. Cut.

Dizziness overcame her brain. Air was at a premium. Her legs gave way and she dropped to the floor. Blackness lapped around her consciousness. "I'm okay, I'm okay," she gasped. "This will pass. Breathe in calm, breathe out fear." She ripped off a Band-Aid and bit the remains of a nail until the pain pushed back the darkness.

She crawled upright and raced to the front door on wobbly legs, snatching up Marley's leash as she ran past. Leaving the front door open, she charged to the car, jumped inside, locked all the doors, then started the engine. She shot down the drive, gravel flying. *OhLordohLord.*

She floored the gas, fishtailing onto the road. Her hands shook so hard she could barely grip the steering wheel. Though the air conditioner was on high, drops of sweat slithered down her neck. Marley frantically jumped back and forth between the front and back seats, barking.

Wait! There's a patrol car!

A white squad car shot past her on the narrow two-lane road, going the opposite direction. He flew away so quickly she didn't have time to wave him down. She caught a glimpse of a strong jaw and heavy shoulders.

Reaching over, she steadied the frantic dog. "It's going to be okay. We'll turn around and catch up with him. This road dead-ends less than a mile from John's house, so he can't be going far."

Marley stopped barking but trembled under her hand.

Her eyes burned. "I'm sorry about John. You know, it's entirely possible someone else found the body and reported it. That would explain the patrol car. If that's the case, we can simply leave and not get involved." The road widened and she pulled over. Marley gave a husky bark.

"What if I'm wrong? No, I can't leave John's murdered body where it is." She sighed and turned the car around. Driving more slowly, she checked each house in case the policeman had pulled into one. When she reached John's driveway, she could see the patrol car parked between the landscaped trees. Something about the squad car . . . She squinted, but the angle didn't give her a clear image.

"Everything's fine." She glanced uneasily in the rearview mirror. "See? Someone *did* find John and report his murder. We'll get out of here before that cop notices." Checking behind her for traffic, she put the car into reverse, then glanced at the house.

The officer had opened the car's trunk. He disappeared, then reappeared hauling John's body over one shoulder. He shoved the body inside the trunk, then slammed it shut.

Marley barked.

The officer spun toward the gate and stared at Tavish.

She gasped. Her hand flew to her mouth.

He pulled out his service pistol and aimed it at her.

She stomped the gas pedal, spun the wheel, and shot out of the drive. Something pinged her car.

Her heartbeat hammered in her ears. Her shaking hands could barely cling to the steering wheel. *He's shooting at me! Oh my Lord, once he turns around, he'll catch up with me. I can't pass out.*

Marley continued to bark as Tavish floored the gas and looked for another road. All she spotted were the occasional dirt driveways.

Glancing in her rearview mirror, she checked for any sign of the cruiser. She pinched herself hard to keep the panic attack at bay.

Up ahead was a paved driveway. *Good. No telltale dust.* She slowed to make the turn. At the end of the lane was an attractive adobe rancher. The drive skirted past the house to the right. She followed it around to an open garage. A cobalt-blue pickup was parked on one side. She pulled in next to the truck, grabbed Marley, and shoved her to the floor, then ducked down.

The dog wiggled under her grasp.

"Shh, please, Marley, I'm sorry, but that man can't find us," she whispered. The dog seemed to understand and stilled.

Above her ragged breathing came the unmistakable sound of the garage door closing.

She remained motionless, pressing down on the small dog, and tried to control her chattering teeth. *I'm okay, this will pass, breathe in calm, breathe out fear. I'mokay,thiswillpass,breatheincalm, breatheoutfear.*

Shortly brakes squealed, a car door opened, and male voices carried through an open window. "No, Officer, I haven't seen a white car, but I've been watering the plants over there and didn't notice anyone. Should I be concerned?"

"The woman's wanted for breaking and entering."

Tavish shivered. Marley licked her hand.

"I'll keep an eye open. Do you have a card or some way I can call you?"

"No. I . . . uh, I'll swing back later. Thanks." A car door slammed and an engine revved, then silence followed. Footsteps. A door squealed open nearby. More footsteps.

"You can sit up now."

She jumped, then righted herself.

A thin man about her age stood next to her car. He was wearing jeans, a torn Wisconsin Badgers T-shirt, gardening gloves, and a green baseball hat. He smiled, exposing deep dimples. Eyes as cobalt blue as his truck crinkled at the corners. "You don't look like a burglar."

"I'm not—"

"Well then, why was that creepy-looking cop after you?"

"He has a body in the trunk of his car. John Coyote. I saw him put it there."

The man rocked back on his heels and stared at her for a moment. "That's not the answer I expected. Maybe you should come inside and tell me about it over a glass of iced tea. I'm Kevin, by the way."

"Tavish," she answered automatically. "I don't know—"

"I remind you, Tavish, that *you* pulled into *my* garage. I hid you from the police. I'm technically your accomplice. The least you can do is tell me more about this body." He glanced at Marley. "And your Rastafarian friend is welcome too." He nodded toward the door to the house and stood aside as she got out with Marley on the end of the leash. Before leaving the garage, she stepped to the rear of her Audi. Her left rear bumper sported a neat bullet hole. She licked her suddenly dry lips. *Just a few inches higher . . . I'm okay. I'm okay.*

Inside the house, the decor was vintage 1980s, with pastel blue-and-peach chintz fabrics, tiled countertop, and harvest-gold appliances. "Your mom's house?" Tavish asked.

Kevin grinned at her expression. "Yeah. She passed away six months ago. I got here last week to tidy up and put it on the market."

"I'm sorry for your loss."

He shrugged. "It was sudden. She'd remarried and we hadn't been close for the past couple of years. Have a seat."

She placed Marley by her feet and sat at a light-colored, faux-wood table in a small dining area off the kitchen. A sliding glass door opened to the desert-landscaped backyard. Her gaze kept drifting to the window overlooking the driveway. She folded her hands to keep them from shaking and to hide her disastrous fingernails.

Kevin poured two glasses of iced tea and placed them on the table, then added a spoon and several packets of sugar. She reached for the glass. His gaze lingered on the Band-Aids, but he didn't ask any questions. He placed a bowl of water next to Marley before sitting down. "I'm all ears."

While Marley scooted the water dish across the room with her nose, Tavish told him about the dog's microchip registered to her name, finding John's body, and her escape. "He was shooting at me. Thank you, by the way, for not turning me in. Why didn't you? You couldn't have seen the bullet hole."

"The look of terror on your face as you drove in. And that so-called 'cop'"—Kevin made quotes in the air—"was driving a squad car without any law-enforcement marking—just the word *sheriff* on the side panel."

"That was it! I knew there was something wrong with the car, but didn't hang around long enough to figure out what."

"Do you think he's the one who killed your friend?"

Beads of moisture slid down her glass and puddled on the table. She resisted the urge to bite her nails while she thought. "I don't know. I think he was concealing the murder."

"And the reason your name was registered to your friend's dog?"

"I don't know that either." Her voice rose and she took a sip of tea.

He reached behind him, grabbed some paper towels, and placed them under the glasses. "It sounds like your John Coyote was tied up and tortured to get the combination to that safe. I bet he somehow got loose and made a run for it. The thief panicked and . . ."

Tavish heard a buzzing in her ears and the room dimmed.

"Are you okay? You just turned sheet white."

She put her head down for a moment. "Just woozy. Give me a minute."

"I'm sorry. One thing for sure, you'll need to call the police. A murder, robbery, someone hiding the body and impersonating a law-enforcement officer . . ."

"The police." She bit her lip. "Maybe you could call?"

"*You're* the one who found the body."

She stood and stepped toward the phone sitting on the counter. He put out his arm to stop her. Marley left her dish and dove between them. "You'll have to find a place where you get cell service. Mom's landline was disconnected."

She slumped back to her seat. "Which makes this a bigger problem—my cell's broken. I'll have to drive somewhere to make that call, and he's out there looking for a white sedan."

"Did he see *you*?"

"I was inside the car, so I'm pretty sure he couldn't see my face. Not clearly at any rate."

"You could wait him out. I mean, stay here until dark. He's got to get rid of that body pretty soon. In this heat . . ."

She clutched the iced-tea glass and tried not to vomit.

"I'm sorry." Kevin leaned forward. "This John fellow was a friend of yours?"

"He commissioned me for a painting. He is . . . was a very nice man. And I can't stay here. I have artwork to deliver and a gallery opening at four that's pivotal to my art career. I've been working on this for almost year. Oh, what a mess!"

"I could drive you straight to the police."

"No."

"Cab? Uber?"

"No again. I don't have the time to get involved in a murder investigation." She glanced at her watch. "And the last time I went to the police about what I thought was a murder . . . they said it was suicide and . . . well . . . I made quite a pest of myself and . . ." Her voice caught and she cleared her throat. "I'll call, but I'll do it anonymously."

"The police can trace calls. Caller ID and all that. You could send an email. Secret-witness kind of stuff. They have free internet access at the library. I'll give you Mom's library card."

"That might work. But there's still the problem of getting out of here." Silence stretched between them. The old refrigerator kicked on, and Marley barked at the noise.

"Marley, shush."

The dog quieted but turned her back on both of them.

"I have an idea." Kevin sat up straighter. "The pickup in the garage was Mom's. Take it, go to the library, and email the police about the murder. Then take care of your art and go to your opening. When the coast is clear, drive back here and switch vehicles."

"That's generous of you—"

"Hardly generous. I'm loaning you a beater 1978 Chevy pickup and you're leaving your late-model Audi. But just so you won't think I'm going to steal your car, take the keys when you go."

"That's very thoughtful, but I'll leave the keys in case you have to move it. How can I ever thank you?"

He looked away. "Maybe you would . . . um . . . go out with me to dinner or something?"

She stared at him for a moment. There was no way he would be asking her out for her money. How could he know about it? That left the way she looked, and she hated it when people took pity on her. She shook her head. "I'm sorry. My life is . . . complicated right now."

"That's okay." He stood. "Take the truck and bring it back when you can."

"I wonder if I can ask you for another favor? Do you think you could keep Marley here for a while? I'll pay you, of course—"

"Sorry. I'm camping out here enough as it is. I don't have time to take care of a dog. And I'm flying out at the end of the week."

"I just thought I'd ask." She stood.

He stared at her hair. "Even though you don't think he saw you, maybe you should change your appearance . . ."

She grimaced. "I didn't think about that."

"Here." He handed her his baseball cap, then pulled out a woman's purse from a cupboard. After rummaging in the black leather bag, he lifted out a wallet and removed a library card. "Here. And there's a pair of sunglasses in the truck. It's not much . . ."

"Thank you." Her pulse raced as they headed for the garage. She almost forgot to get her artwork out of the Audi. She'd have to deliver the pieces to the gallery looking like she had a hangover. What if the killer recognized her in spite of the disguise? Maybe she should just stay put. *But what if he decides to return and really look for me?*

CHAPTER 4

Tavish slumped in the seat of the pickup to appear shorter and kept checking the rearview mirror. At any moment she expected the patrol car to race up behind her, lights flashing, and pull her over. The steering wheel slipped in her damp hands, and she wiped them on her slacks. A few nibbles on a fingernail kept the attack at bay. Marley peered at her through her topknot of corded fur, then stared out the window as if watching also. *What on earth have I got myself into? I just tried to save a dog from euthanasia, and now I've witnessed a murdered man and someone's trying to kill me.*

She made it as far as the intersection before she saw him. He'd parked in the shade of a massive ponderosa pine. She slid farther down in her seat, allowing the steering wheel to partially block her face. "Stay low, Marley," she whispered. The dog crouched.

Holding her breath, she carefully signaled, then turned right toward Albuquerque. She concentrated on staring straight ahead, but her gaze darted between the street and the side mirrors. The road curved, and the patrol car dropped from sight.

Turning at the first intersection, she pulled over and waited until she could get control of her breathing. Marley hopped into her lap. She patted the dog, then returned Marley to the seat. "Your owner was a very nice man, but I can't live in fear like this. I'll do my duty, but then I'm through. It's up to the police. And I'll find a home for you."

Marley licked her cheek.

How many germs are in dog spit? She pulled a small bottle of hand disinfectant from her purse and rubbed it on her face.

Turning around, she headed for the library, choosing the downtown main branch. The more people, the less chance she'd be remembered. Parking diagonally across the street in the parking garage, she reasoned that the temperature seemed cool enough to leave Marley in the truck with the windows cracked. The dog barked her protest.

As she crossed the street, she could almost see the police department, less than two blocks away.

As always when entering any room, she felt like everyone in the library was staring at her, judging her clothing, weight, and hairstyle. She resisted the urge to tug down her shirt and check her hair. She found the computer section, located a vacant machine, and composed the email.

I found John Coyote, a retired archaeologist, dead in his home at 75644 Loco Drive. The house was ransacked and the safe broken into. The body was placed into the trunk of a car by a man posing as a cop . . .

She pictured the "cop." *Brown hair, average height, thick shoulders, strong jaw . . .*

That description wasn't helpful.

She drummed her fingers on the desk surface until the man seated nearest to her glanced over. She stopped.

Tugging out the small sketchpad she kept in her purse, she drew a thumbnail sketch of the fake cop's face. She scanned the drawing, attached it to the email, and sent both off to the police. Resisting the urge to dust off her hands, she stood, glanced around to see if anyone was paying her any attention, then left, dropping the library card in the trash on the way out. Civic duty done. She'd watch the news to see how John's murder investigation unfolded—from a safe distance.

Of course, her fingerprints were on John's phone. Maybe she'd left other evidence . . . Her cell phone! Maybe John's telephone recorded her number. *Don't worry. There isn't anything I can do about the phone, and it looked pretty shattered.* As for the fingerprints, she'd been in his home when she'd met with him about the commissioned art. She could explain it.

A fresh set of teeth marks gouged the plastic steering wheel. "Oh, great, Marley. That was rude! This pickup belongs to someone else, who probably saved our lives."

Marley refused to look at her as she drove to Hogarth and Montgomery Art Gallery.

Traffic was mercifully light, and a parking spot appeared right in front. Tavish slipped the nylon leash on the dog, grabbed the two framed drawings, then got out of the truck. The next time she left the Puli, the dog would probably eat the seat.

Marley circled Tavish as if herding her legs, making walking difficult. Keeping the leash straight was almost impossible.

Lambert, the clerk, looked up and glared at her. "You know Mrs. Hogarth doesn't allow dogs—"

"I . . . um . . . she's a therapy dog. I'm leaving just as soon as I drop these off." She placed the two drawings on his desk. She was pretty sure Lambert enjoyed various illegal substances and wouldn't have been surprised if he made connections through gallery "patrons." She noticed an upturn of college-aged students whenever he worked. They wouldn't be able to afford the art, and they never seemed to even be looking at the paintings. Plus, his car was too nice and his clothing too expensive for someone living on a manager's salary.

"You have a package upstairs," Lambert told her. "Looks like a paper order. You can pick it up tonight after the show. Mrs. Hogarth locked it up. And she told me to tell you we are not a mail service." Lambert picked up the drawing of the old man. "Skillful, I suppose."

Skillful? I've seen his sketches. He couldn't draw blood with a knife.

"What's this?" He held up the second framed piece.

"An elephant."

"An elephant?"

"Well, okay, an elephant's leg. Up close. Just the hide. See? Here's the elbow . . ."

He was staring at her with his mouth open.

She gave him a tight smile, pivoted, and left. *I have an original take on an overused subject and no one gets it. No wonder Van Gogh lobbed off an ear.*

The sight of a police SUV on the street made her pause. They should have her report and sketch by now. Maybe they'd put out a . . . what did they call it? APB on the fake cop. No one should end up in the trunk of a car bound to be dumped off in the desert somewhere. *Poor John.* She'd met the man at one of her mother's parties a couple of months ago. When he'd found out she was an artist, he'd asked her about a commission—a painting of himself with Marley. He was a delight to work with, though picky. He knew a lot about art and seemed to like what she did, although in the end he'd changed his mind about the painting. He'd paid her in full anyway. She'd hoped this would be the start of numerous commissions, but no further work was forthcoming. The offer of a gallery opening was her last hope. After that . . . what? Back to her accounting company? *No.* She'd buried that life. Literally.

Checking her watch, Tavish shook her head. She just had time to change her clothes and get back to the gallery before her show opened.

She glanced at the dog as she drove home. There wasn't time to find a boarding kennel. She'd have to leave Marley in the house. "Looks like you're going to be my guard dog—at least for tonight. So here are the rules. No chewing shoes. No piddling on anything. No barking unless you see a crook or Fake Cop. Um . . . try to think like Lassie. Faithful guardian. With a touch of Doberman."

Marley had curled up on the seat and was fast asleep. Her legs twitched in pursuit of her dream kitties.

Tavish currently resided in the guesthouse of her mother's sprawling estate. She'd had a small apartment, but following Andrew's death, her mother insisted she move in. It was a disagreeable situation, but the free housing made it possible for her to turn her back on the old job and take what solace she could from her art. Art was what she needed, especially when grieving.

She parked, grabbed the leash in one hand and her purse in the other, and trotted to the guesthouse.

Tavish's outfit for the gallery opening had been the last one she'd purchased while shopping with her grandmother. Wearing it would be like having Grandma at the opening. She'd add a four-strand necklace of turquoise, coral, garnet, and pearls, with a large, orbicular jasper crystal on the bottom. Her research showed this stone to be an excellent talisman to transform her life to a more desirable state.

During their short time together, Andrew had taken a great deal of interest in her appearance, encouraging her to get a new hairstyle, makeup, and wardrobe. Upon his suicide she'd reverted to her standard jeans and T-shirt, although Maria kept everything pressed and her mother made sure they were designer. Tavish didn't really care what she wore.

She undressed and pulled on the heavily embroidered maxi skirt. It slid down her hips and threatened to fall off. It had fit at the store. How had she ended up buying the wrong size? A large safety pin took care of the extra fabric, but where should she place the pin? If she gathered it in front, she'd look pregnant. Bunching the extra fabric in the rear would work if fashion ever brought back the bustle. Maybe two pins and go with wider hips? She ended up with two pins front and back. Slightly pregnant with a big rear end.

The beige eyelet-knit pullover hid a multitude of fashion sins, like safety pins. The boots were covered with studs and belts.

They were new and pinched like a girdle on a hot day, but super cute. After she put on the earrings that matched the necklace, she spun around for Marley to see, then did a fan kick. "Ha! Still got it. What do you think? Classy, or over the top?"

The Puli whined. While she'd been getting dressed, the dog had raided the dirty-laundry basket. A neat row of socks, underwear, and one sneaker lay on the floor behind her. A second sneaker was between her front legs.

"Let me get this straight. If I leave you behind, you'll eat your way through everything you see, chew on anything you don't eat, and probably bark continuously, right?"

Marley spun, then did a dance on her hind legs.

"That's blackmail." She grabbed the leash. Marley's barking would swiftly bring her mother to investigate.

Maybe if a few of the drawings in her exhibit sold, she could consider herself officially an artist. When she turned thirty, she'd receive the bulk of the estate her grandmother left her. She could move out to Santa Fe, with its lively artists' community, or even out of state. She'd be photographed in black and white with a mysterious expression on her face—like Georgia O'Keeffe. They'd even call her the reincarnation of O'Keeffe. Her work would command millions, but she'd seldom let a piece go. She'd have all the latest security to discourage art thieves. She'd become one of those wealthy reclusive artists, living alone, with no one around to complicate life.

No one around to hurt me.

She shook her head to empty the thought.

After parking more than a block away from the gallery so she wouldn't be seen driving the junker pickup, she tried to look cool and elegant strolling up the street. Unfortunately Marley was determined to herd her legs and kept running behind each step. Blisters had already formed on both heels. *But the boots are cute.*

Lambert was arranging Oreo cookies on a silver platter as she arrived.

Cookies? She'd hoped for pâté or caviar with champagne. What next? Wine in a box?

Moving to the special showing area of the gallery, she stopped dead. Lambert had hung colorful watercolors between her graphite drawings.

A gray-bearded man approached. "You must be Evelyn McTavish. I'm Rick Stevens. We're sharing this show—isn't that exciting?" He beamed at her, then glanced at Marley. "Cute dog. My getting this opportunity was last minute. I just walked in with my work and Mrs. Hogarth said she had space to hang everything . . ." He kept babbling, but Tavish didn't hear him. She was to have had a one-woman show! A solo. That was the agreement. How was she ever going to establish a reputation when her name was lumped in with others in group showings?

Mrs. Hogarth drifted past, then did a double take on Marley. "Tavish—"

"She's a therapy dog."

Mrs. Hogarth raised her eyebrows. "We'll address this later." She gave Tavish a small shove. "Go mingle with the guests. And smile."

People had been filtering into the room, plastic cups of wine in hand, and wandering around the works. Rick had buttonholed a couple and was jabbering away at them. He nodded at Lambert, who strolled over and put a tiny red sticker on the mounted art label. A sale. His work had sold at *her* show.

Mrs. Hogarth caught her gaze and nodded toward a man standing in front of one of her drawings. Right. She'd have to talk to him. Make a sale.

She swallowed hard and bit the edge of a fingernail. *Just ask him what he thinks or if he has any questions.* Her stomach twisted.

This shouldn't be hard. It wasn't . . . *Don't think about Andrew.*

The man had his back to her and was studying her drawing of the elephant leg. He had to be over six foot four—actually taller than her own five foot ten. She moved next to him and gestured to the piece. "What do you think?"

She moved to see his expression.

She blinked. Up close he proved to be divinely good looking, in a Hugh Jackman–like way. His deeply tanned skin contrasted with his bright blue eyes and brown hair bleached light by the sun. He wore a khaki-colored long-sleeved shirt rolled up to the elbow and tucked into olive-green cargo pants. His well-worn hiking boots were covered in dust.

Her hands grew sweaty.

"Huh?" He continued to study the art.

"I . . . I was wondering what you thought?"

"About what?"

"About the drawing."

"Oh, um . . . what is it?" He glanced at her, then did a double take. "Hello there."

"Hello." She cleared her throat. "It's an elephant's leg."

"Don't see many of these." He bent over and scratched behind Marley's ear. The dog closed her eyes in bliss.

"Elephant legs?"

"Pulik. Cute dog."

Tavish gulped in air. "So . . . what do you think of the drawing?"

"Now that I know it's an elephant's leg, my next question would be, why?"

He was decidedly the handsomest man she'd ever seen, and she longed to claw his eyes out. "Why not?" she said stiffly. "No one draws elephant legs."

"There's probably a reason why that subject hasn't been explored in the fine-art world." The man's gaze drifted to the gathered fabric at her waist.

Her eyes burned. *Not the skirt. The boots. Check out the boots!* The cumulative effects of the day caught up with her. A giant lump formed in her throat. She tugged Marley's leash, moved to the table holding the wine and cookies, and snatched a plastic cup. It almost slipped from her hand. *Don't cry. Don't let anyone see how you feel.* It wasn't the end of the world that someone didn't like her art. That he didn't like her art. She just hadn't developed the thick skin needed for critics in the art scene.

She concentrated on the clerk.

Lambert moved around the room with a package of crimson dots, applying them to most of the watercolors. Sold, sold, sold, sold.

She drained the wine. *I try for original. I get sarcasm.* Earcutting time.

Mrs. Hogarth frowned at her from across the room.

Tavish deliberately picked up a second cup of wine and raised it in a toast to the older woman. Good-bye, art career. Her throat closed up. She couldn't swallow. She placed the second untouched glass of wine on a nearby table. Who was she fooling? The whole art experiment had been a waste of time. Maybe she *should* go back to rearranging paper clips at that stupid accounting company. *Maybe this is how Andrew felt. No place to go. The world closing in, doors slamming shut . . .*

Turning to leave, she glanced at the handsome stranger.

He'd been staring at her.

Her face burned. She bolted from the gallery.

CHAPTER 5

Agent Sawyer Price had surreptitiously watched the clerk move around the room placing red dots on placards—apparently noting those paintings had sold. His constant sniffing, red nose, and dilated eyes pegged him as a cocaine user. *Maybe cocaine dealer?* Sawyer glanced at the gallery business card in his hand. The card had a maple leaf on the back—possibly indicating a source for illegal drugs. Drugs could be the link in the case he was working. He needed to talk to the man.

He glanced around the gallery and spotted a familiar face. A man from the joint drug task force he'd met during one of his many meetings with the local law enforcement. The officer was watching the clerk's movements as well. *If they have the clerk under surveillance, it probably wouldn't help if I blew their sting operation with a public scene in the middle of a gallery show.*

He stared sightlessly at the drawing in front of him. *Maybe if I look interested in the art, the clerk will come over.*

A woman's voice intruded on his thoughts. "Huh?"

"I was wondering what you thought?"

"About what?"

"About the drawing."

He realized he'd been staring at a pencil drawing. He blurted out the first thing that came to mind. "Oh, um, what is it?" He glanced at her, then did a double take. "Hello there."

The woman was stunning. She moved like a dancer. Her clothes spoke of wealth, her hair and makeup whispered class, and her dog was an incongruent exclamation mark. He didn't care much for the boots.

He had no idea what he said next. Whatever it was, the woman pivoted and stalked away. When she reached the beverage table, she snatched up a glass of wine. Her brilliant blue eyes sparkled with unshed tears as she watched the snobby clerk place red dots on some of the watercolor paintings.

Could she be the pencil artist? *Oh brother, and I probably blurted out some stupid comment about her art. What was I thinking?* Obviously he wasn't. When would he learn to keep his mouth shut?

She glanced at him.

He raised his eyebrows and slowly smiled. Maybe he could explain, apologize, take her to dinner.

Her eyes grew wide while twin red spots appeared on her cheeks. She fled the gallery.

Wow. I've reached a new low in impressing women. That was the side effect of his job. He was always traveling, but seldom to anyplace where he could meet someone—especially a beautiful someone.

The annoying clerk appeared at his elbow. "I noticed you admiring this piece."

"Who was that?" Sawyer didn't look at the other man.

The clerk sniffed. "Evelyn McTavish. Calls herself Tavish. That's her work you've been staring at."

Sawyer turned his gaze to the framed drawing of an elephant leg. The texture of the creature's hide had been captured in exquisite detail. It must have taken months of work. He glanced at the price, then sucked in his breath. That would set him back for a time. What would he do with it? He was living in a dusty tent. In the desert. At least for another couple of days.

The clerk leaned closer, giving Sawyer a good whiff of marijuana seeping from his pores. One of the graduate students probably bought his or her drugs here. "I'm sorry, I didn't catch your name."

"Lambert West."

"Do you work here every day?"

"Yes. Tuesday through Saturday."

Sawyer smiled and nodded. He'd have a word with the drug task force officer to be sure he didn't blow their operation. He could always pay a visit to the clerk tomorrow.

"I overheard what you said about her art," Lambert whispered. "I suspect this will be her last show. She was terrible to deal with." Sniff. "Late, leaving the opening like that, no sales, and that dog—"

"I'll take it."

"Pardon me?"

"The drawing. I'm buying it."

The clerk straightened, smoothed the front of his shirt, and gave a sharp nod. "Of course." He placed a red dot on the art label. "Please step over to the desk so I may record—"

"I'm taking it with me."

"Oh. Most irregular."

Sawyer glared at the man. "I'm leaving town and need to take the drawing with me. If that's a problem . . ."

"No, no, no." The clerk took a step backward, then reached over and removed the drawing from the wall. "I'll wrap it for you." He scurried from the room.

Sawyer strolled to the immaculate desk, which held only a computer. He pulled out his wallet and counted out the total. The clerk returned and placed a bubble-wrapped package on the desk. Lambert typed something on the computer, wrote up the invoice, then carefully counted Sawyer's money.

Sawyer leaned over the desk slightly and read the screen. *Evelyn McTavish, 965 Westwood Estates, Albuquerque*, and her phone number. He memorized the information.

Heading out of town in his SUV, he tried to keep his mind off of what-if scenarios. What if he called Tavish and apologized? What if he asked her out? What if . . . ?

What if I just do my job and forget I've ever seen her? He glanced at the wrapped drawing sitting beside him. Forget her? Never.

≡≡

Tavish didn't remember driving to the cemetery, but when she parked, it seemed the perfect choice.

She carefully avoided looking toward Andrew's headstone. With no family to bury him, at least none who showed up after his death, she'd paid for it all and chosen a site near her grandmother so she could visit them both. All this before the graveside encounter with the pregnant woman.

Her grandmother's grave was a short distance away, near a row of trees. With Marley in tow, she strolled to a shady bench where she could see the headstone. "Well, Grandma, I know you would have stayed at the gallery opening until it was over. You would have been gracious and polite to that awful man at the dog pound. And to Lambert, and even to that good-looking art critic." Under her grandmother's name—Grace Eileen Gordon—and date of birth and death, was *Prov. 3:5*. Grandma had given Tavish a Bible, but she'd never looked up the reference.

"Grandma, I miss you so much." She was silent for a few moments. Her often-married mother had been consumed by her career and hadn't had time to raise a child. Tavish had spent more time with her grandmother than her own mother. Her grandmother's untimely death last year left an aching hole in her life, a hole that art and crystals and food and psychiatrists and even Andrew couldn't quite fill.

Then Andrew died too. Betrayed her and committed suicide . . . A yank on the crystal around her neck pulled her back from those thoughts.

"Grandma . . . I wish you were here. I found poor John murdered. My gallery opening was a disaster. I'm not sure what to do next." She looked down and whispered, "Is being dead so bad? Being alive sure is."

"Excuse me?"

Tavish jumped, then turned.

A casually dressed man in his sixties stood behind her. "I'm so sorry, miss. Is everything all right? I heard someone talking and . . ." He gave a sheepish smile and waved his hand.

"Hi. Sorry. My grandma is here and I visit her every week to talk to her. I didn't mean to disturb you."

"Oh, no, no, no. I understand completely. My dear wife of forty years is over there." He waved at a tombstone with an angel on top two rows over. "I often talk to Ruth. That was my wife. Ruth. My name is Ezekiel Lewis."

Ezekiel had moved closer. His blue shirt was crumpled, his pants wrinkled and in need of pressing. His gray-white hair fluttered around his head, and he absently ran his hand over it, causing it to fluff even more. "Your dog looks like Bob Marley's dreadlocks."

Tavish nodded. "She's a Puli."

"Dogs make good companions." He reached out his arms and Marley jumped into them.

"Oh, I'm sorry." Tavish stood to retrieve the dog. "She's never done that before. I think she misses her owner."

"Not a problem." Ezekiel placed the dog on the ground and patted her.

"She seems to like you. I'm looking for a home for her. Would you be interested?"

"Somehow I think you need a dog more than I do. I should leave you, Miss . . . ?"

"Tavish. Call me Tavish. You don't have to leave." Her gaze drifted toward Andrew's grave. "You were married forty years?"

"Indeed I was. How about yourself?"

Touching her bare ring finger, she shook her head. "Engaged. He's buried over there."

"Oh my. So young. So sad. How did you meet? Sometimes it helps to talk about it."

He reminded her of her grandmother with the same crinkly blue eyes and deep smile lines. "I met Andrew at a gallery. The one where I just had a showing." She wanted to stop but the words tumbled out. "He was so handsome. There were all kinds of beautiful women there, but he paid attention only to me. *To me.* He didn't mind my few extra pounds. He said there was more to love. A cliché, I know, but I loved it. Before I knew it, we were engaged. He wanted to get married right away. He said he didn't want to wait. And he didn't know about my money—"

Not according to the pregnant woman at Andrew's funeral. The thought smashed into Tavish's brain. *She said Andrew was marrying me* for *my money.*

"Anyway"—she glanced into his kind eyes—"he knew I promised to visit my grandmother every week. I thought I could see his grave at the same time. But if I'd only known, really known about him, I wouldn't have put him so near to her."

Tavish snapped her mouth shut. "I'm . . . I'm sorry. I don't usually talk about myself. I'm heading home. It's been a . . . long day."

Ezekiel reached into his pocket, pulled out a card, and handed it to her. "Miss Tavish, if you need someone . . . living to talk to, give me a call." His gaze stopped at the jasper cabochon on her necklace, slid down to the tattered fingernails and Band-Aids, then drifted to her grandmother's headstone. "Proverbs three five." He nodded. "Your grandmother was a religious woman?"

"Yes, but Helen, that's my mother, wouldn't let her talk to me about it."

"Yes. I do believe we should talk." He turned and strolled away.

By the time she returned to the guesthouse, the sun had set. Her mother was waiting in the living room. Tavish mentally groaned.

Helen Gordon McTavish Richmond wore an off-white raw-silk jacket over black slacks and a red cashmere sweater. Her silver hair was swept into a chignon at the base of her neck. The woman's mouth dropped open, then shut at the appearance of Marley. "That looks like a black mop. What is it?"

Tavish turned the dog loose. "A Puli." Marley raced from the room.

"Is that some kind of canine?"

"Yes. I'm . . . taking care of her for a friend." Marley returned with a sock from the dirty-clothes basket. Tavish gingerly removed it from her mouth.

"Get rid of it." Helen looked around.

"Her."

"What?"

"Marley's a female, not an it."

Helen's eyes narrowed. "It. Her. I don't care. Take her to the pound. You know I don't like dogs in my home."

"Marley's not in your home, Helen. And if you'd had a dog five months ago, your gardener wouldn't have been shot and killed and your art wouldn't have been stolen."

"Evelyn!" Her gaze shot toward the kitchen.

Maria, the housekeeper, stood at the doorway. "I . . . I'm finished."

"Thank you." Tavish gave the woman a slight wave.

Helen waited until the kitchen door closed. "My art was recovered."

"Yes."

"Evelyn, would it be so hard for you to call me Mother?"

"When you can call me Tavish, I'll call you Mother."

"But that's not your . . ." Her mother sniffed. "Technically this *is* my home. But I didn't come here to argue. Where have you been?"

"I told you I had a gallery opening."

Helen's gaze went from Tavish's boots to her hair. "Wearing that?"

"Yes."

"I see. You know, ever since your grandmother passed, you've thrown yourself into your art—"

"And that's bad because . . . ?"

"It wasn't just the art. Dance, yoga, crystals, meditation. Strange diets—"

"You sent me to psychiatrists and medication."

Her mother's lips thinned. "I will be so glad when you get this art foolishness out of your system."

Tavish clenched her teeth. *Maybe I am being foolish.* "It was a major gallery opening."

"I noticed you haven't been taking your medication. Some of your prescriptions look untouched. And then I found this." She held up a leather-bound notebook.

"That's my journal." Tavish held out her hand. "Please give it to me."

Her mother ignored the proffered hand and strolled to the window. "I just don't think you're taking your therapy seriously."

"Please return my journal."

Her mother held it up. "The psychiatrist wanted you to write in this every day." She opened the book. "But you wrote in this only one time."

"I *never* promised I'd maintain a journal."

"Just listen to this—"

"I know what it says. I wrote it—"

"*Write how you feel today. I feel stupid writing in this journal. What new discovery did you have today? There's a patch of dead lawn that bears a striking resemblance to Lyle Lovett. What is something positive today? I'm positive it looks like Lyle Lovett.*"

Her mother looked over at her. "What is that all about?"

"Lawn care." Tavish retrieved the journal from her mother and placed it on the table.

Helen moved to the built-in bookshelves. "Anyway, I just bought a piece of pottery and thought it would look nice in here." She pointed to a new piece she'd strategically placed, having shoved aside a book on drawing figures.

"I don't have the same security as you. Aren't you afraid someone will steal it?"

"It's insured."

Tavish pulled a Band-Aid off her pinkie. The finger was red and raw.

"We've just about made a decision on that job offer at Softmode Testing." Her mother adjusted the pot. "You've shown no indication you want to return to the accounting firm, and this might be a good fit. You won't get another chance at it if you don't decide now. We're starting a major testing with the homeless and could use your math background." The older woman straightened a line of leather-bound books. "Quite frankly, you need to think about doing something. It's not healthy for you to just mope around and sketch. And you shouldn't believe your grandmother's estate will be sufficient in this day and age—"

"We can have this discussion at another time. I have things to do."

"What do you have to do?"

Tavish clenched her jaw. *I'm twenty-five. I don't need to tell my mother what I'm doing.* "Things."

"What things? You know how I worry about you ever since—"

"What did you want?" *I hate the way she makes me feel like I'm five again.*

"I have an extremely important . . . and delicate situation. I'll need your presence the day after tomorrow."

"What is so important and delicate?"

Two red spots appeared on Helen's cheeks. "It's nothing."

"Then it can't be important and delicate."

Helen stared at a point above Tavish's head. "It has to do with the stolen art."

"I thought the police—"

"Not the police. The insurance company. They're sending an investigator."

"What's to investigate? Five months ago you had a robbery. Your gardener was killed. The art disappeared, was recovered and returned. End of story."

"Apparently not. He wants to talk to me. I have nothing to say, and I especially don't want to talk to him. So will you please be there?"

Tavish nodded.

"Cocktails by the pool at four. Wear the Armani dress I got you. It's hanging in your closet. And put your hair up." Helen started for the door.

"You're throwing a cocktail party for an investigator?"

"No, I just told him that's when he could come. It will give me excuses to avoid him."

"Then why do you need me?"

"I'm the victim of a crime, Evelyn. Being investigated by an insurance company makes me look guilty. Is it so hard for you to stand by me? I will not have my good name sullied by gossip and innuendo. Try to remove the Band-Aids and keep your hands out of sight."

Slowly Tavish sank into the sofa, her legs too weary to hold her. A weight settled into her chest. Was she simply her mother's bodyguard? A bad artist? Only desirable because of money—

Someone rang the doorbell.

Go away. She pulled off her boots and massaged her feet.

The doorbell rang again.

"Who would be calling at this time of night?" Helen strolled over and opened the door.

A man with black hair, even features, and dark eyes held up a gold badge. He wore a sports coat and slacks. "I'm Detective Mike Mullins, Bernalillo County Sheriff's Department."

Tavish pulled her legs up on the sofa and wrapped her arms around them.

"I'm following up on the report of a murder."

Helen's hand flew to her mouth. "Murder?"

Detective Mullins's eyebrows drew together. "A report came

in today." He looked around the room, his gaze eventually resting on Tavish. "I'm wondering what you knew about that."

Tavish couldn't meet his gaze. "How . . . Why did you think I emailed you?"

"I didn't say emailed. I said a report came in."

Tavish's face grew warm.

Her mother glanced back and forth between the detective and her daughter. "What's this all about?"

Detective Mullins raised his eyebrows. "May I come in?"

Helen clutched the door as if debating whether to slam it shut. "I suppose."

Mullins entered and continued to stare at Tavish. "Technically you didn't email us. You contacted the Albuquerque Police Department. They passed your message on to us, as the address you gave was outside the city limits. And as for your identity, a colleague of mine was at your gallery opening and commented on your drawings. You included a composite with your report. He thought he recognized your drawing style. You just validated our hunch. Pretty easy sleuthing on our part."

Tavish unwrapped her arms and sat up. "I just . . . didn't want to be involved."

"I'm afraid you are involved, Miss McTavish. You turned in a false police report."

"Oh no." Helen stared at Tavish. "You're not doing that again, are you? You're determined to ruin my reputation."

"Doing what again?" Mullins asked. "And you are?"

"Helen Richmond. My daughter's been under a lot of stress." Helen smoothed her jacket. "Her fiancé committed suicide a couple of weeks ago and she was convinced it was murder—"

"That's not the case here, Helen." Tavish's face felt hot. She addressed the detective. "I realize you didn't find the body. I told you in that email that John Coyote was placed in the trunk of a fake police car, but there should have been blood—"

"Miss McTavish, you said there was a murder at 75644 Loco Drive."

"Yes. As I told you, his name was John Coyote."

"We drove over there. It's a rental handled by a property management company. They've never heard of John Coyote. No one currently lives there."

CHAPTER 6

Tavish's mind blanked for a moment. "What do you mean?"

"I mean," Detective Mullins said, "that we followed up on your report by sending a deputy over there and found nothing. No blood. No signs of disturbance."

"Then he was at the wrong address. Or the fake cop came back and cleaned up the blood. But you can check that, with that stuff you spray on and it lights up—"

"Luminal."

"Yes." She licked her dry lips. "I'm sure you'll find blood if you just look."

"Miss McTavish, we were at the right address. Are you sure *you* were?"

"Of course!"

He glanced at her mother. "Why did you go there?"

"To return his dog."

"That dog? The one that hasn't left your side?"

"Well, yes—"

"Look, you sound sincere, but I think you're . . . confused."

Tavish leaned forward. "I'm not confused. I'd been to the house before. And there's a witness to the fake cop. A guy who lives down the street. I was afraid the fake cop would come after me again, so he loaned me his mom's truck and her library card—"

"What's his name?" Mullins pulled out a small notebook and pen.

"Kevin."

"Kevin what?"

"I don't know. It would be the same as his mother . . . No, wait . . . He said his mother remarried." Tavish placed her pinkie in her mouth. It tasted of old copper. "You'd have her name from the email I sent."

"Those are anonymous."

"I used her library card."

Detective Mullins put the pen back into his pocket. "Okay, bring me the library card."

"I threw it away, but you could go to her house."

"Address?"

"I don't know. But her truck—"

"Miss McTavish, I would strongly recommend you stop watching too many police shows and refrain from filing reports unless you really want to be charged. We're stretched too thin as it is with all the Antifa protests—"

"But—"

"Stay out of police business. Do I make myself clear?"

"Yes," Tavish whispered.

Detective Mullins nodded at Helen, turned, and left.

Tavish clutched the arm of the sofa.

"Evelyn—"

"Don't. Don't say a word. I'm not crazy. I know what I saw." She shoved herself up and headed for the kitchen.

Her mother followed. "Maybe you should go back to that psychologist again. Look at your fingers. You're practically bleeding. I just think with your grandmother, then losing your fiancé—finding his body like that—has pushed you over the edge. You haven't been yourself since."

Tavish spun toward the older woman. She could barely choke out the words. "I didn't 'lose' my fiancé." She made quotes in the air. "He died. And I don't know who I am now, so I'm not surprised I'm 'not myself.'" She clenched her fists. "And I know I saw John's body, so if you'd please just leave . . . I need to be alone."

Her mother stiffened, then turned.

"Wait. I'm sorry—"

The door snapped shut behind her mother.

Go after her. Apologize. She's only trying to help. Tavish walked to the door, then wandered over to an overstuffed armchair and sank into its depth.

Marley jumped into her lap and ran a wet tongue up her cheek. "That's disgusting. You really need to be less physical." She pushed the dog to the floor, picked up a hand sanitizer from the end table, and rubbed some onto the spot. "I know you believe me. You were there."

The dog sat facing away from her.

"I'm not crazy and I don't need a shrink." She'd never told anyone about the woman at Andrew's funeral. The pitying stares after Andrew's death had been almost more than she could handle. What would the rumors and gossip have been had any-one found out about her fiancé's pregnant lover?

She stood and paced, ending up looking at the bowl her mother had brought. Another of her endless Native American purchases. This one was chipped. She wanted to throw the bro-ken bowl away. Instead, she took it into the kitchen and put some dried onions into it. Bowls should be useful.

Marley followed her into the kitchen, whined, and pawed the air.

"What?"

She licked her lips.

"Dinner? I guess I forgot. I'm not hungry . . ."

The dog moved to the refrigerator and stared intently.

Tavish opened the door, then closed it. "I guess there's no good way to break this to you. I'm vegan."

Marley tore her gaze from the refrigerator to Tavish's face.

"Don't look at me like that. We'll find something for tonight. Tomorrow we'll go to the store." She opened the refrigerator again, pulled out a container of hummus, a package of tofu, some carrots and zucchini, and a container of soy milk. "I can make you a tofu manicotti, maybe some hummus with homemade flax, chia, sunflower, and oat crackers. That would be gluten-free . . ." She glanced at the dog, sighed, then returned the ingredients to the refrigerator. "You win. Come on, let's get some kibble."

After changing from her skirt to jeans, pulling a baggy, aqua-colored cotton sweater over a pink jersey tank, and grabbing a hooded jacket, she headed for the truck.

The weather had turned cool with the smell of rain. Clouds gathered over the Sandia Mountains, and lightning slashed the evening sky. The rain held off while Tavish picked up a bag of gluten-free, grain-free, organic dog food at her favorite store, but a light smattering of droplets began as she returned to the truck.

The dog whined and pawed at the passenger-side window.

"Now what is it? I bought you food."

Marley let out a low howl.

The sound raised the hairs on the back of Tavish's neck. "I can't bring John back. I did all I could. You heard the detective. No one even believes me. *I* don't believe me—"

Marley howled again.

"How can I prove anything? There's no body . . ."

The dog sniffed the dashboard, then sat.

Dashboard. Glove box. There should be a license and proof of insurance in the truck with the name of Kevin's mother. That would have an address.

The glove box was empty, but the idea of driving to Kevin's place stuck in Tavish's brain. He had seen the fake cop. Her car still had the bullet hole, and maybe the bullet could be recovered from somewhere inside. She could *prove* to that detective she wasn't nuts.

The fake cop wouldn't still be watching the road, so the coast would be clear.

The rain stayed steady as she turned toward the Tijeras Canyon. Marley took turns staring out the front, then the side window, as if she knew the way home.

They soon reached the house where Tavish had hidden in the garage. She stopped before turning in and checked the time. "It's a bit late, but this is important."

The dog whined.

"We won't stay long." She pulled into Kevin's driveway. No lights appeared at the front windows. She followed the drive around to the garage in the rear. The garage doors were closed. "Good idea. Keep my car hidden."

She parked the truck and turned off the headlights. The patter of the rain sounded like drumming fingers. The house remained dark.

An uneasy shiver danced between her shoulder blades. "He was working hard. He must have gone to bed early," she whispered.

This is ridiculous. She started to get out of the truck, but Marley insisted she be included. Tavish headed for the garage and peered into the window. No Audi.

The uneasy prickle turned into goose bumps. Her stomach tightened. *He just moved my car, that's all.* With Marley herding her legs, she strolled up to the back door and tapped.

No answer.

She rapped again, this time louder, wincing at the clatter.

Again no sound came from the house.

She tried the door. Locked.

Pulling the hood of her jacket over her rapidly frizzing hair, she left the back door and moved toward a patio door barely visible in the dim light. This door was unlocked.

She slid the door open and stuck her head inside. "Hello? Kevin? It's me, Tavish." Her voice echoed off bare walls. Nudging the door wider, she called, "Kevin? Are you okay?"

Marley shot past her, yanking the leash from her hand, and disappeared into the house.

Tavish abandoned politeness. She fumbled around the wall until she found a light switch. The light revealed the same

1980s-era kitchen and an empty dining room. She licked her lips. "Kevin?"

Marley's nails clattered on the bare floor somewhere in the house. Tavish moved toward the sound. "Kevin? Marley?" A hallway split the structure, with doors on either side. She found the light, then opened each door in turn. Empty rooms. In the bathroom, empty shower curtain rings hung on a rod. Through the illumination spilling from the hallway, she could clearly see the barren living room. A faint scent of bleach made her nose twitch. Marley was sniffing a spot in the middle of the floor.

"This doesn't mean anything." Her voice sounded high and shrill as it echoed off the bare walls. "Kevin said he was cleaning out the house. I only saw the kitchen, so all I can be sure of is the dinette is missing."

And my car. And Kevin.

CHAPTER 7

Tavish wrapped her arms around herself, clamping her cold hands under her armpits. *Don't panic.* The house could have been empty when she drove up earlier in the day. All but the table and chairs. Dishes. He'd served her iced tea. And given Marley water in a bowl.

She rushed to the kitchen and opened the first cabinet, then all the drawers and cupboards. Nothing remained. Next she checked the refrigerator. No sign of the pitcher of iced tea, but the light came on.

Iced tea. Ice.

She checked the freezer. The ice maker was full and still churning out ice cubes. "You left the ice maker on. What else did you miss?"

In the living room, she flipped the light switch. The anemic overhead fixture barely illuminated the room. Small nail holes next to the wall confirmed that the deeply scarred oak flooring had been covered by wall-to-wall carpeting. As she approached the spot Marley had inspected earlier, the odor of bleach grew stronger. Dropping to her hands and knees, she sniffed, then studied the wood. The color was lighter, and something had caught between the wooden slats. As she ran a thumbnail along the crack, a dark, flaky substance emerged. "Blood?"

If they killed him here, they could have ripped the plastic shower curtain down, wrapped his body in it, and dragged him from the house. That's what Norman Bates did in *Psycho*.

Marley barked from another room.

Tavish stood. "Good idea. Let's get out of here."

Marley was in the kitchen barking at the old refrigerator. Tavish snatched up the trailing leash, then bolted outside. The rain had stopped while she'd been investigating. "Kevin's gone. My car is gone."

Marley whined as Tavish climbed back into the truck and started it up.

"Yes, I know. Kevin told me to take the keys. I trusted him. I swore I'd never trust anyone ever again. I don't know if anything he told me was true. Maybe he was robbing the house and I interrupted. Or maybe he's dead too. Maybe that fake cop has Kevin in the trunk of his car along with John." She turned up the heat and shivered.

Marley cocked her head. Tavish backed down the driveway, then turned in the direction of John's house.

"No. I can't call the police and say that *maybe* my car's been stolen, but then again, I gave someone my key, and *maybe* Kevin's been killed because *maybe* there's blood in the living room of an empty house, and *maybe* this is all related to the murdered John Coyote and Fake Cop, except they don't exist. I don't believe it and I was there."

She had only the detective's word that they'd found nothing at John's house. She'd broken her cell phone. There'd be glass on the front walk.

A light was on in John's living room and the gate stood open. "I *knew* the police were wrong!" Tavish pulled forward until she could clearly see the front of the house. She drove as far off the road as she could, turned off her headlights, and watched. No activity seemed to be going on. She rolled the window partway down to see better. Maybe John had left his lights on. She hadn't thought to check. Of course, the one lamp was on the floor, broken—

A man materialized next to her window.

She jumped. Marley lunged at the man, barking wildly.

Before she could roll up the window, he pointed a finger at her. "What do you think you're doing, casing the place?"

"No, I—"

"Then if you don't want me calling the police, go away."

She stared at him a moment, memorizing his face. Midthirties, with a black mustache waxed into Salvador Dali–like points, gray T-shirt, and jeans. "Well . . . um . . . who are you?"

"I am none of your business."

She flipped on the headlights, pulled into the street, and turned around. Marley stared out the back window at the rapidly disappearing house.

"I should have stood my ground. Confronted him. Asked him if he knew John. Asked him what *he* was doing! Maybe he was casing the house." She clenched the crystal hanging around her neck. Marley nuzzled her arm. "I'm sorry. I know you wanted to go home, but if I stayed any longer, that man would have called the police." She gnawed on her thumb for a moment. Her watch said 10:34. "It's late and I've had a bad day. Let's go home and get some rest. We'll do something about my car in the morning."

An SUV passed her. The driver looked like the man who'd just confronted them.

"Now where are you going this time of night?" The SUV had already disappeared up the road. Switching on the headlights, she pressed down on the gas, hoping to catch up with him when he stopped at the intersection.

She reached the stop sign, but his SUV was long gone. *So much for all my Nancy Drew sleuthing.* She turned the truck toward home. After parking on a nearby street so she wouldn't have to explain the truck to her mother, she let Marley out. As they approached the house, the dog released a sharp bark. She caught a soft glint on the blinds covering her kitchen window.

Someone with a flashlight was inside her house.

Call the police. Yanking on the leash, she raced up the side-walk to the truck, jumped in, and locked the door. *Use the phone at Mother's house. No. Don't involve Helen.* She started the engine.

Marley cocked her head, then lay down.

As always, the convenience store a mile from her home was doing a steady business. A woman gassing up her car gave Tavish a quizzical glance when she parked by the old pay phone, then ignored her.

For a change, the phone worked. "9–1–1. What's the nature of your emergency?"

"There's someone in my house with a flashlight." She gave the address.

"I'll send a patrol car right over. Please stay away from the dwelling until the police clear it. Do you have a cell number I can contact you on?"

"It's broken. I'm driving an older Chevy pickup. I'll drive over and stay in the truck until it looks like they've arrested the burglar. Okay?" She disconnected before the dispatch operator could comment.

Tavish parked a block away where she could see the flashing lights. She grabbed Marley's leash and her purse, then walked the final distance on foot. Although part of her mother's sprawling estate, the guesthouse opened to the street and appeared as a separate dwelling. An officer stopped her near the front door. "Are you the homeowner?"

"Yes. I called it in."

A second officer walked up to them. "No one was here. Your front door was unlocked and open. Probably some kids saw the open door and went in to investigate."

"But I'm sure I locked the door . . ." *Did I? I don't remember.*

The officer raised her eyebrows. "I see. Well, nothing seems to be disturbed, but you should go in and have a look."

"Could . . . would you go inside with me?" She glanced at the officer's name tag. "Officer Perez?"

Perez nodded and trailed Tavish up the walk and into the house. Tavish strolled from room to room, flipping on lights and glancing around.

"Nice place." The female officer's gaze went from the handmade Navajo rugs covering the stone floor to the caramel-colored leather furniture and finally rested on the bronze sculpture of a buffalo on the fireplace mantel. "Do you see anything missing?"

"No . . . no." She let go of Marley's leash. The dog shot into the bedroom and barked.

Perez pulled her pistol and signaled Tavish to stay put. She disappeared for a moment, then returned. "Nothing."

Tavish checked the kitchen. The bowl her mother had left earlier had been moved. "In here!"

The two officers charged into the room.

Tavish pointed. "That bowl was moved."

"Bowl?" Perez asked.

"The one holding onions." Tavish's lips could barely move. "Yes. I put it over this way farther."

"I see. Someone walked into your house and instead of stealing any of your art, antiques, or other valuables, they moved a bowl of onions." Her gaze focused on something behind Tavish.

Tavish turned in time to catch the other officer twirling his finger around his ear.

Tavish shook her head. "I'm not crazy. I know what I saw. Someone was in my house looking for something."

The male officer shrugged. "Okay. You might want to lock your doors this time."

The two officers made their way to the front door.

"Wait."

They paused.

"I'd like to report a stolen car."

"Did you just now remember this?" Officer Perez glanced at her partner.

"No. I mean, I was going to call it in."

The male officer pulled out a notepad. "Describe your car."

"A white 2019 Audi A4—"

He stopped writing. "There's an Audi parked on the street over there." He jerked his head. "Did you just forget where you parked?"

She stared at him with her mouth open for a moment. "Ah . . . no . . . I mean . . ." She brushed past him and ran to the street.

Her sedan was tucked under a streetlight, the bullet hole still marring the bumper.

The two officers had followed her outside.

Tell them about the fake policeman who shot at you. Show them the bullet hole.

"Well?" Perez asked.

"It's my car . . . Wait a minute! I drove here in a truck, a pickup owned by Kevin's mom."

"Kevin's mom?" The male officer's gaze slid to Perez, then back to Tavish. "Does Kevin have a last name?"

"Of course, but—"

"Tell you what." Perez nudged her partner. "We need to get going. If you need us for anything, give us a call." Both officers turned and left.

Tavish's stomach churned. She clenched her fists. She didn't try to stop them but marched to the Audi and opened the door. She found the keys on the floor. She took the keys, locked the car, and slowly walked to where she'd parked the truck.

As she expected, it was missing.

CHAPTER 8

Marley was sitting by the door in the living room when Tavish returned. She flopped to the floor, sitting cross-legged facing the dog. "You knew the truck would be gone, didn't you?"

The dog blinked at her.

"This whole thing started with you." She shook her head. "Or maybe it started with John. He put my name as your owner in the microchip."

The Puli whined, then headed for the kitchen.

"Kibble! Oh, Marley, I still haven't fed you and the dog food was in the truck." She glanced at her watch. Almost midnight. Her favorite store would be closed, but the poor dog had to eat. And she wasn't going to be able to sleep anyway.

Marley tore into the room at the sounds of Tavish collecting the leash, bowls, a bottle of water, purse, and car keys.

The night had become progressively cooler, and Tavish was shivering by the time she reached her car but decided not to go back for her jacket. She still took a few moments to walk around the sedan, looking for any damage. Outside of a bit of dust, everything looked the same.

The only change to the interior was the position of the seat, which had been pushed back. She didn't remember the exact odometer reading, and the various settings hadn't been altered.

As Tavish drove to the store, Marley investigated every inch of the car, paying particular attention to the back seat. Tavish adjusted the rearview mirror to watch the dog while she drove.

The grocery store's parking lot held few vehicles. She parked under a light and stayed in the car a few minutes to be sure they hadn't been followed.

Marley dug at the seat.

"Stop it! I'll take a look." Taking a deep breath, she stepped from the car and opened the rear door. Marley ignored her and continued to pay attention to the seat.

Or more precisely, the crack between seats where they folded to open up the trunk space.

She hadn't looked in the trunk.

Call the police.

Oh, sure. She could just imagine what they'd say this time. *So, lady, you want us to look in your trunk because the dog barked in that direction? Should we look under your bed for monsters as well?*

No police. She'd just open the trunk.

A puff of wind, heady with the scent of rain, sent a plastic bag twirling across the deserted lot. The light overhead cast a jaundiced illumination over her car. She clicked the button on her car key twice. The trunk swung open.

Empty.

She exhaled and leaned closer to check.

A faint scuff mark marred one side of the interior. She ran her hand over the carpet, feeling a slight grittiness. Something, or someone, had been in her trunk.

Tavish slammed the lid, then ran for the store. The harshly lit interior and too-loud Muzak grated on her. She grabbed the first bag of dog food she came to, two bowls, and a couple bottles of water, threw cash at the startled clerk, and raced for the car. Once inside, she tore into an already shredded nail with her teeth as fast as she could while searching for a paper bag.

Marley jumped into her lap.

She was going to shove the dog away but clutched her instead. *I'm okay, this will pass, breathe in calm, breathe out fear. I'mokay,thiswillpass,breatheincalm,breatheoutfear.*

Someone tapped on the window beside her.

She screamed and released the dog.

The supermarket checker's eyes were wide open. She held a handful of bills. "Your ch-change, ma'am. Is everything all right?"

Tavish rolled the window down far enough to take the cash. "Yes. I'm sorry. It's . . . complicated."

The woman returned to the store, glancing backward at Tavish every few steps.

Tavish opened the dog food bag and placed a handful in one of the bowls she'd brought. Some of the bottled water went into the second bowl. Both went on the floor. Marley happily munched on the kibble.

She started the engine. "The police aren't going to believe me until I can show them something tangible." She looked at the dog. "And that means finding out about your owner, John Coyote. And I need to find you a home."

She turned the car toward Interstate 25 and Santa Fe. "John said he still spent time at the Kéyah site even though he was retired. Maybe I can locate a colleague who will vouch for his existence."

The dog continued to eat.

"He only mentioned one name, an associate, Pat Caron. That would substantiate my report. If I can find this Pat . . ."

The dog paused and gave a sharp bark.

"I suppose that's why he kept changing his mind on what he wanted included in the final painting. He might have wanted another person in it besides you and himself. I know that's just speculation. But it's reasonable. Maybe he had a girlfriend."

Marley barked again.

"Just because you didn't meet her doesn't mean he didn't have one. Why couldn't Pat be Patricia? I think you're jealous that you weren't the only female in his life."

The dog huffed and returned to her kibble.

Tavish concentrated on the road. The more she thought about a girlfriend, the more she thought about Andrew, and the more she thought about how women made men do strange things. Her theory fit with John's strange behavior in the last few weeks. What if he was going to make the art a gift? And the girlfriend was married? What if her husband was Fake Cop . . . ?

That didn't fit either. A jealous husband wouldn't necessarily want to hurt, rob, and kill, would he? She sighed.

"At any rate, John told me how to get to the dig." She glanced at the dog. "Well, okay, he told me the exit and nearest gas station."

Only semitrucks and an occasional car populated the four-lane highway, so she made good time. "Once I get close to the site, I'll ask directions."

Marley finished the food and settled on the seat next to Tavish.

She should just turn around and go home. She really didn't know who John Coyote was, or why there was no record of him renting that house, or why he was murdered. It had nothing to do with her.

Except Marley. He'd made sure she'd be notified if anyone found his dog. A dog that he could turn loose if he expected trouble. Could he have hoped that Marley would be found and she'd be notified before his message came from beyond the grave?

She rubbed her neck, trying to smooth the prickling sensation. The exit appeared, and she stopped for gas at the all-night gas station. While her car was filling up, she asked the clerk, an older Native American, for directions to the Kéyah site.

"You one of the students?" he asked.

"Students?"

"The university is always sending students to work up there. A steady stream of them. They don't seem to stay very long." He shook his head. "Pretty smart if you think about it. Not just free labor. The students actually pay to be part of the dig." He pulled out a copy of a hand-drawn map. "Here's what I give anyone who asks. The university made these up." With a grubby finger he traced the route she had to take. "Lots of potholes and dry washes. And it's been raining off and on. You got a truck or four-wheel drive?"

"I'll be okay." She tried not to think of her clean little Audi grinding up the dirt roads.

He grunted. "Just take it slow."

She purchased an extra-large cup of scalding coffee. It

smelled old, so she doctored it up with sugar and powdered creamer. It turned grayish-brown, confirming her original assessment. Map and coffee in hand, she joined Marley in the car. The dog greeted her as if she'd been gone for a week, then settled back onto the seat.

On her way, the light sprinkling of rain turned into a steady downpour. In several places, a small stream crossed the road, and the potholes were filling with water, making it hard to gauge their depth. She crawled along for several hours. The rapidly cooling cup of brew she bolted down made her hands shake and heart race, but at least she was wide-awake.

Daybreak arrived with a gradual shift from black to gray, revealing red-and-cream-colored rolling hills with scruffy vegetation between the rounded rocks. The rain was constant now. The road was little more than a worn-down track with water streaming down each side. She was about to stop and turn around when she crested a small rise and saw two vehicles, an SUV and pickup with the university's logo on the side, perched beside several tents and covered areas.

Tavish switched off the lights, put the car into park, and turned off the engine. Marley sat up and looked around. "Oh boy. Now what?" She checked her watch. "I can't exactly go barreling into camp demanding answers. And they're probably not going to be in any hurry to get up in this rain."

With the engine off, the interior cooled rapidly. In the distance, a gas-powered generator rumbled softly.

She shivered in the dampness.

Marley crawled into her lap.

Tavish hugged the dog, feeling her warmth. "Just for now,

little buddy. We can't make this a habit." Shifting her weight to find a comfortable angle in the bucket seat, she closed her eyes.

Bang, bang, bang!

She jumped. Marley barked furiously at the window next to her. A man stood beside the car. The rain had stopped, and tepid sunshine peeked through the windows. She unlocked the door, leaped from the car, and faced the man.

"You!" they both said in unison.

The man from the gallery, the one who'd said those nasty things about her art, stood in front of her—with a pistol.

She sucked in air and put up her hands. "Don't shoot."

He gave her a slight smile.

Her face burned.

He tucked the pistol into his waistband and glanced down. Marley danced around him on her hind legs, giving him a doggy grin.

Tavish put her hands down. "Traitor," she muttered at the dog.

"Miss McTavish." The man scratched the dancing Puli. "What are *you* doing here?"

"You know my name."

"I asked." He folded his arms. "What are you *doing* here?"

"I should ask you the same thing." She shoved the wisps of hair from her face. She'd kill for a cup of coffee . . . and a toothbrush.

"I work here. I'm an archaeologist. Your turn."

Why does he have to look so good? Even needing a shave and with tousled hair, he was stop-dead-in-your-tracks-and-stare handsome.

"Answer?"

She realized she was gawking at him. "Um . . . question?"

"What, Miss McTavish, are you doing here at the Kéyah site?"

"I'm trying to find some answers about the murder of John Coyote. I believe he has an associate here, a Pat Caron."

The man straightened. "John Coyote? Murder?"

"Yes. It's just, well, his body is missing. I'm trying to locate someone who knew him. Maybe a girlfriend. Or Pat. He might corroborate my story."

The man looked behind him at one of the tents. "When did this happen?"

"Yesterday. I think."

"I see." He furrowed his brow. "She's never mentioned a John Coyote to me."

Now it was Tavish's turn to frown. "She?"

"Professor Patricia Caron, PhD. She's in charge of this dig. Did you want to meet her?"

"Yes. John said he visits Pat out here a lot. I need her to help me prove—"

"A lot?"

Tavish tried to think back to her last conversation with John. "Most recently just a few weeks ago, I think."

The man shook his head and shoved his hands in his pockets, then turned toward the tents. "Well, I hate to break it to you, but I've been working at this site for months, and I've never met anyone named John Coyote in that time."

CHAPTER 9

Sawyer Price had risen at his usual early hour and stepped out of his tent. He spotted the dusty white car immediately. He returned to his tent, picked up his Glock and tucked it into his elastic bellyband, then quietly approached the vehicle.

He'd broken the news to the professor that his investigation here at the Kéyah site was over. The brief flurry of thefts came under the jurisdiction of both the Native American police as well as the FBI. Once he'd shown up, even though undercover, the thefts had stopped. Something still nagged at him about the entire setup, and he'd been hypervigilant because of it. He hoped the unexpected appearance of the car was just another lost scholar looking for the graduate-student campsite.

He'd pulled out his Glock and tapped on the tinted window. When Evelyn McTavish had leaped from the car, his mouth dropped. *Now that's what I call a great early-morning wake-up call.*

Wisps of hair floated around her face, her clothes were wrinkled, and her lips held a slight bluish tinge from the cold.

She was trembling slightly in the early-morning air. Now, as he led her toward the site, he said, "We'll figure this out. Let's get you warmed up and some breakfast in you."

She didn't argue when he lightly touched her elbow to guide her to the campsite. The meal tent was fifteen by twenty feet, open-sided, and held the food and cooking supplies. Several resin folding tables and chairs were scattered about, and blue plastic water containers were stacked at one end. Quickly he filled the enamelware percolator with coffee and water, then set it on the freestanding propane cookstove. While the coffee brewed, he retrieved a jacket from his tent and brought it to her. "I'm Sawyer Price, by the way."

"Thank you, Mr. Price." She pulled it on.

"Call me Sawyer."

"If you call me Tavish. Stupid of me to forget a warm coat."

The coffee finished brewing and he poured two cups. "This is my special coffee, shipped in from Germany. Cream? Sugar?"

"Black is fine." She wrapped her hands around the mug as if absorbing the heat.

"You drove all the way out here to investigate a murder? I thought you were an artist."

"I am."

"Why didn't you tell the police?"

"I did. But . . . well, it's complicated." She sipped the coffee. "This is good."

"I told you so. Tell me about your homicide."

"Oh my. Murder?" A slender, gray-haired woman entered the tent. She wore khaki slacks, a thick overcoat over a salmon-colored sweater, and hiking boots. A leopard-print scarf encircled her neck. She smiled, adding a dozen more wrinkles to her well-lined face.

"Professor Caron, this is Evelyn McTavish." Sawyer poured the woman a cup of coffee. "Tavish, meet Dr. Caron."

Patricia took the chair across the table from Tavish and leaned forward. "This makes for an interesting start to the day. Who's dead?"

Tavish blushed but explained the microchip, discovery of John's body, Fake Cop, missing Kevin, reappearing car, and home break-in. Patricia propped her elbows on the table and rested her chin on her hands. Every so often she'd shake her head.

Sawyer pulled eggs, bacon, and butter from the portable refrigerator. Marley had decided he held more promise for handouts and was sitting beside the camp stove. He dropped the dog a day-old biscuit.

Tavish finished and slumped in her chair. "I know this all sounds crazy—"

"Some of it sounds decidedly singular." Patricia straightened, took a sip of coffee, then cleared her throat. "You said this John Coyote claimed he worked at this dig and was an archaeologist, a peer of mine. Why did he tell you that?"

Tavish explained the commissioned art. "At our last meeting we met at his house in the Tijeras Canyon. He pointed to some photos on the wall of the Kéyah site and said he wanted to—how did he put it?—'weave some of his past into the negative space.'" She made quotes in the air. "He couldn't decide what he wanted, so eventually he asked to hold on to the preliminary drawing so he could ponder it. He paid me in full."

"I see. Describe his home."

"Pueblo Revival–style."

Dr. Caron nodded. "Was the address of the house 75644 Loco Drive?"

"Yes, but how—"

"I own that place." The older woman frowned. "Your description sounded similar, and the photos on the wall were the final clue." She glanced at Sawyer, then back at Tavish. "When I started this project, I secured an agency to rent it out for me. I had no idea this all would take close to two years. For the past couple of months, I haven't even had a tenant. I should have just sold it."

"So you think Coyote found your empty house and moved in, made up a story?" Sawyer added bacon to the sizzling cast-iron pan, filling the tent with mouthwatering fragrance. "I want to think about that some more." He put a lid on the spattering bacon. "What about the man Tavish said was outside the house when she went back to check? The one with the mustache?"

"I don't know. Could be a neighbor. You didn't actually see him in the house, did you?" Patricia took a sip of coffee as Tavish shook her head.

"I'm glad at least one part of this mystery has a logical answer," Tavish said. "But what about the murder? The microchip with my name on it? Kevin's disappearance? What could they be looking for at my house? And what about—"

Sawyer placed a plate of bacon, eggs, and hash browns in front of her. "What about some breakfast?" He placed a second plate in front of Patricia.

"I'm vegan," Tavish said softly.

"Not today." Sawyer joined them with a mound of food. "Dig in."

Tavish tried to smile at him. "I appreciate all the work you went through to cook this. I'll just grab a bite to eat on my way home—"

"Not today." Patricia touched her mouth with a napkin. "All that rain last night will have flooded the road."

Sawyer grinned at Tavish's expression. "You're stuck here until things dry out, which should be sometime tomorrow."

"Tomorrow?" Tavish grew pale.

"Yep." He took a bite of bacon.

Tavish picked up her fork. "Maybe I will eat the hash browns..."

"Cooked in butter. Yum." He grinned at her. Even looking cold and tired, she was the best bit of landscape he'd seen since coming to New Mexico.

She slowly lowered her fork.

Patricia reached over and rapped him on the arm. "Stop torturing the poor girl. I think we have some fruit, and she can lie down on my cot and catch up on some sleep. I'm sure her car wasn't that comfortable to nap in."

He was about to protest his innocence, but the look of gratitude on Tavish's face shut him up. "Fine. We talk more about the murder when you get up, okay, Tavish?"

She nodded, then yawned.

"Come along." Patricia popped the last piece of bacon into her mouth, stood, and motioned to Tavish. "If that walking black mop over there is your dog, bring her too."

Patricia reached into the small refrigerator, pulled out an apple, and handed it to Tavish. Grabbing her purse, Tavish followed Patricia toward the professor's personal tent. Tavish devoured the apple before they arrived.

Sawyer stood and started cleaning the breakfast dishes. Shortly Patricia returned, helping herself to another cup of coffee. "What do you think of her story?"

He left the dishes soaking in a bucket of hot water, dumped the last of the coffee into his cup, and joined her at the table. "I don't know what to think."

"We have today to try and sort it out. None of the students and volunteers will be able to get up the road to work. The ground is too wet even if they could."

"I figured as much."

"This will delay your departure as well." Patricia smiled at him. "I can't say that's a bad thing. I enjoy your cooking . . . and your company."

"In that order?" He smiled back. The sun made a brief appearance through a break in the clouds and just as quickly disappeared. The scent of some flowering desert plant perfumed the air.

"I didn't ask you how it went in Albuquerque."

"The business card was to a real art gallery, and the clerk there easily could have been providing drugs to the students. I spotted someone from the drug task force watching him, though, so I backed off until I can talk to them."

"You didn't arrest the clerk for selling drugs?"

He patted her hand. "Not my jurisdiction. Only in certain cases does the FBI step in. But as far as the sting operation here and stolen artifacts, that gallery business card seems to be a dead end. No sign of any Anasazi pottery, either legal or stolen." He stood. "I did widen my search and came up with a few cases I'd like you to look at. See if any of the recovered items could be related to this site." He headed to his car and pulled out his briefcase, then returned to the tent. He placed the briefcase on the table and removed a few case files containing photographs.

She took the photos from him and studied each one, finally setting two on the side. "These are possibilities. Where are they from?"

"About three or four weeks ago there was a shootout up in the Four Corners section of New Mexico. The thief was killed. Several stolen paintings were recovered and those two pieces of pottery. The timing is about right. The paintings were returned, but no one had circulated the pottery photos until a few days ago. They just came across my desk. The thief was killed, so if he was fencing these for someone else, I have yet another dead end, if you pardon the expression."

Dr. Caron nodded. "I suppose I should be grateful that the stealing has stopped."

Sawyer leaned back in his chair and drummed his nails on the table for a moment.

"What are you pondering?"

"I was just thinking about the strange coincidence that a business card would lead me to that gallery, where I'd meet Tavish, who *just happened* to see a murdered man in your house. I don't believe in coincidences."

"What are you going to do?"

"Quite frankly, there's not a darn thing I can do. Everything Tavish told us is a matter for the local police."

"Who don't seem to be all that interested."

"Unfortunately. But once again, I can't just jump into something that isn't my jurisdiction without an invitation. At this point I'm mopping up loose ends on this case unless something else turns up. I've checked out almost all the students who've worked here in the last eight months. I'm finishing that in the next day or so. The only fenced pieces positively identified have been recovered, and the scumbag is enjoying the view of his jail cell." He held up the photos. "I'll put out an inquiry on these two pieces and see what shows up."

They were silent for a few moments. A coyote yipped in the distance.

Patricia jerked her thumb toward her tent. "Do you think she might be . . . unstable?"

He thought about her actions at the gallery. "Not unstable. Under a lot of stress."

"She's wearing a crystal. It could be just jewelry, but she might be into some New Age stuff. Conspiracy theories, Elvis sightings, and maybe she thinks the rest is alien abductions."

He grinned at her. "You're kidding. All that from just a necklace?"

"Don't you ever listen to late-night radio? Ask her about the crystal at any rate."

"I will."

She straightened in her chair. "*If* she's unstable, could she be dangerous?"

He patted Pat's arm. "Unless that dog is a Rottweiler in disguise, no, I don't think she's dangerous. But just to reassure you, I'll check out her car while she's sleeping."

Patricia gave him a quick grin. "Can you do that legally?"

"Probable cause? I'll figure out something."

"Thanks. I'll be in the work tent if you need me." She headed toward the largest of the structures at the campsite where she kept her notes, research, maps, computer, and other equipment. All recovered artifacts were recorded, photographed, and kept locked up and away from the actual excavation. The stolen artifacts were not taken from the formally recovered items, which were so carefully documented. They'd been looted from the periphery of several established archaeological sites.

He still hadn't figured out how the looted items had been transported from the individual sites without being detected.

He thought about Tavish's odd story for a moment. *Jurisdiction or not . . .* He took out a small notepad, opened it, and jotted down *Do a background check on John Coyote. And Evelyn McTavish.*

Sawyer stood, finished washing the dishes, then sauntered to Tavish's Audi. Though now covered in dust, it appeared she usually kept it immaculate. She'd also left it unlocked.

A crime-scene team would be able to fingerprint, vacuum, sweep, photograph, and go over every square inch of the car. He didn't have that luxury. He found the bullet hole in the bumper as she'd described. No sign of the bullet inside the car, but the trunk had scuff marks and a dirty area, also as she'd pointed out. Inside the car, he searched under the seats, opened the glove box, and pulled out the contents. Her registration and insurance form, service record, and receipts were neatly arranged in a leather book . . . but the registration card was upside down in its plastic window. He replaced everything.

On a hunch, he ran his hand under the dashboard. His fingers swiftly discovered a tiny tracking device. "Well, well, well." He removed it and placed it in his pocket.

So far her story checked out. Of course, she could have come up with the details to match the evidence. But someone wanted to know where she was going. It might be interesting to see who showed up. The tracking device wouldn't work here, but it would resume once off the mountain.

The sun burst through the clouds, spotlighting the surrounding hills and painting them red under cloud-shaped Prussian-blue shadows. A light breeze rustled the pale yellow grasses. At this rate the water would rapidly recede off the road—a fact he planned on keeping from Tavish.

He had a lot of questions he needed to ask her.

CHAPTER 10

Tavish gradually opened her eyes, then blinked. The ceiling overhead was moving. *No, it's not a ceiling. It's fabric. A tent.* And she was . . . on a cot, a ridiculously hard cot. Groaning as she shoved out of the bed, she tried to orient herself.

Marley pranced over and barked sharply once.

Of course. The dog. John's body. The missing Kevin. Patricia. The campsite. Sawyer.

Sawyer.

She reached up and touched her hair, then groaned again. The rain had frizzed her hair into a mop worthy of a Puli. If her hair weren't blond, no one would be able to tell them apart. Her breath would probably drop a fly, and her twenty-four-hour deodorant was on hour twenty-eight.

Wait a minute. Why should she care what she looked or smelled like? Sawyer was a cretin when it came to art. Who was *he* to judge her?

And he'd waved a pistol in her face. How many archaeologists were armed?

There are snakes in the desert. It's probably for that.

At any rate, he needed a shave, was dusty, rude, and . . . and . . . there was probably something else wrong with him.

She checked out Patricia's tent. The older woman slept on a canvas cot hard enough to satisfy an ascetic monk. Opposite the bed, a folding table held a large water container, a thermos, several notebooks, a blue enamel coffee cup filled with a collection of pens and pencils, and a laptop. A storage container at the foot of her bed contained neatly folded clothing and underwear. *Snoop.* She quickly closed the lid, then did a series of stretching exercises to work out the kinks.

A mirror attached to a tent pole showed just how bad her hair had gone. She found several tortoiseshell hair clips in the bottom of her purse and fastened the wilder strands off her face. Calling Marley over, she clipped the dog's topknot back from her eyes. As Tavish left the tent, she pulled Sawyer's jacket over her shoulders. It felt good, even if its owner was a cretin.

Billowy clouds punctuated the lapis-blue sky, and the rain had scrubbed the air clean and perfumed it with sage. She took a deep breath, admiring the view across the mountains. She hadn't really been on any kind of road trip since . . . She shook her head.

Marley examined the ground, finally selecting a spot to relieve herself.

No one was in sight, but a portable blue plastic outhouse was tucked into the hillside. Once finished, Tavish climbed slightly higher above the camp to an east-west ridge. Just beyond was the actual archaeological project. Plastic tarps had been placed in several areas, apparently in anticipation of the rain. A canopy in one corner covered a table and a line of five-gallon plastic buckets. Sawyer had strategically placed one bucket at the edge of the canopy and was pushing the tarp upward to empty the collected rainwater. His aim was nearly perfect and he partially filled the bucket. He spotted her. "How'd you sleep?"

"Well, thank you. Do you think the road's clear enough so I can leave?"

"Do you see any students?"

"No."

"Then the water is still dangerously high." He picked up the bucket and approached. "We tell the students to stay away after a rain. Just six inches of water can sweep you off your feet, and a foot of water can float your car. Heaven help you if you're in a slot canyon or dry riverbed."

He'd reached her by this time. He'd shaved and combed his hair. He grinned, flashing white teeth against the deep tan of his face.

She put her hands behind her back and pulled on a hangnail. The sting made her eyes water.

Strolling past her, he headed for the kitchen tent. "We've a little extra water here if you'd like to clean up."

I do stink. Tavish cupped her hand over her mouth and blew, then sniffed.

"Your breath is fine," he said without stopping or turning around.

Her face burned. There was no way he could have seen or heard her.

She waited until he'd reached the kitchen area before

following. Without asking, he filled a water bottle from one of the large containers and brought it to her. "We're over six thousand feet here. Dehydration and altitude sickness are always a problem."

"I see you're up," Patricia said as she entered. Sawyer handed her a glass of water as well. The two of them exchanged glances.

Great. They've been talking about me and are convinced I'm a nut. Her face continued to feel warm.

"I checked your car." Sawyer took a chair near her. "You do have a bullet hole in the bumper, and I saw the other things you mentioned. I assume you usually put your registration and proof of insurance in the holder so they can be easily read."

She stared at him. "You had no right to be snooping in my car." *While I snooped in Pat's storage locker.* She looked down so he couldn't see her face.

"Tavish, we are in the middle of nowhere"—Sawyer leaned forward—"without cell service or any way to contact people, and you show up with a strange story about missing bodies, missing people, missing cars . . . We had to check you out as best we could."

She raised her head, slipped her hands below the table, and dug at a nail. He leaned forward and placed a small black plastic rectangle on the table in front of her. "I did find this."

"What is it?"

"A portable, real-time GPS tracker."

She nudged it with her finger. "Is this like some kind of spy—"

"No. You can pick one up on Amazon quite easily." He turned it over so she could see the display. "Shows location on a map and coordinates. Someone wanted to know where you were going. Any ideas?"

Mother. That was the kind of thing she'd do. Not that Helen cared what happened to her, but she wouldn't want Tavish to embarrass the family name. The other possibility chilled her. Kevin. Or whoever took Kevin.

"How long has it been in my car?"

"That's hard to say. You probably would have seen it the next time you vacuumed the floor. When did you last clean your car?"

"Technically I don't clean my car. I have it cleaned every week." *By Mother's staff—easy enough to plant a tracker.*

"Well? Any ideas?"

"I'd guess whoever took Kevin and returned my car." *Don't mention Mother.* She kept her gaze on the tracking device so Sawyer couldn't see she was lying.

"I see." He placed it in his pocket. "It won't work up here, so you're safe from whoever is needing to keep an eye on you."

Tavish looked up in time to see Patricia glance at Sawyer, then back at her. The man leaned away and rubbed his chin, then shook his head briefly. Patricia cleared her throat. "That's a pretty necklace you have. What's the stone?"

Tavish held up the minty-green and lavender crystal. "Fluorite."

"Does it have any meaning?"

"Well . . . it harmonizes spiritual energy and can assist the upper chakras to link the mind to universal consciousness . . ."

Patricia and Sawyer had exchanged glances again.

Great. They didn't believe in, or understand, the power of crystals.

A dog barked in the distance.

Marley. She'd forgotten to watch the dog. Jumping from the chair, she rushed outside. "Marley? Marley!"

The Puli appeared briefly at the entrance to Patricia's tent, then disappeared back inside.

Patricia and Sawyer joined her, then the three of them entered the tent.

Marley danced around on her hind legs, her attention on the table.

"I'm sorry." Tavish picked up the dog. "I should have been watching her. She's looking at the water container, so I'd bet she's thirsty. She's probably hungry as well."

Patricia zipped her tent shut after they left, then headed toward the outhouse.

While Marley slurped down a bowl of water, Tavish stared at the photos of the recovered pottery. "What's this?"

"Nothing. Just some photos of a case—"

"Case? I thought you were an archaeologist."

"Not quite. I'm an agent with the FBI—"

"FBI?" The words were a whisper. "Then you're like all the others who don't believe me." She rose from the table, but Sawyer caught her wrist.

"No, Tavish, I'm not like the others. I believe you."

His hand was warm. His touch shot up her arm, making her catch her breath.

"I've been working undercover here for several weeks." He let go.

She slowly sank back into her seat, placing her hand over her wrist to preserve his touch. "If your being here is a secret, why are you telling me?"

"My work here is over." He patted the case files on the table. "The rest of this is follow-up."

Her gaze drifted toward the files, then sharpened. She picked up a file.

"Sorry." Sawyer tried to take it from her. "Those are law-enforcement sensitive—"

"Why do you have this one?" She held up the file.

"Why are you asking?"

"The paintings."

"What?"

"The stolen artwork. My mother."

"Tavish, you're not making sense." He reached for the file again.

She placed it on the table. "About five months ago my mother, Helen Richmond, had three paintings stolen. A gardener was killed. The paintings were recovered after a shootout with the thief. So why do you have this file?"

Sawyer stared at her. "Helen Richmond is your mother? I didn't make the connection."

"She's been married a few times," Tavish said dryly.

"I see." He tapped his upper lip with a finger. "Connections. Not coincidence."

"Now *you're* not making any sense."

"Probably not. Tavish, somehow this dig, stolen artifacts, Dr. Caron, John Coyote, and you are all connected. Why do you think John Coyote put your name on the dog's microchip?"

"I don't know. I hardly knew him. At the time, everything seemed normal—I'm commissioned for a painting, I meet with the patron a few times, create the preliminary sketch—"

He snapped his fingers. "That's it!"

"What's it?"

"You're an artist—"

"How quickly you forget."

"Draw him. Them. Do a sketch of John Coyote, then one of the fake cop, and one of Kevin."

"Why?"

"Identification. It's a place to start."

"Start?"

He reached over and lifted up the file on the shootout. "As of now, the FBI is officially interested in your case."

"Then you'll help me find out who killed—"

"Correction. I will investigate. You will steer clear."

She stared at him for a moment. *Just like Detective Mullins. Stay out of police business. Steer clear.* She looked down at her fingers and poked at a cuticle. Easy for him to say. But she was the one with a stray dog, a bullet in her bumper, and a tracking device in her car. This was way too personal to steer clear.

CHAPTER 11

The sun was sinking on the horizon, casting deep blue shadows across the rusty orange of the mountains, before Sawyer finished up his final on-site report to the SAC—Special Agent in Charge. He'd left Tavish at the meal tent working on her sketches.

Standing, he thought about going for a run to shake off the excess energy. *Don't kid yourself. You want to run to get Tavish off your mind.*

Focus. He needed internet access to look up some background information, but he thought he'd written a compelling supplemental update as to why the FBI needed to expand the investigation to include Tavish's information. Once back in Albuquerque, he'd personally hand it over to the SAC.

"Thank you for the rains, Lord. They kept Tavish up here long enough for me to get this lead. And thank you for Tavish," he whispered.

He headed to the dining tent to start dinner. He'd fallen into the habit of cooking for the professor and an occasional grad student after experiencing Patricia's culinary skills.

He found Tavish still bent over a table, sketchbook in front of her. She'd already completed two drawings. He picked one up and studied the face. "Which one is this?"

"John Coyote."

"He looks Native American. Maybe Navajo."

"That's what I thought when I first met him." She continued to draw. She'd french braided her hair, but wisps had escaped two tortoiseshell clips and floated around her face. Marley, lying at her feet, wore matching clips. A smattering of light freckles crossed Tavish's nose and cheeks. She'd removed the jacket and sweater and now wore a pale-pink tank, exposing slender, tanned arms.

He tore his gaze from her and pulled three steaks out of the refrigerator. Vegan or not, she wouldn't be able to resist his herb-butter-basted, pan-seared ribeye steak. After chucking three cleaned potatoes in the camp oven, he assembled the salad. Without looking at her, he asked, "Where did you learn to draw like that?"

"Growing up, I had tutors. One of them was also an artist."

"You didn't go to private school?"

"I didn't go to school at all. I had asthma and a mess of food allergies, so I spent a lot of time getting shots and medications, seeing doctors . . ." She shrugged. "I finally just outgrew it."

"That's a blessing."

"My grandmother used to say the same thing."

He glanced at her. Her eyes glittered with unshed tears.

He wanted to take her into his arms, hold her tight, and whisper everything would be fine. Instead, he returned to chopping tomatoes. "You mentioned John took your preliminary sketch and paid you in full, but canceled the painting. Why do you think he canceled?"

"At the time, I thought he was undecided as to what he wanted and didn't want to keep me on hold. Hopefully it wasn't because he didn't like my artwork."

"I think you're a terrific artist."

Her cheeks grew pink. "Thank you. After your reaction to the elephant leg at the gallery, I kinda thought you didn't care much for my drawings."

"I bought that drawing."

She stared at him, mouth open, cheeks now flaming red.

The urge to kiss her grew. He cleared his throat. "How did he pay you?"

"Cash."

He busied himself covering and placing the assembled salad, minus the dressing, into the refrigerator, then sat across the table from her. "How did you meet? Gallery?"

"No. This was before I had a showing. I met him at one of my mother's frequent soirees a couple of months ago."

"So your mother knew him?"

"I assumed so. She invites what she calls 'interesting' people to these get-togethers. Usually for a cause. Or business profit." She pushed a piece of paper across the table to him. "Here's Kevin. I already drew the fake cop and sent the scan of it to the police."

Sawyer studied the drawing. She'd neatly written Kevin's name under the sketch. The FBI taught that most people remember only four to five facial features. If John and Kevin were simply a figment of her imagination, why did they have such detail? She hadn't drawn the faces like a typical composite—facing forward—but rather as if they'd been caught unposed in a moment of time. She had another drawing in her sketchpad. "Who's that?"

"It's . . . it was my fiancé."

A weight settled in his stomach. His gaze shot toward her left hand. "I didn't know you were engaged."

"I'm not. Not anymore. He died."

"I'm sorry."

She bit her lip, tore out the sketch, and crumpled it up.

Sawyer raised his eyebrows. "Not such a good memory?"

"I drew this some time ago. Before . . . well, before." She stood and dropped the drawing into a garbage container, then returned to her seat.

After tapping a finger against his lips, he finally asked, "Did you talk to John while he was sitting for you?"

"Some." She took the three drawings and placed them into her sketchpad.

"What about?"

She leaned back in her chair and absently played with a kneaded rubber eraser. "A lot about art. Some crafts—"

"What kind of crafts?"

"Woodworking. He smelled of turpentine once and that started the conversation. Marley, of course. Living in New Mexico. Helen."

He hesitated. "Why do you call your mom by her first name?"

"That's how I think of her. We aren't close."

Patricia strolled in and greeted them. The professor moved to a side table, opened a bottle of red wine, and poured three glasses. She handed one to Sawyer, then brought the other two to the table. "Cheers."

Tavish raised her glass.

"You set out three steaks," Patricia said to Sawyer. "Hoping to convert our young vegan here?"

Tavish choked and began coughing.

He stepped over and patted her on the back. "Who knows?" He liked the warmth of her skin through the thin shirt. He realized she'd stopped coughing but he was still stroking her back. Patricia gave him a pointed look and he snatched his hand away. "Maybe she hasn't been a vegan long and is apt to fall off the wagon."

"I changed my diet shortly after my grandmother passed away." She absently pulled a Band-Aid off her finger and began to nibble on the nail.

"When did you become interested in crystals?" Patricia asked.

"Around the same time."

Conversation ceased while he prepared the meal. He watched Tavish out of the corner of his eye. As the sun dipped, the temperature dropped. She pulled on her sweater, then the jacket he had loaned her. A light breeze spread the aroma of grilled steak around the tent.

Without asking, he prepared all three plates with a baked potato slathered in butter and a steak next to it. He placed dinner in front of Patricia and Tavish, then set the salad on the table. Bowing his head, he said a silent grace, adding a prayer for Tavish.

Tavish was staring at him when he looked up. "You're religious?"

"I have a relationship. A walk."

Frowning, she stared at her steak. Her stomach let out an emphatic rumble. Two red spots appeared on her cheeks. She picked up a fork, then put it down. Marley whined at her feet, then licked her chops loudly.

He ignored her and sliced off a chunk of meat, shoving it into his mouth. As he slowly chewed, the heavenly flavor made his own stomach growl.

She glanced at him, looked away, then burst out laughing. Her mirth was contagious.

He joined her.

Patricia looked back and forth between the two of them, shrugged, and continued her meal.

Tavish sliced a sliver of meat and tasted it. She closed her eyes and slowly chewed. The next bite was larger. And the one after that. "You were right. It's a good thing I didn't promise myself I'd stay a vegan. I never break my promises."

By the time they'd finished dinner, the sun had retired over the mountains, and the high-desert, evening chill penetrated his khaki shirt. Before cleaning up, he retrieved a spare coat.

"I'll help you clean up," Tavish said.

He shook his head. "Better yet, over there is a fire pit. Firewood's nearby, and matches should be in a tin by the log." She strolled away, hugging his jacket around her slight frame.

He scrubbed grease off the skillet. *Lord, please direct my steps.*

She screamed.

He tore over to where she'd started building the fire. She was standing on a log, hands over her mouth, sucking in air. She pointed.

A scorpion peeked out from under a piece of firewood.

Reaching over, he grabbed the shovel kept by the fire pit, used the shovel to flip away the firewood, and smashed the scorpion into a pancake.

"I hate bugs, and snakes, and especially scorpions!" Tavish allowed him to help her down. She trembled in his arms. He wanted to leave them around her, but she stepped away.

"That little guy was a striped-tail scorpion. His sting would hurt like crazy, but not kill you. Not like a bark scorpion, which can be deadly."

"I hope I never have to know the difference."

He reluctantly returned to the dishes.

⇒⇐

After Tavish built the fire, she tried to regret the steak she'd wolfed down, but she had to admit it was the tastiest thing she'd eaten in some time. So much for concentrating on a healthy lifestyle. Marley had gobbled down a few scraps, then sat up and begged for more. *Wait!* Would table scraps upset the dog's digestion? Would she puke all night and get the squirts?

Tavish reached down and touched the dog currently sprawled across her feet. "Well, Marley, now what?" she whispered. "Forget I saw a dead man? That an empty house once held a man named Kevin who stole my car, then returned it? That someone broke into my home?"

She stared at the shifting flames. Sawyer believed her, but everyone else thought she was delusional.

A tiny voice in her mind whispered, *Prove them wrong.*

"You built a great fire." Patricia joined her. "Do you camp out often?"

"No. I watched a television show on survival in the wilderness. It showed how to construct a campfire."

"What, if you don't mind my asking, do you do for a living? Is your art full time?"

Tavish held out her hands to the flames to warm them. "It is now. Or was. I . . . had an accounting company."

"Did you sell it?"

"No. I just . . . stepped away." Tavish tugged on her necklace.

Patricia cleared her throat. "Have you ever heard about or listened to Dusty Rhodes on the radio?"

"Is that a place, show, or person?"

"Person. I would guess the answer is no."

"Correct. Why did you ask?"

She nodded at Tavish's crystal necklace. "He talks about crystals—their healing power—and a lot of other topics on his late-night call-in show."

"How do you know about him? He doesn't sound exactly . . . scholarly."

Patricia smiled. "He's fun to listen to when I'm driving up here late at night. I was first turned on to his show when he called me about this dig. Wanted to know more about it for a show. I answered his questions, but when he aired that segment, I was stunned. It was all about spirits of the dead haunting this place, causing mischief, taking things, scaring the students. I got angry, but it turned out the show brought in extra funding for our work. Who'd have thought?"

"Is it?"

"Is what?" Patricia asked.

"Is the Kéyah site haunted?"

The professor indicated Tavish's necklace. "I'm sorry, my dear. I don't believe in such things. Crystals, hauntings, or even that God that Sawyer prays to."

Tavish gave her a half smile and focused on the fire. "So what is around here? What are you digging up?"

"This is one of the Ancestral Puebloan, or Anasazi, sites, roughly from the twelfth century BC. It's a newly discovered location and relatively unknown. The Anasazi vanished suddenly, at least from sites like this."

Tavish looked around. "Is that why people think this place is haunted?"

Patricia shifted and chewed her lip for a moment. "No. It's because of the discovery here that was a bit like the excavation at Cowboy Wash."

"Cowboy Wash?"

"In Colorado. Twelve human skeletons were recovered, five of them buried. The remaining seven showed signs of cannibalism. We found two sets of skeletons here showing the same signs."

A small shiver coursed through Tavish. "Cannibalism?"

Patricia patted her knee. "The more important finds here are not so ghoulish. Mostly pottery and a few tools."

"So they must be valuable to have an FBI agent investigating the thefts."

"Important enough."

=≡=

Tavish had the fire blazing by the time Sawyer finished washing the dishes. He poured two paper cups of wine and brought them over. Patricia had joined Tavish by the fire, which was unusual. The older woman generally spent the evenings working on her project. It was almost as if . . . he needed a chaperone.

Maybe I do. Tavish was staring at the flames, one hand cupping her chin, the other poking the blaze with a stick. More wisps of her blond hair had escaped their clips and swirled around her head like a halo. Her skin was a flawless warm beige, with peach highlights on her cheeks.

He sucked in his breath.

Patricia glanced at him, then moved closer to Tavish as if to make room for him.

He grinned at her, then moved to the other side of Tavish and squeezed onto the log. Both women slid over. "Nice fire, Tavish."

Patricia stood. "Well, I tried. Be careful, my friend." She headed for her tent.

"What was that all about?" Tavish asked.

"Patricia can be a little . . . motherly at times." He handed the young woman a cup of wine.

"I wouldn't know." She poked at the fire, sending sparks dancing into the air, then sipped the wine.

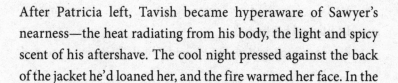

After Patricia left, Tavish became hyperaware of Sawyer's nearness—the heat radiating from his body, the light and spicy scent of his aftershave. The cool night pressed against the back of the jacket he'd loaned her, and the fire warmed her face. In the distance a pair of coyotes yip-howled. Marley sat up and looked at her. "No. Coyotes would look at you like Hungarian goulash. You don't need to check it out."

The dog lay back down.

She placed the wine cup beside her on the log. *What would I do if Sawyer put his arm around me?* The thought made her heart speed up. She started to pick at a hangnail. He caught her hand and gently stroked it. His touch was like warm liquid running up her arm and over her body. He carefully placed her hand back on her lap.

She offered him her other hand.

He turned it over, brought it to his lips, and kissed her palm.

Her mind went blank. The night disappeared. There was only Sawyer. This was what it felt like. Excitement. Joy. Anticipation. Love. She'd felt only . . . gratitude with Andy. He'd found her attractive—or so she had thought at the time. She hoped this moment with Sawyer would continue forever.

Marley jumped up and danced in front of her on her hind legs.

Sawyer let go of her hand. "I think someone is jealous."

"Maybe *I'll* turn someone into Hungarian goulash," she muttered.

Sawyer stood and added another log to the fire.

She folded her arms.

He sat and nodded toward her hands. "When did you start doing that?"

"My fiancé . . . Andrew James . . . um . . . died. He committed suicide. I found his body."

"But you don't believe he killed himself." His eyes seemed

to reach inside her head, exposing thoughts she'd spent the last month burying.

She looked away. "I believed he was murdered. At first."

"What changed your mind?"

She glanced at him, then stared at the flames. She'd built a wall around Andrew's memory. Mentally she added yet another brick, then deliberately studied the fire. *I'm okay.*

After a few moments he asked, "What are you thinking?"

"Do you really want to know?"

"Yes."

She pointed. "I was thinking the way those logs cross each other makes it look like Gumby playing a Rickenbacker bass."

"So you've built a wall around Andrew's memory?"

Her face burned. How could he have known that?

He cleared his throat. "It just looks like burning logs to me."

Much safer topic. "Don't you ever lie on your back, look at the clouds, and see things?"

"Things?"

She waved her hand upward. "Patterns? Animals, people, shapes?"

"Not really."

"I see shapes, patterns, faces, animals everywhere. In swirling marble on the floor, rock formations against a hill, even in a patch of dead grass."

"And you find unusual things to draw, like elephant legs."

She nodded.

Sawyer turned slightly and raised his eyebrows. "Is it because you're an artist?"

She stared at him. The firelight lit up half his face in warm oranges and gold, accentuating his strong jaw and cheek.

He grinned. "Yes?"

"And . . . um . . . I forgot what I wanted to say."

"Something about being an artist?"

"Oh, right. We study negative shapes."

"Negative?" He leaned closer to her. "That doesn't sound good. Are you going to tell me you're into feng shui?"

His nearness seemed to thin the air. She took in a deep breath. "Not in a metaphysical sense. John Coyote and I had this conversation, and he gave me a great illustration." She held up her hand. "My hand is a positive shape. The negative space is the shape between my fingers. If I focus on the negative space, I will always draw the positive shape correctly." She pointed at a shrub nearby. "Most people would look at the pattern formed by the leaves. I look for the pattern both in the leaves and in the negative space between the leaves."

"Is that what brought you here? Looking for a pattern in the negative spaces?"

She wrapped her arms around her bent knees. "Interesting way of phrasing it, but I suppose I am looking for that pattern in yesterday's events."

They were both silent for a time, absorbed in the dancing flames. Eventually Sawyer reached over and patted Marley. "How about you? Are you a wounded spirit like your owner?"

The dog wasted no time jumping in his lap and giving him a quick swipe with the tongue. "I see. Unlike your owner, who keeps people at arm's length, you make friends."

She stiffened. "I have friends."

"Have you met any of her friends, Marley?"

The dog whined.

"Traitor," Tavish whispered. Picking up a stick, she pushed a log farther into the blaze. *Don't tell him about the other woman. He'll think I'm a gullible fool, or worse, so undesirable that my fiancé would find another to love. And that he'd kill himself rather than choose to love only me . . .*

"What is it, Tavish?"

The way he said her name warmed her all over. Could she . . . Should she tell him? Marley jumped off his lap and sat in front of her, head cocked. The tiny voice inside her whispered, *What difference does it make? He'll find out sooner or later, if his investigation takes him to the police reports.* She took a deep breath. "A woman showed up . . . at Andrew's funeral. She was beautiful and . . . pregnant. She claimed my fiancé was the father. That she made him choose . . ."

"Who was she?"

"I don't know. I never saw her again."

"Tavish."

Something in his voice made her look at him.

"I need you to do one more drawing. Draw the woman who showed up at the funeral."

Tavish sighed. "Why do you want me to do these drawings?"

"They're concrete evidence to take to the police—"

She jumped up. "I've been to the police. To the sheriff. Nobody believes me. Sometimes *I* don't believe me."

Sawyer stood. "I'm just saying—"

"Good evening." A voice came from the other side of the bonfire.

Tavish stepped away from Sawyer. "Who's there?"

The man moved forward into the light. Detective Mike Mullins.

Marley barked. Tavish's hand flew to her mouth. "Quiet, Marley," she gasped.

"Well, well, well," Mullins said. "I see we meet again, Miss McTavish. May I ask what you are doing here?"

"You found his body?" she asked.

"Body?" His eyebrows rose.

Her stomach twisted and she felt like throwing up. "J-John's—"

"Excuse me." Sawyer slipped his hand around Tavish's arm and gently pulled her behind him. "Who are *you* and what are you doing here?"

Mullins reached inside his coat.

Sawyer put his hand behind his back, resting his hand on a small pistol.

Tavish swallowed hard.

Mullins's gaze followed Sawyer's movement. He opened his jacket wide, slowly drew out a wallet, held it up, and flipped it open. A gold badge glinted in the firelight. "Detective Mike Mullins of the Bernalillo County Sheriff's Department."

Sawyer let his arm drop to his side, then moved to where he could see both Tavish and the detective. "You two know each other?"

"We've met." Mullins stared at her, then pulled out a small notebook and opened it. "I'm here to speak to a Professor Patricia Caron."

"May I ask what this is all about?" Sawyer asked.

"You may, but I'll be telling Professor Caron."

Sawyer stared at Detective Mullins for a moment, then said, "I'll go get her." He strolled away.

Mullins moved closer. "Miss McTavish, I'll ask you again, what are you doing here?"

"Why do you ask?"

"Just answer my question."

"Am I under arrest?"

"Should you be?"

Tavish shook her head and folded her hands together to keep from chewing on a nail.

Sawyer and Patricia returned quickly.

"I'm Dr. Caron." Patricia approached the man with a proffered handshake. "May I help you, Detective?"

"I have you listed as the owner of a house at 75644 Loco Drive." Detective Mullins read the address off his notebook.

Patricia glanced at Tavish, then back to Mullins. "Seems to be a lot of activity going on at my house. Yes, I own the place and rent it out through Sandia Way Management."

"We tried calling you, but couldn't get through. I'm sorry to tell you your home's been destroyed."

"What?" Patricia could barely get the word out.

"Looks like a gas leak. It took out a total of four homes. We're still investigating." Mullins closed his notebook. "No one was home at the time—at least not at your house. An older woman and her cats . . . Well, anyway, we'll want you to drop into the department to make a statement. I'm sure your insurance company will need our report." He turned to Tavish. "I'd like for you to come in as well. We'll have some questions for you."

"I've been up here since early this morning."

"I didn't ask you if you have an alibi."

She dug at a cuticle. "Okay, um, the road is open?"

"Some pretty full potholes, but yes." He pulled out his wallet and extracted several business cards. "Here's my information for the insurance." He handed one card to the professor, one to Sawyer, then one to Tavish. "You know how to reach me." Nodding to Sawyer, he headed away from the campfire toward the parking area.

"I hope you didn't have a lot of irreplaceable things at your house," Sawyer said to Patricia.

"Not really." Patricia slumped to the log. "Some photos, but most of my things have been in storage."

Tavish looked from Patricia to Sawyer. *Could they really be buying the notion of a gas leak?* "Don't you think the timing of the explosion is a little strange?"

"How so?" Patricia asked.

"It neatly destroys any trace evidence of John's death."

"I'll look into it," Sawyer said. "I need you both to stay clear and stay safe."

Tavish removed Sawyer's jacket and handed it to him. "I don't think I can stay safe until John's killer is located." She snapped her fingers at Marley and trotted toward her car.

"Where are you going?" Sawyer called after her.

"To find the truth."

CHAPTER 12

Tavish gritted her teeth to keep them from chattering until the heater in the car kicked in. *Oh yeah, brave words. But how am I going to find out the truth?*

In the dark, it was hard to avoid the potholes. Marley whined.

"I know. I shouldn't have told him about the pregnant woman, but hey, how could I have made things any worse?"

Marley nudged her arm as she steered.

"What do I mean? I have no career, I'm living with my mother, I have panic attacks that practically knock me out, and now the handsomest man I've ever met probably believes I'm toxic."

The little dog barked sharply, then sat up.

"You cutie." She swiped at her eyes. "Yeah, I am indulging myself in a pool of self-pity." Driving for another mile, she thought over what Detective Mullins said. She'd bet one of the houses destroyed was Kevin's.

So what did she actually have for facts? One bullet hole in

the bumper of her car. One Puli dog with a microchip registered to her.

She could go back to the shelter, find that nasty man, Mr. Brown, and get more information on the microchip. She could also place a call to all the veterinary hospitals to see who may have done the procedure. Both actions would have to wait until morning, as nothing would be open this time of night.

She turned on the radio, then pushed the search button until she got a clear station. A man was speaking.

". . . and I'm telling you that there is mind control. The U-ni-ted States government is controlling the minds of people. I had to tinfoil over the winders to keep out them there waves they're sending out—"

"Let me break in here, Bob, and tell you that just could be true." The second male voice was apparently the show's host. "Back in the fifties to the late sixties, a CIA-run program called MK-ULTRA experimented on people using LSD."

"LDS? The government used Mormons?"

"LSD, Bob, LSD. Some of those waves may just be breaking through your living room." Music swelled. "Gotta go to break now, folks, but stay tuned. This is Dusty Rhodes, station KZRT, the voice of enlightenment here in Bernalillo, New Mexico." A commercial followed.

"Hear that, Marley? I bet that caller's name was Bubba or Jim Bob, he lives in a rusty trailer with seven cars and trucks up on blocks, and he's been probed at least once by aliens." She was about to shut off the program when the host came back on. "Thank you for tuning in to my show. We've been discussing mind control by the government. Let's go to the next caller. Hello, Eunice, this is Dusty Rhodes and you're on the air."

"Oh my heavens! I'm so excited—"

"What's on your mind, Eunice?"

Tavish slowed to cross a small stream across the road. Her headlights spotlighted several jackrabbits munching under a sage bush.

"The mark of the devil, Dusty, written about in Revelations. The plot for the government to plant tiny microchips in our bodies. Like they do dogs . . ."

Tavish sat up straight and turned up the volume.

"It's all related to the New World Order," Eunice continued. "Agenda 21 and the Illuminati. They want to track, control, regulate, and spy on people. And the head honcho—"

"Let me guess, Eunice. The Antichrist."

"Right! Revelation chapter thirteen. 'And he had power to give life unto the image of the beast, that the image of the beast should both speak, and cause that as many as would not worship the image of the beast should be killed. And he causeth all, both small and great, rich and poor, free and bond, to receive a mark in their right hand, or in their foreheads:'"—her voice rose and became shrill—"'And that no man might buy or sell, save he that had the mark, or the name of the beast, or the number of his name. Here is wisdom.'" Her voice dropped to a whisper. "'Let him that hath understanding count the number of the beast: for it is the number of a man; and his number is Six hundred threescore and six.'"

"Thank you for your call, Eunice. That's an interesting subject. We do microchip dogs, cats, and horses. Why not chip people?

We could locate missing children, track felons, locate fugitives. In 2009, the British scientist Mark Gasson put a microchip into his hand that contained a computer virus. He used it to infect other computers. At least one company announced they would begin offering microchip implants to their employees. Here in Albuquerque, we . . ." The signal faded out.

"No!" Tavish adjusted the dial, trying to get the station again.

Finally the host's voice returned, albeit faint. ". . . Industries, Nanoace, Ichip, and Cryprochips are a few of the nationwide companies. Going to our next caller. Hello, Steve, this is Dusty Rhodes, and you're on the air."

"You talked last night about the crazy and violent Antifa movement, the anticapitalists who have tied up the police and sheriff's departments the past month in Albuquerque. What I want to know . . ."

She turned down the sound. "Did you notice something, Marley?" Tavish glanced at the dog. Marley looked like a dreadlock wig tossed onto the seat. Gentle snores rose from the heap of fur. "Okay, I'll tell you anyway. The people calling in were . . . well, let's just say on the fringe. But his comments were grounded in facts. He seems to know something about microchips." She tapped the steering wheel. "Maybe I can stop at the next gas station and call in? No. I don't want him to put me on the air. I wonder how hard it would be to locate his station? Bernalillo's less than thirty miles from Albuquerque. It's on our way home. And it's something I can do tonight, not wait until morning." Marley grunted and shifted in the seat. "Never mind. I'll just look for the radio tower or ask directions. I have a few questions for Dusty Rhodes."

Sawyer waited until Tavish's taillights disappeared before moving. With only one road up to the camp and one highway leading to Albuquerque, she wouldn't be hard to follow.

All he needed to do was grab the change of clothing and his sleeping bag he'd kept out to pack up in the morning, and he could leave the Kéyah site.

Patricia raised her eyebrows when she saw him loading his vehicle. "So you're heading out tonight?"

"My job's done here. I thought I'd head—"

"After a particular young woman?" She grinned. "You really like her, don't you?"

"I think she's the most interesting, talented, beautiful woman I've ever seen."

"In that case, you'd better hurry. I'll miss your company, but maybe I can convince my son or daughter to come and visit. It gets pretty lonely at night when all the graduate students head back to town."

She suddenly looked older and more vulnerable. Sawyer paused. "Will you be okay here? Alone? And considering your house . . ."

Patricia waved him away. "I've been alone for a long time now, ever since my husband died in Iraq. Go on with you. I'll be fine. I'll drive down tomorrow to talk to the sheriff."

Just before climbing into his SUV, Sawyer patted his shirt pocket. The tracking device he'd removed from Tavish's car was still there.

The road had standing water in places, but nothing his

vehicle couldn't handle. He drove slowly, not wanting to catch up to her. When the lone gas station appeared, he slowed even more to be sure she hadn't stopped.

He finally spotted her Audi outside of Santa Fe. The traffic had picked up, and he let a few vehicles pull between them. He rolled down the window to let the cool evening air rush through the SUV. *She's probably going home.* In that case, he'd make sure she arrived safely and no one lurked nearby.

Could she have followed him to the site from the art gallery? He turned that possibility around in his mind. That didn't fit. Maybe she'd call it karma that they would meet. Divine intervention fit better. "So, Lord," he whispered, "besides getting her home safely, what particular plan did you have in mind?"

The Lord remained mute.

He pulled a notebook out of the briefcase on the seat beside him, opened it, and jotted *dog, microchip, John Coyote.*

Had she mentioned the name of her fiancé? He thought about their conversation. Andrew . . . Andrew James. Under *dog, microchip, John Coyote* he wrote *fiancé Andrew James.* Then there was her mother and the stolen art. He'd get ahold of the department that had jurisdiction over that Four Corners shootout. They might offer him more insight than the file could. Tavish was three cars ahead of him when she signaled a turn at the small town of Bernalillo. He slowed and made the same exit. She turned into a service station, but instead of pulling up to a pump, she parked at the front and went inside. He drove around the building and stopped where he could watch her and not be seen.

$$\Longrightarrow\Longleftarrow$$

Using her smattering of Spanish, a variety of hand signals, and finally tuning the store radio to station KZRT, Tavish got the store clerk to draw a map to her destination. The location wasn't far. She was grateful Marley hadn't had time to do any damage to the car's interior.

As she approached the station, her palms grew damp on the steering wheel. She didn't know radio station protocol. Should she have made an appointment? Talked to the station manager? Would they turn her away? To slow her whirling thoughts, she bit a nail until it hurt.

The store clerk had drawn what looked like a cow with an arrow pointing right. She'd been too embarrassed to ask him what that meant. Longhorn Lane? Bovine Boulevard? Udder Alley?

Her headlights picked out a sign for a dairy on her right. The pungent odor of manure seeped through the closed windows. She turned at the sign. The pavement quickly gave way to a gravel road, then dirt, then dirt and potholes.

"This can't be right." Searching for a place to turn around, she arrived at a 1970s gold-and-white camper trailer held up by cinderblocks. Only one of the two doors had wooden steps. A chunk of plywood leaned against the second door. An ancient orange VW minibus was parked in front. A metal shed on the right stood near a rusted gravity fuel tank. A tiny glow of light peeked between the slats covering the trailer windows.

Marley sat up and glanced around.

"Yeah, I agree. I think we need to get out of here ASAP." A small trail to the left seemed to lead back to the county road. She turned in that direction, but before she could drive away, lights blinded her on all sides. A booming voice on a loudspeaker crackled out, "Do *not* back up. Severe tire damage will result. Place your hands on the steering wheel where I can see them. Your license plate has been recorded. Remain in your vehicle. I am armed and have a rifle pointed at you."

Marley jumped from front seat to back, barking wildly. Tavish clutched the steering wheel with both hands.

"I'm okay, this will pass, breathe in calm, breathe out fear."

Out of the corner of her eye, she glimpsed a younger man with wild, dark hair in need of a shave with headphones wrapped around his neck. "I'm-okay-I'm-okay-I'm-o—"

He rapped on her window.

Tavish jerked away.

Marley lunged at the window barking frantically.

She released the steering wheel and covered her head. The noise, the lights, the banging on the window receded. Her pounding heart roared in her ears, then it, too, receded. Blessed darkness wrapped around her mind.

CHAPTER 13

Tavish was vaguely aware of movement, being carried, a soft surface under her cheek, a calloused hand brushing her hair from her face. *What a strange dream. Blinding lights, barking . . .* The nostril-burning reek of ammonia made her eyes fly open.

"She's coming to." Two men crouched in front of her. The wild-haired man reached forward with the reeking ammonia smell.

"No!" Tavish covered her nose and struggled to sit up.

"Just stay put." Sawyer placed a firm hand on her shoulder.

Sawyer? "Wha . . . what are you doing here?" she croaked.

"Never mind that. What happened to you?" He sat on a metal kitchen chair.

"Panic attack." She managed to sit upright on a threadbare sofa. She couldn't meet his gaze. "I thought I'd stopped having them. At least that severe. I feel like an idiot."

Marley wiggled out of Sawyer's arms and jumped up beside her on the sofa.

The wild-haired man scrunched his face. "Hey, lady, I'm sorry. I'm security conscious out here, ya know, with all the fringe crazies who call me up and claim Martians have invaded earth or the government is using mind control. I'm Dusty Rhodes, by the way."

"Evelyn McTavish. Call me Tavish," she said automatically, then offered her hand.

Dusty shook it briefly while studying her face, then said, "Any relation to Helen McTavish Richmond?"

"My mother. Why do you ask?"

Instead of answering, Dusty turned to Sawyer. "And you are?"

"Sawyer Price."

"Are you two together?"

Tavish opened her mouth to answer, but Sawyer beat her to it. "She was recently visiting the Kéyah archaeological site doing a bit of . . . research. I was making sure she made it home safely."

She stared at him. There was no doubt he'd followed her. The question was why.

Dusty sat on a yellow lawn chair. "Okay. Do ya want to explain what you're doing here? Or were ya lost?"

"I was listening to your show . . . Wait, aren't you doing your show right now?"

Dusty jabbed a thumb in the direction of a small kitchen. It had been turned into a radio station. "Prerecorded. Go on. You were listening to my show . . . ?"

"You don't sound the same as you do on the radio."

"Ah, you mean like this?" Dusty's voice deepened and his words became clipped. "Good evening, folks, and welcome to station KZRT."

"Amazing. Anyway, you mentioned microchips and placing microchips into people—"

"Ya don't actually believe that stuff, do you?" Dusty shook his head.

"*You* don't believe it?" Sawyer asked. "But it's your show."

Dusty waved away Sawyer's comment. "My topics are like my radio voice. For effect. It's a paying gig. Entertainment. It was about all I could do for work once I got out."

"Out?" Sawyer asked.

"Of prison."

Tavish was suddenly grateful for Sawyer's presence. She took in her surroundings. The trailer had stained wood-paneled walls, ripped avocado shag carpet, and a half-empty bucket resting on a chunk of plywood under a ceiling drip. It smelled of mildew and spoiled milk. She tried not to look too closely at the sofa.

"So, Miss, um, Tavish, how can I help you? Why are you interested in microchips?" Dusty spoke softly.

Marley had placed her two front paws on Tavish's lap, rested her head on them, and was watching Tavish's every move. "A man by the name of John Coyote had a microchip placed in his dog—this dog—but put my name as the contact. I barely knew him and had just drawn a portrait for him. He was murdered."

"Okay, ya have my attention. Tell me about this guy who got murdered."

"She drew his picture," Sawyer said.

Both men looked at her. "I'll go get it." She started to rise, but Sawyer placed a hand on her shoulder. The room spun for a moment. She sank back down.

"Tell me where it is and I'll get it," Sawyer said.

"Back seat, in the black bag, tucked into a sketchpad."

Sawyer nodded toward the door. "Do you think you could turn off all the bells and whistles?"

"Oh, sure." Dusty stood, stepped into the kitchen, flipped a switch, then returned to the lawn chair.

After Sawyer stood and left the trailer to retrieve her sketches, she explained further about the murder, Fake Cop, neighbor, tracking device in her car, and gas explosion.

"You're sounding like someone who would call me," Dusty said, "and that's not a compliment."

Tavish squeezed her hands into fists. Why was it so hard to convince anyone of the truth? "I thought you might have an idea what was going on."

Dusty shifted in the lawn chair, sending out a metallic twang. "Microchips, the ones we put into animals, are designed to be read from a short distance. They don't transmit. You can't track anyone with them."

"But you told that lady on the radio that she could be on to something."

He made a *pffff* sound. "I said it was an interesting subject. Like I said, entertainment."

"You mentioned companies that were making microchips—"

Dusty snapped his fingers and jumped to his feet. "Now we're getting somewhere. Your mother. Microchips." He moved to the kitchen, retrieved an old grimy laptop, and returned to his seat. After tapping on the keypad for a moment, he turned the computer around so she could see the screen. It displayed a long list of names. She recognized several at the top from the list he'd recited on the radio. Nanoace, Ichip, Cryprochip.

She looked up at him. "You read some of these names? Microchip manufacturers."

"Keep reading."

Her gaze returned to the screen. She saw the name in the third column. *Softmode Testing.*

She blinked. The name remained. "I don't understand."

"I think you're beginning to. Your mother, Helen McTavish Richmond, is the owner and CEO of Softmode Testing."

"My mother owns many companies," Tavish said through stiff lips. "She's an astute businesswoman. That particular enterprise does product testing. It has nothing to do with microchips."

"And you know this because . . . ?" Dusty asked. "Does your mom tell you about the inner workings of her companies?"

She started to look for a handy hangnail to work on, but Marley slipped into her lap. She hugged the dog instead. "No. But she offered me a position with this one."

"How much do you know about Softmode Testing?" Dusty asked.

"They have a large building on the edge of town. I've been there a few times. They get contracts to do custom tests on different products. Um . . . not much else. Why?"

Dusty stared at the mottled ceiling for a moment. "I've heard rumors. That's all. I've heard your mother has expensive tastes."

Tavish wrinkled her nose. "What does that have to do with anything? She makes a lot of money."

"And spends it. I heard about her art collection."

Marley sat up, whined, then jumped to the floor. Tavish bent forward to retrieve her before she could explore the trailer.

The windows and door exploded in a torrent of gunfire.

CHAPTER 14

Sawyer stepped from the trailer and moved forward in the moonless night, banging his shin against something. *Confound it!* He closed his eyes and waited until the pain receded and his vision adjusted to the dark. He'd run into the edge of a discarded refrigerator lying on its side. *Classy place.*

Ahead of him was an orange VW minibus. Tavish's white Audi was on the other side. Before he could take a step, he smelled cigarette smoke. He ducked down and slipped his 9mm Kimber from the ankle holster. Allowing the bus to shield him, he silently crept to a battered metal building on his left.

He'd made a mistake in telling Dusty to turn off the warning system. Worrying about Tavish had definitely interfered with his usual caution.

Scanning the area, he started looking for the telltale glow of a burning cigarette. Was this one of Dusty's fringe listeners? Or Tavish's tracker? The inexpensive unit he'd found in her car was typically accurate to only forty feet. He'd tucked his car into the trees, so whoever might be following the signal would see the Audi, not his SUV.

On the other hand, the smoker could be nothing more than a late-night neighbor out walking his dog.

Yeah. Right.

A pack of coyotes in the distance yipped a discordant melody. A breeze rustled the piñon pines and junipers. The cigarette smoke disappeared. In the gloom, he could barely make out a slight movement near the edge of the clearing. Whoever it was, they were not walking a dog.

Clat-clat-clat-clat-clat-clat-clat-clat!

He dove to the ground as the semiautomatic fired overhead. Windows shattered. The trailer rocked as hundreds of bullets raked across the building, punching holes in the side. *Tavish!*

Pushing away from the storm of bullets, he crawled as quickly as he could out of the line of fire. With the barrage of shooting, he would circle around behind the sniper. Surprise was an equalizer when faced with superior weapons.

Boom!

The blast and fire from the exploded fuel tank engulfed the trailer.

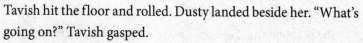

Tavish hit the floor and rolled. Dusty landed beside her. "What's going on?" Tavish gasped.

Dusty didn't answer.

She glanced at him.

His eyes were wide open in a look of infinite surprise. The rest of his face was a mass of blood.

She screamed. Her voice was absorbed by the din of gunfire.

Holes opened in the wall above her. Broken glass sliced her hands.

The *clat-clat-clat-clat-clat-clat-clat-clat* came in bursts, raking the sofa she'd been sitting on a moment ago.

Marley dug with a frenzy at the plywood on the floor.

Tavish grabbed for her, but she scurried sideways, not stopping. The plywood moved a scant inch.

A puff of air came from a crack under the wood.

Still lying flat on the filthy, glass-covered carpet, Tavish slid closer and added her weight to moving the wood.

Another inch, then another. A small hole in the camper shell appeared.

She shoved the bucket aside. It tipped over, soaking the floor and her with dirty water. The plywood moved aside easily without the weight of the bucket. The rusted hole in the floor was tiny.

The gunfire stopped, then resumed, now striking lower on the wall, moving toward her.

Tavish exhaled and pulled herself through the opening. The fit was incredibly tight, and the metal gouged her skin.

Marley howled.

Tavish gave a final shove, tearing both skin and rusted metal. She dropped to the ground under the camper.

Marley jumped on top of her.

She grabbed the dog and crawled away from the sniper. Once free of the structure, she crawled forward using her elbows. *Please don't let there be scorpions. Or snakes.*

Marley wiggled in her desperate grip. Once the firing paused, she'd run—

Boom!

The blast deafened her, sending scorching air over her back, and launched her into a small ditch.

She curled up around the dog, trying to breathe. *Sawyer.*

Sawyer retreated from the conflagration. His chest was tight and swallowing was difficult. There was no way Tavish could have survived that attack and fire. The trailer had two doors, both on the same side. She hadn't escaped from either, nor would she have made it outside through a window.

She'd been telling the truth all along. Now she was dead.

He would find her killer.

An engine roared to his right in the distance.

Sprinting toward the sound, he caught a glimpse of a white sedan as it shot down the gravel road. He raced to his own SUV and took off in pursuit.

Tavish didn't want to move, but she was too near the fire and the heat was intense. The inferno roared and crackled, sending up billows of black smoke.

Keeping the burning camper between herself and the sniper, she clutched a shaking Marley and limped away from the conflagration.

Her vision was blurred and scalding tears rolled down her face. Sawyer would have walked directly into that gunfire.

"I'm okay, this will pass, breathe in calm, breathe out fear," she whispered. Would the killer wait until the fire burned down to see if her body was inside?

No. The blaze would attract people. He, or she, would want to be as far away as possible. Sure enough, the faint sound of a racing engine reached Tavish's ears. At least she wouldn't be shot. *This time.*

She needed to go . . . where? *Away.* She couldn't be found at yet another homicide. Or double homicide.

In the distance, the scream of sirens split the night.

Away quickly.

She broke into a limping run, angling toward her car. Her hands and knees burned from the glass cuts, and her side pounded from the gouging metal floor. Her legs barely supported her. Marley ran with her, this time without trying to trip her. *How far to my car? Pleasepleaseplease give me strength.*

Rounding the corner of the metal building, she spotted the Audi, looking orange in the fire's glow. She couldn't drive out the way she'd come in—the fire engines and police would soon be tearing down that road. Deliberately keeping her gaze from the area where she knew Sawyer's body would be found, she opened the door, scooped Marley into the passenger side, and jabbed at the start button. Her hands trembled so badly it took three tries to start the engine.

The sirens and flashing lights were almost there. She pulled out, aiming for the small trail she'd spotted on the way in. She drove as fast as possible with just the parking lights. The narrow road passed scrubby growth, two more trailers, each more rusted and forlorn than the previous, and a structure leaning impossibly sideways.

Stopping after the last single-wide trailer, she cut the parking lights, then waited until her eyes adjusted to the dim light. The red-blue-white strobes from the fire truck and police flickered on nearby vegetation.

Tire tracks.

She should have stopped long enough to sweep her tire tracks leading away from the fire. How long before they would investigate the cause of the fire? Putting the car into drive, she moved forward scarcely above an idle speed. The track she followed, a slightly lighter patch of earth, gently curved until the fire was in the distance on her right.

Marley stood silently in the back seat, watching the flashing lights and leaping flames.

The steering wheel was wet with blood and sweat. Her knees throbbed and her side pounded with the beating of her heart. She concentrated on driving, forcing her mind away from the deaths of Sawyer and Dusty. Not deaths. Murders.

She shivered and turned up the heat. It didn't help. *Three murders.* If she added Kevin, the man who'd lent her his truck and later disappeared, to the list, up to four people were dead or missing.

Or could it be five? How strange was it that Andy would commit suicide at roughly the same time all these mysterious events started happening?

Could she have been right in the first place about Andy being murdered? The police hadn't wanted to look into it, but she'd been so sure at the time that he wouldn't have committed suicide.

She had only the word of that pregnant woman that Andy was the father of her child.

Am I trying to connect something that isn't connected? What am I missing?

Headlights passing back and forth ahead indicated she would soon reach the main road. She'd need a break in traffic to slide onto the street unnoticed. She crept forward as close as she dared, hoping the headlights from a passing car wouldn't pick out her vehicle as they swept past.

Finally the road cleared. She gunned the engine and shot off the dirt track, keeping up the speed until she'd put some distance between herself and the dust cloud she'd raised.

Marley jumped to the front seat and whined.

"I agree. We've been shot at, almost burned alive, witnessed two murders, and barely escaped. We need to hide out until my brain can make sense of all this. I haven't got enough money on me to get a motel room, and I don't know if anyone could trace us through a credit card. Assuming we were the targets just now."

Marley curled up in the seat, exhaling a deep sigh.

"Go home?" Tavish nodded. "That might work. No one would expect that. I can park the car in Helen's garage, then cross to the guesthouse through her garden, where no one can see. We can hide in plain sight. If someone was actually trying to kill me, they should believe they've succeeded."

CHAPTER 15

By the time Sawyer reached Interstate 25, the white sedan was gone. In all probability, the driver had turned toward Albuquerque. Sawyer dialed 9-1-1 as he headed south toward the city and increased his speed. The shooter would think he'd shot or blown up everyone and was home free. There'd be no reason for him, or her, to draw attention by speeding.

The call center answered, "9-1-1, what is the nature of your emergency?"

"This is FBI Agent Sawyer Price. I'm in pursuit of a white sedan heading south on Interstate 25. I'm reporting a shooting and explosion." He described the location, then hung up. They had his cell number and would soon get back to him. He approached the edge of town without encountering the sedan. At the first intersection, he turned off the interstate and pulled over. He'd head back to the camper and fire. Identify himself as a witness and find out exactly what was going on. He needed to find the connections between stolen artifacts, the shootout at the Four Corners, a dead man, a fake cop, a missing neighbor, a microchip in a dog . . . and Tavish.

≫≡≪

Tavish circled the block around her mother's house, then checked out several blocks in all directions, looking for anyone lurking nearby. She had been given a remote for the garage door but she'd never used it. Wincing at the sound of the opening door and light spilling out to the street, she pulled in between her mother's Mercedes and the Toyota truck she kept for the staff. She pushed the close-door button even before putting her car into park, shut off the engine, and waited to see if Helen would investigate.

As her car engine cooled, she watched the door that led to the workout room. It didn't open. She relaxed for the first time, peeling her white-knuckled grip off the steering wheel.

The garage itself was a tribute to her mother's various pastimes—bicycles, skis, and snowshoes hung from their respective holders on the wall. Perfectly neat. Everything in its place. No wonder Tavish was such a disappointment to her mother. She was neither neat nor in her place.

After waiting a few moments, she picked up the bag of dog kibble and her sketches. Snapping her fingers at Marley, she slipped from the car and headed outside.

After the theft in January, her mother had installed a new major security system to protect her extensive art and Native American collection. Her three Georgia O'Keeffe paintings alone were worth millions, and her rare kachina dolls, pottery, and weavings would fill a museum. Fortunately most of the security involved the interior of her home. Her exterior precautions were limited to motion-sensor lights and the private security patrols, which Tavish knew how to avoid.

They skirted the pool, Marley staying close to Tavish's heels. The night was mild, fragrant with blooming flowers from the previous rain. Any other time Tavish would have appreciated the evening's offerings.

Once inside her house, Tavish turned on the alarm system, leaned against the front door, then slid down until she was sitting with her back to the carved wood. Marley raced through the house, returning with a sock that she placed on Tavish's lap.

"That's so sweet, Marley." She stayed on the floor until the pain of her injuries forced her to rise and hobble to the bathroom to clean up. After a long shower, which stung like the dickens on her wounds, she applied antibacterial cream and Band-Aids to the still-seeping cuts.

She left all the blinds drawn and curtains closed and used the night-lights to move around. After filling the dog's bowl with food, she pulled a container of yogurt from the refrigerator and sat down to eat.

The first mouthful almost made her throw up. The events of the evening washed over her. She dropped the spoon and covered her face. Her breathing became ragged. *I'm okay, this will pass, breathe in calm, breathe out fear.*

I'mokay,thiswillpass,breatheincalm,breatheoutfear—
Marley barked at her.

"Shhhhhh." *I'm okay, this will pass, breathe in calm, breathe out fear*—
The dog barked again.

Tavish took her hands away from her face and looked at Marley. "Be quiet. I'm—"

The canine spun in a small circle, barking.

"Marley, be quiet!"

Marley shot out of the room, returned, spun, and raced out again, barking insistently.

"Shhhhhh! Quiet! Someone will hear you—"

Marley flew into the room and launched herself into Tavish's lap. Tavish caught her before the dog could cover her face with a wet tongue. "What is the matter with you?"

The dog calmly dropped to the floor, trotted to her food dish, and began crunching the kibble.

Tavish stared at her a moment.

The phone rang.

Tavish jumped. She checked the time. One thirty a.m.

The phone rang three more times before the answering machine picked up. Her mother's voice came from the machine. "Evelyn? Are you home? I thought I heard a dog barking at your place. Well, anyway, don't forget my little get-together later today. Cocktails by the pool at four." *Click.*

Won't you be surprised when the police show up today at your little soiree to tell you I was shot and burned up in a ratty trailer . . . Wait. No one except the killer knew she was in that trailer.

She started shaking. She had almost died. Marley saved her life by digging at that chunk of wood on the floor. "Marley, you really are a dog hero."

The dog didn't look up from her bowl of chow.

"Tomorrow, or make that later today, I'm going to buy you a

toy. Whatever you want." She took a shuddering breath. "I don't know how to say thank you to a dog."

Marley stopped eating, sauntered over to Tavish, sat, and offered a paw. Tavish sat next to her on the kitchen floor and took the proffered foot. "That's it? A handshake? Such a simple thing for such a grand act." She stroked the cords away from the dog's eyes. "Marley Coyote . . . make that Marley McTavish, you are the best friend I've ever had."

The dog sneezed, then returned to her food.

Tavish stood, turned on the television, and found a local all-news station. A newscaster standing in front of the dying trailer fire was in mid-report.

". . . fire had fully engulfed the trailer by the time the firefighters arrived. No word yet if anyone was inside."

No mention of finding Sawyer. She pulled a bottle of water from the refrigerator, opened it, and took a drink. Sawyer's voice rang in her head. *"Dehydration and altitude sickness are always a problem . . ."*

"No," she whispered. "Don't think about it. You were a fool to let him get close." An itchy, nervous restlessness settled over her. She checked all the doors and windows to be sure they were locked, then checked a second time. She turned off the television, but the silence amplified every squeak of the floor and distant car engine. She turned the television back on, this time to the music station.

Her spiral-bound journal still lay on the table. She snatched it up and opened it to a clean page. Maybe writing down the events would get them out of her brain and she'd stop going over them again and again in her mind.

John Coyote murdered.
Body picked up by Fake Cop.

That wasn't right. She had to go further back. The microchip in Marley. But that was probably because she met John.

Events:
Met John at Mother's soiree.
(ask Helen how she knew him)
- Deliberate?
- John must know Helen.

When was that soiree? She tapped her pencil while she pictured the scene. Lots of people, as usual. Sun glittering off the brilliant blue of the pool, making her blink and turn away. The paintings hadn't been recovered . . . *Of course.* Her mother had received the insurance money. She'd installed the new security system and was looking forward to buying replacement art. That would put the party around mid- to late March. The artwork was stolen January 1, while they were attending a New Year's Day bash across town. At the party in March, her mother told her to mingle with the guests. John was by the edge of the pool . . . Andrew was to have attended and met her mother that day, but he'd canceled.

John lists my name as owner of Marley.
- Insurance?
- Because of Helen?
John murdered.
- Why?

Body picked up by Fake Cop.

The last entry was the easiest. Get rid of the evidence. Did the Dali-mustached guy have anything to do with this? And how did the killer clean up the evidence so fast?

Maybe he'd been sloppy. Hence the "gas leak."

She circled *Helen* several times, then added *Softmode Testing?* She'd have some questions to ask her mother.

Writing did help. She was finally drowsy enough to get some sleep. She headed for bed.

≥≤

A sheriff's deputy stopped Sawyer near the dairy. "You'll have to turn around, sir—"

Sawyer flashed his FBI credentials. "I have information about this fire."

The deputy pointed up the road toward the smoldering trailer. "You'll want to speak to Lieutenant Hammen."

Sawyer slowly approached the mass of fire and police vehicles. When a deputy strolled over, he rolled down the window and asked, "Lieutenant Hammen?"

The deputy pointed to a place for him to park, then jerked his thumb at a lean man with light-colored hair and a mustache. He was currently talking with several firefighters.

Sawyer parked his SUV, then approached. The lieutenant dismissed the first responders and turned. "Yes?"

Holding out his credentials, Sawyer stopped in front of the man. "I was here earlier."

"Were you the one who called this in?"

"Yes."

"Then you can tell me what happened."

After Sawyer explained the sniper attack, his pursuit, and the white sedan, the lieutenant asked, "Were you here on official business?"

"No. I had just finished working on location on a case."

"So was someone after you or Dusty?"

"You knew Dusty Rhodes?"

"Hard not to know him. I put him in prison."

Sawyer rubbed his chin. "Do you think this shooting had something to do with his criminal activity?"

"No. We're looking into someone from Antifa. They left a calling card in the bushes over there." The lieutenant held up a sheet of paper inside a clear plastic holder. "Dusty had been talking about them on his show. Guess one of them got mad. Unless you were the target and were investigating them . . ." He raised his eyebrows.

"No. That wasn't something I was working on."

"In any case, I'll need you to get me a statement."

"Will do. Also . . ." Sawyer didn't look at the other man. "There was a young woman here as well. She wanted to talk to Dusty about one of his shows. I believe . . ." He swallowed. "I believe you will find her body inside along with Dusty."

The lieutenant stared at him. "I think you and I need to have a long talk about what exactly you were doing here tonight."

"I already told you. The young woman, Evelyn McTavish, stopped here to talk to him. I was keeping an eye on her."

"So you were following the young woman?"

"Yes."

"And she was driving . . . ?"

"A late-model white Audi."

"I see. But if she died in there, where's her car?"

CHAPTER 16

*T*avish sat next to Sawyer, staring at the fire. *He slowly reached over to her, brushed her hair back from her face, leaned forward, and licked her nose.* Opening her eyes, Tavish stared into a wad of hair. The hair parted and a wet tongue emerged, swiped up her nose a second time, then disappeared.

Tavish jerked upright, scrubbing at her face. "Marley! You have got to stop the licking thing."

The dog cocked her head.

"Yes, I'm talking to you. Dog spit has germs."

A soft noise came from the other room.

Tavish's heart jumped. *He found me.* Her gaze darted around her bedroom, seeking a weapon. Shoes, padded clothes hangers, lamp?

"Marley," she whispered. "I need you to be brave. You need to go out there and bark at the intruder. Maybe bite an ankle. Distract him. Okay? I'll make a run for it."

Marley rolled onto her back.

"I don't think exposing yourself is enough of a distraction."

The noise came again.

Tavish slipped from the bed, softly padded to the door, and carefully eased it open.

Maria, the housekeeper, sat on the sofa, quietly sobbing.

"Maria?" Tavish opened the door wider. "Is everything okay? Are you okay?"

"*Sí, señorita. Lo siento te desperté.* I am sorry." She stood and hurried from the room.

A bad time for staffing problems. Tavish glanced at the clock.

"Oh no!" Helen's soiree started in a half hour. She wouldn't be able to privately ask her mother about Softmode Testing. Or how she knew John Coyote.

Sawyer.

She charged across the living room and turned on the news station, leaving it on as she stepped into the bathroom. News of the fire came on as she was brushing her teeth.

"The fire that burned a mobile home last night took the life of late-night talk show personality Dusty Rhodes. Further information is being withheld as the sheriff's department investigates, but inside information reports the fire was not an accident . . ."

Are they withholding Sawyer's murder as well?

She stared at her reflection in the mirror. Her face blurred.

"Don't be ridiculous," she whispered. "You didn't cry for your fiancé. Why would you cry for a man you barely knew?" Turning on the faucet, she splashed cold water on her face.

The phone rang.

She let the answering machine pick up.

"Evelyn." Her mother's voice was tight. "Be sure you are here before four." *Click.*

Tavish swiftly pulled her hair up, applied makeup to hide the bruises from the night before, and slipped on the black Armani dress she had worn to her grandmother's funeral. It hung on her like a flour sack. And it was sleeveless, exposing arms peppered with bruises and cuts.

That left the outfit she'd worn for the opening at the gallery. The sleeves were long enough to cover a portion of her hands. A swift sniff at the armpits proved the outfit to be reasonably odor-free. And the safety pins were still in place.

Marley watched her intently.

"You have to be good. I'm not going to this party for fun. I need information. Your job is to guard the house. Pretend you're a Rottweiler. Think teeth."

The dog looked unmotivated.

Tavish left, followed by Marley's mournful howl, and headed to the pool. The party looked to be in full swing, with uniformed waiters offering trays of drinks to brightly dressed guests chattering in small groups. The spicy odor of a southwest buffet scented the air. She circumvented several groups before one of the guests accosted her.

"Evelyn! I mean Tavit, isn't that right?" The woman's face barely moved from all the cosmetic surgery. Her eyes were open in a permanent look of surprise. "It's so good to see you."

"It's Tavish. It's nice to see you, Mrs. Coombe." Tavish kissed the air in the general direction of the woman's cheeks, then peered over her head, looking for her mother.

"I heard through the grapevine that you had a gallery opening. How lovely to have a nice hobby."

"She just displayed some sketches in a quaint little gallery." Helen had come up behind Tavish and gripped her elbow. "You'll excuse us, Nan dear, my daughter needs to meet some guests. Come, Evelyn." Helen didn't wait for Nan Coombe to respond. She hustled Tavish out of earshot and hissed in her ear, "Where have you been? Why are you wearing that hideous outfit? What's wrong with your face? And why do you reek of smoke?"

"I fell. I need to ask you about Softmode Testing—"

"If you're taking me up on that position now, I told you to let me know quite some time ago. We hired someone just this morning. See that woman over there? With the pearls and silk dress? She has the job you should have taken. And stop changing the subject." She turned and waved at a distinguished-looking man.

"Actually, I was just wondering what sort of things you test."

Helen gave a small nod to someone behind Tavish, then moved closer and lowered her voice. "This is neither the time nor place to ask that."

"Why?"

"Look around you."

Tavish glanced at the well-dressed partygoers. "So?"

Helen moved closer still and whispered, "So many of these are potential clients. What we test, how we conduct these tests, is highly confidential. If anyone even heard your question, we'd lose credibility."

"What about a man named John Coyote? Was he a client of yours? I met him here."

"Not now, Evelyn! Now make yourself useful. I'm going to show a few people my art collection. If anyone . . . unknown to you shows an interest in me, point him out."

"Watching your back?"

"Yes."

"That insurance adjuster you mentioned? But you arranged to meet with him here. What's the big deal?"

Helen didn't answer.

"Help me understand all this. Everything is all settled. Your artwork was recovered. You returned the insurance money . . . didn't you?"

"We'll discuss this later. Now keep your eyes open." She grabbed Tavish's arm and pulled her toward a strikingly handsome couple. "Camron and Leah! So glad you could come."

"We wouldn't miss one of your famous parties for the world." The man took Helen's hands in his own. "Rumor has it you've been adding to your collection." He kissed both of her cheeks, his lips actually making contact.

"For once the rumor mill is right." Helen stepped away and nodded at Tavish. "You remember my daughter, Evelyn."

The woman, in a Dulce & Gabbana silk dress, held out a manicured hand. "Of course. How are you doing? Is your fiancé here?"

Tavish automatically shook the woman's hand. "I'm afraid my fiancé . . . passed away."

"Oh, I'm terribly sorry!"

"About a month ago."

"Oh." The woman put her hand over her mouth. "Oh dear."

Helen patted the woman's arm. "You've been in Europe for a while. You couldn't have known. Come inside and let me show you my recent acquisition. I decided to step outside of pure New Mexican art and invest in a Frida Kahlo."

"How on earth did you manage that? It must have cost a fortune."

"It did. Evelyn, did you want to follow us and—"

Tavish shook her head. Seeing her mother's art collection would remind her that the return of the paintings after the theft had been more important than being with her daughter at Andrew's funeral.

As Helen led the couple toward the house, she glanced back at Tavish and motioned her toward the rest of the guests.

Before Tavish could make her escape, a burly man cornered her. "Evelyn! I haven't seen you around for a bit."

Tavish smiled, but someone caught her attention—a man in khaki slacks with a salmon-striped polo, moving around the edge of the partygoers, searching.

". . . I was just telling your mother . . ."

The man was heading for the patio door, slipping between guests. He had what looked like a professional camera around his neck and carried a briefcase. *He looks familiar. I saw him recently. Where?*

". . . stunned when I heard—"

"Excuse me. Do you know that man over there?"

The man stopped speaking and stared first at her, then in the direction she was pointing. "Which man?"

"That one."

He'd paused by a table.

"I can't say that I do. Why?"

"I'm wondering if I know him."

"You probably saw him at one of your mother's businesses. She's quite . . . avant-garde in her invitations."

The man glanced around.

Tavish gasped. He had a black, Salvador Dali–style mustache.

He spotted her, then did a double take. She did know him. He'd been at John Coyote's house the night she'd gone back to check it.

CHAPTER 17

Before Tavish could move, someone grabbed her arm. Helen.

Tavish tried to pull from the woman's grasp. "Who is that man?"

"Did you see someone snooping?"

"Not exactly snooping. I saw a man with a camera and briefcase with a Salvador Dali mustache. Is that the insurance investigator?"

"I don't know. I've never met the man."

"Just what have you got yourself into, Helen?"

"Nothing. Filthy lies. Don't make a scene."

"Let go!" Tavish glared into her mother's tight-lipped face. "*You're* making the scene."

Helen glanced around. "If he's an insurance investigator, just meet with him and get it over with. He's right over . . ." He was gone. The guests continued to mingle and chatter with each other in small groups.

"He's gone." Tavish again looked at her mother. "We have to talk."

"Later."

"But—"

"We will talk in the morning. Go." Her mother released her arm, stepped back, and said—loud enough for nearby guests to hear—"Of course I understand. Teaching art to underprivileged children should come first."

Tavish stared at her mother a moment, turned, and walked away, her legs feeling like she'd run a marathon. The farther she got from the poolside party, the faster she pushed herself. Thoughts bounced around in her brain.

What does the man at the party have to do with anything? He reacted when he saw me. Maybe because he saw me near John Coyote's house? What was he doing there? And why is Helen acting so strange? Is any of this related to last night and the shooting?

By the time she reached her house, she was running. *How is my mother involved? She couldn't be aware of the attempt on my life or she would have acted differently when I showed up at the party.*

If Dali-mustache is the insurance investigator, what is he investigating? The artwork is here. Why did Helen say "filthy lies"? Insurance fraud? Did she arrange to have her own artwork stolen?

Tavish slammed the door shut and leaned against it. The crazy thoughts continued to swirl in her brain.

Dusty Rhodes suggested her mother had expensive tastes. Helen had avoided answering her question about returning the insurance money. Could Helen be in financial trouble? If so, the money Tavish was set to inherit would come in mighty handy.

For once Marley hadn't emptied the dirty-clothes hamper. Tavish swiftly pulled on a pair of jeans, good running shoes, and a loose-fitting T-shirt. She grabbed a hooded sweatshirt and jacket. The phone rang, but she ignored it.

She needed to drop out of sight until she could figure out who was trying to kill her. And why.

I can drive to . . . Wait . . . Her car was still parked in Helen's garage. She couldn't retrieve it without being seen by the guests. She dropped the jacket and sweatshirt on the sofa.

The gathering wouldn't last forever. No one would try anything in broad daylight. She could relax. Maybe do . . . something. Think about the timeline of events. Review the facts. She paced across the living room and back. *I drew their faces. Someone should recognize one of the sketches. I need to call about Sawyer. Find out what happened to him.* She paced faster. *Does any of this have to do with Softmode? Microchips—*

"Umph!"

She fell.

Marley yelped and raced from the room.

"Oh, Marley, I'm sorry. I didn't see you."

The dog trotted into the room and sat.

"Okay, I'll stop pacing. Action, I need to take action." She picked up the phone book and looked up the sheriff's number. She really needed to replace her cell phone.

It took a few minutes for her to figure out the town of Bernalillo was not in Bernalillo County, but Sandoval. She dialed the Sandoval County Sheriff's Department. After a stream of recorded information, a human finally answered.

"I'm calling about the two murder victims found last night

at Dusty Rhodes's trailer. One of them was Dusty Rhodes. The other was"—she swallowed hard—"Sawyer Price."

"I don't know anything about a Sawyer Price. Let me connect you to Lieutenant Hammen."

In a few moments, a man answered. "Lieutenant Hammen."

"Yes. I'm calling about the two murder victims found last night at Dusty Rhodes's trailer."

"Two? Who's calling, please?"

She disconnected. That was stupid. He now had her number. Sure enough, the phone rang. She picked it up.

"We must have been disconnected. Who am I speaking to?"

"Evelyn McTavish."

"And are you one of the dead people?"

"Excuse me?" Tavish gripped the phone.

"An FBI agent—"

"Sawyer!" Tavish gasped. "He's . . . dead?"

Lieutenant Hammen paused for a moment. "Um . . . maybe we need to talk in person."

"So he is dead." Tavish swallowed hard.

"Miss McTavish, this is an active investigation, and I'm not at liberty to reveal details to you. I can tell you that an FBI agent reported *you* as dying in the shooting and fire."

Only Sawyer would believe I died in the fire. He's alive!

". . . As your car was missing, and no female bodies were found, we thought—we hoped—you might just show up. We put out an APB on your car. I'll cancel that, but I need you to come in to our office for an interview and statement as soon as possible. You're a witness."

"I didn't see the shooter."

"We need to have you come down to our office and tell us exactly what you did see. And hear. And did."

"Who did this? Do you know?"

"Not yet. We believe it's someone connected with Antifa."

"Antifa? But I thought—"

"We need you to come in and share those thoughts. If transportation is a problem, I can send an officer to pick you up."

"No. I'll come there."

"When can I expect you?"

"Could you get word to Sawyer that I'm alive and . . ." *Want to see him? Have him hold me?*

Lieutenant Hammen sighed. "I'll tell him when I see him. When can you come in?"

Sawyer said he was investigating. She trusted him. Not so much the sheriff's department. If she didn't come in, would they arrest her?

"Miss McTavish, do you want me to come to you? Or shall I—"

"I'll be there in three hours." She crossed her fingers and didn't look at Marley.

"Do you know how to find the department?"

"I'll get there." She disconnected.

Marley was still sitting in the same place.

"Don't say a word about my lying. We have three hours to figure this out and disappear for a bit. It's hard to kill someone you can't find."

She moved to the kitchen table, Marley hot on her heels. "I'm not going to be a victim. Or an innocent bystander, or collateral damage, or an unfortunate accident." She pointed at the dog. "Got that?" The spiral notebook still rested where she'd left it.

"I'm tired of being shot at, attempted incineration, accused of being nuts, car stolen, someone in my house, told by my *mother*!" Her voice had reached a shout. She took a deep breath and lowered her tone. "That 'we'll talk about it in the morning.'"

She opened her sketchbook and laid out the drawing she'd done of John Coyote, then retrieved her laptop. It took a moment to boot up the machine and look up Happy Tails Dog Shelter. After checking the time, she dialed. "Hello, is Mr. Brown working?"

"No," a pleasant woman said. "May I take a message?"

"He called me about, um, my dog. He found me through a microchip, and I was wondering if I could get more information."

"That's not a problem. Give me your name and address and a few minutes. I'll look it up."

Tavish did as asked. After being put on hold, the woman returned. "I found it. What information did you need?"

"When Mr. Brown first called, he gave me some numbers. Could you give them to me?"

"Certainly. Thirty-five, zero three, seventeen seventy-nine, then your name and address."

After jotting the numbers in the notebook, Tavish asked, "Are the numbers separated by spaces or dashes, or are they all run together, like three-five-zero-three-one-seven-seven-nine?"

"Good question. Spaces between every two numbers."

"By any chance did the information list who put the microchip in?"

"Usually no, but this one listed Mountain View Veterinary Hospital."

Tavish thanked her and disconnected. Opening her spiral notebook to a clean page, she wrote:

Met John at Mother's soiree.
John listed my name as owner of Marley.
Placed numbers with name—35 03 17 79.

The numbers were odd. A phone number would be seven digits, nine with an area code. Zip codes were five or, with the extension, nine. Not a date. Lock combination? She typed the numbers into her laptop. Keno numbers, sessional papers, astronomical observations, labor statistics. Whatever it was, John wanted her to know because he put it with her name. She sighed and continued to write.

John commissioned drawing.
Murdered (by?)
Body removed by "cop."
Kevin disappears.
Car disappears.
House broken into.
Car reappears—with tracking device?

Her pencil skidded on the last entry. If someone wanted to keep tabs on her, would they have put something in her home? Was she being watched now?

She hunched her shoulders and shivered. If she was being watched, they'd know she had survived the shooting and explosion. Gritting her teeth, she continued to write.

Kevin gone.
Dali-mustache man shows up at John's house.

She had only her mother's comment that the man at the party might be the insurance investigator. But her mother hadn't even seen the man. Was Tavish making a bad assumption? Could more than one person be watching her?

"This is ridiculous." She stood and moved to the center of the living room. Slowly she turned, staring at each surface and object. Nothing looked out of place. She didn't even know what to look for.

She'd have to assume someone was watching. After checking her watch, Tavish peered toward the pool. The soiree seemed to have ended. The catering service her mother used was busy cleaning up. They'd be done in about an hour.

She'd work until the coast was clear, then head out to . . . somewhere.

The prickly feeling was stronger than ever.

She returned to her notes. Under the last entry, she continued to write.

I was followed to Dusty Rhodes's trailer.

How could she have been followed? More likely, Sawyer had her tracking device with him, and *he'd* been stalked—with the shooter believing it was her. Of course, all of that was an assumption. She couldn't be sure it wasn't one of Dusty's psycho listeners who'd finally snapped.

Dusty murdered. Antifa?

She stared at the name, then drew a line through it. "That's what whoever is behind this wants the police to think."

Attempted to kill me.

Dali-mustache at Helen's party.

She'd need to sketch the Dali guy and add it to her growing pile of drawings.

She could link two people to her mother—John Coyote and Mr. Dali-mustache—and the start of the events seemed to be the party in March.

Tavish had set up a drafting table in the second bedroom. Collecting her notes and the sketches she'd already completed, she moved everything to the taboret next to the drafting table.

The sketch of the Dali-mustached man took a little more than an hour. She added it to the other drawings and placed them all in a small portfolio along with her notes. She tapped the small pile of evidence, picked up the phone, and dialed. The recorded voice informed her it was after hours for the FBI, but she could leave a message.

She disconnected without saying anything.

What if Sawyer can't help me? The thought left her gasping for air. He was a federal law-enforcement officer. Nothing that had happened was a federal crime, was it?

Outside of Sawyer, who could she really trust?

Maybe the question should be *what* could she really trust?

Money. She looked down at the dog. "For your information, Marley, I have scads of money. Well, maybe not scads, but enough to hire a bodyguard, or a bunch of bodyguards, and pay for a private investigator. And maybe a lawyer."

Marley sniffed.

"If Sawyer . . ." Her voice caught. "If Sawyer can't get involved, I can pay for my own protection."

Marley barked.

"Of course I know what time it is. The bank's closed, as is the post office, UPS, and FedEx. I can't get funds or mail the evidence until morning." Whoever tried to kill her knew her car, where she lived, everything. The car problem wasn't an issue— she'd just take the staff pickup.

What if she put her materials someplace safe, then called Sawyer and told him where he could collect them? If he refused, she could hire someone and do the same thing. She could go away until the killers were arrested and the coast was clear.

She paced across the living room. Her mother's home was secure, but it had been broken into this year, as had hers.

A face flashed through her mind. The man at the cemetery— Ezekiel Lewis. No one had been around when they met, and he'd offered to listen to her.

Can you trust him?

I have to. She retrieved his card and dialed the number. He answered on the first ring. "Hi, Ezekiel, it's Tavish. I don't know if you remember me. We met at the cemetery and you gave me your card."

"Tavish! Of course I remember you. Did you decide to take me up on my offer?"

"Sort of. I'd like to drop by, if that's okay with you. I . . . might need some help."

"Absolutely. I'll see you soon."

Checking the pool area, she saw that all seemed to be quiet. She gathered dog chow, bottled water, and bowls into a cloth bag.

In a roller bag, she packed enough clothing for several days, toiletries, the portfolio, and all the cash she had around the house. She'd cash a check tomorrow. At the last minute she added a blanket and pillow.

Taking one last tour of the house to be sure she had everything, she pulled on her sweatshirt and jacket and quietly slipped outside, Marley in tow.

Most of her mother's lights were out, with only her office illuminated. *Good.* The office was on the opposite side of the house from the garage. The truck keys were under the windshield wiper. She still winced when the garage door opened, and it wasn't until they'd driven two blocks away that she could breathe normally.

The old man lived at the base of the Sandia Mountains in a beautifully maintained, single-level patio home. He met her at the door. Marley wagged a greeting and was rewarded with a scratch behind her ear.

They didn't speak until he'd shown her into a well-appointed living room smelling faintly of lemon oil. Photographs of a plump woman with a generous smile covered the top of a grand piano in the corner of the room. The hardwood floors gleamed where they peeked out from under priceless oriental rugs. She sat on a sepia-colored leather sofa, and he sat opposite on a matching chair. He studied her face for a moment.

"Why, Tavish, are you running for your life?"

CHAPTER 18

Sawyer was drained by the time he finished his statement and interview at the Sandoval County Sheriff's Department. The process had taken most of the day, and the vending machine candy bar he'd eaten for lunch had long since worn off. He'd turned the tracking device over to Lieutenant Hammen, even though Sawyer wanted to follow up on it, but he did extract a promise that if something showed up, they'd let him know. He had no idea how Tavish survived the blaze. They hadn't found her body, and Hammen had put out an APB on her car.

He wasn't used to being on the victim/witness end of an investigation, and it made him itch to be part of the action. The part that irritated him the most was the lack of access to information. The lieutenant had made it plain he wanted Sawyer to stay clear.

Of course, that didn't mean he would follow the lieutenant's advice. Sawyer tried calling Tavish several times before remembering she had no phone. He stopped only long enough for a burger and gas before racing down the road to Albuquerque.

He placed a routine check-in call to his department, then regretted it when his unit chief insisted he attend a late-afternoon meeting on policy changes regarding retirement funds.

Once freed of the department, he drove over and finally located Tavish's home. *If this is just her mom's guesthouse, what kind of palace does her mother live in?* A drive around the area answered that. Helen's home and estate sprawled over four city blocks. The driveway curved around an impressive fountain and meticulously maintained plantings. Major money. *Major out-of-my-league.*

He parked next to the garage attached to the main house and peered in the window. Tavish's Audi was parked next to a Mercedes.

He briefly closed his eyes in relief. She'd made it home. He drove around to Tavish's home, parked, and strolled to the front door. All the lights were off. He rang the doorbell. The chimes carried clearly through the heavily carved door. No barking.

Frowning, he rang again. Marley would be barking like crazy if she were home.

He slowly went around the house, peering in windows. Most of the blinds had been pulled, but he could see into the corner of a bedroom. A pillow was missing off the bed, and the closet door was open.

Checking for any passing security staff or patrolling police, he used a credit card to slip open the kitchen door. A swift race through the house showed no sign of either woman or dog or any sign of a struggle. Her purse was missing.

Maybe she'd done as he told her—decided to stay low and let him work on the case. Maybe she was in the main house, which probably had better security. He left his business card on the table with his private cell phone number on the back. He'd return in the morning.

≡≡

Ezekiel waited patiently for Tavish to answer his question. *Why am I running for my life?*

"I don't know. I think my mother, or at least one of the companies she owns, may somehow be connected to all the events of the past few days. And she may be involved in something to do with insurance fraud. And other things as well. Maybe even murder. I need to stay out of sight for a bit until I can figure out what's going on. And I need a place to store this information until I can get word to Sawyer Price, an FBI agent, to pick it up."

"I'm happy to help, but what exactly *is* going on?"

She'd brought her portfolio in with her. "I'll show you. Could I use your table?" She pointed at a large oak table in the dining room that opened to the living area.

"Be my guest."

Tavish laid out the drawings and her notes. While she explained, Ezekiel picked up each drawing in turn and studied it. When she finished, he held up the sketch of John. "Who did you say this is?"

"John Coyote. I think he was trying to send me a message through Marley's chip."

Ezekiel, still holding the sketch, wandered to a desktop computer in the corner of the room, muttering, "My, oh my, oh my.

We do have a conundrum." He sat down. "And you said your mother's company, Softmode Testing, may have some connection with the rest of what's going on?"

"I don't know. That's just speculation."

He nodded. "I suppose. I suppose. Would you do me a favor? Go into the kitchen, right through that door, and pour us a couple of glasses of water."

Tavish headed to the spotlessly clean kitchen, a cream, terracotta, and turquoise–colored room. The glasses were logically placed near the sink. After filling two glasses, she returned to find Ezekiel seated back in the living room.

"Ah, thank you." He took the water and sipped. "What do you know about Sandia Labs, or the work at Los Alamos?"

Tavish sat, placed her drink on a coaster, and rubbed her arms. "I know Los Alamos was home to the Manhattan Project, where scientists developed the bombs dropped on Hiroshima and Nagasaki at the end of World War Two. Sandia Labs is connected to Los Alamos and . . . um . . ."

"The Lawrence Livermore National Laboratory in Livermore, California. Very good."

"May I ask what you're getting at?"

"Certainly. Oh my, yes. I'm retired, you see, from the Sandia National Laboratories. I can't tell you what I did—very hush-hush, you know—but Sandia didn't just develop nuclear weapons. They worked on defense systems such as Star Wars, national security, and nanotechnology."

"Nanotechnology? Like the microchip placed in Marley?"

"Well, something like that, though the microchip, about the size of a small grain of rice, would be well over 100,000 nanometers thick. Nanotechnology is less than 100 nanometers. It's on the molecular scale."

"Then I don't see—"

"This man"—he held up the sketch of John Coyote—"I had to look him up to be sure. His picture was there, just as I thought. Can't trust the ol' noggin these days. Anyway, he used to work at Sandia Labs, a design engineer working in nanotechnology. He was fired about three years ago. His name is, or was, Dr. John Begay."

"I can't believe you know, or knew him!"

He shook his head. "Sandia employs more than thirteen thousand full-time people, not including the contractors. I hardly know even a small percentage of them, but the ones where the labs could have potential issues with . . ." He held up the sketch. "These I get to know very well. Begay was fired. Ergo, he was on my radar."

Tavish made a deliberate effort to relax her fists and breathe normally. "Do you know why he was fired?"

"No. That sort of thing would be like everything else at the lab." He put his finger to his lips. "Shhhh. National security. Top secret. But it wouldn't be because he was selling secrets or anything like that. That would be treason. Sandia is a contractor for the National Nuclear Security Administration."

"Then how would you get fired? What kinds of things?"

"The usual, of course. Not showing up for work. Not doing the work assigned. Maybe lying or falsifying data. Total insubordination."

"Insubordination? I doubt that. He seemed like a nice man."

"Yes, and a design engineer is given a great deal of latitude on attitude. Oh my, sounds like a song. Latitude on attitude."

Tavish stood, too restless to sit. "What about the rest of the sketches? Did any of these people work for Sandia? What made John reach out to me? Why would he change his name? What possible connection could I have with him? Do you think—"

"Tavish, my child, sit down and stop pacing. Let's reason this out."

She sat and tugged on her crystal pendant. "What do you make of the numbers he put in Marley's chip?"

Ezekiel stared at her hand, then reached over to a coffee table with a shelf underneath. He pulled out a small black book. He opened a drawer, withdrew a strip of fabric and placed it into the book, then handed it to her.

She opened it. A Bible. "What's this for? I'm not religious."

"Keep it. You also have a bookmark. Look up the verse on your grandmother's headstone sometime. Read it when you get a chance."

She tried to hand it back, but he held up his hands. "Take it. I have others. You need to read it. You'd be surprised at how much of what we do, and say, today are in there."

"Okay, I'll read it."

"Do you promise?"

"I promise."

He lifted his eyebrows.

She raised her right hand. "I promise, and I always keep my promises."

"I do believe you do."

After tucking the Bible into the pocket of her jacket, she took a deep breath. "What do you think John wanted me to know?"

"You do have those numbers. I'd start there."

"But they don't mean anything."

"Anything that you know of *now*. What else did he give you?"

"Cash for the art. Um, passcode to the gate. His phone number so I could reach him."

"Anything written? Notes? That kind of thing?"

She furrowed her eyebrows. "The preliminary sketch had some notes on it, but no numbers."

"Where is that?"

"He asked to keep it, then decided he wasn't going through with the painting. He paid in full for the artwork, so I didn't ask for the sketch to be returned."

"Did you copy or photograph the drawing?"

"No. I didn't think about taking a photo. I expected him to return it with final notes before I started the painting."

"Any other papers or packages he wanted you to keep?"

"No."

"How did you meet him?"

"At my mother's party a couple of months ago."

"I take it he was introduced as John Coyote, not John Begay?"

"He introduced himself to me as John Coyote. But my mother couldn't have known him by that name or she would have reacted when the detective showed up after I told them about his murder."

"Did you ever ask him or your mother how they knew each other or why he was a guest at her party?"

"I tried asking her earlier today, but she was too busy to answer." *Or she knew the answer and was just putting me off.*

Ezekiel tapped a finger on his lip for a few moments. "You seem to remember meeting Begay pretty clearly. I assume you meet a lot of people through your mother's parties. Why did you remember meeting him so well? Did you talk about the commission then? Or perhaps you discussed how you met at some point during the project?"

Closing her eyes, Tavish pictured their meeting. "I remember the sun on the glittering pool. It was a warm day, and I was wearing a long, floral skirt and sleeveless top. Andrew had picked it out for me to wear on this special day."

"Why was the day special, Tavish?"

"Andrew was to meet my mother for the first time. Helen was furious with me for getting engaged without her approval, not to mention denying her the big church wedding she would have insisted we have. We—Andrew and I—decided she wouldn't throw a hissy fit in front of her guests, and Andrew would have a chance to charm her."

"I sense a *but* coming in here."

"But Andrew didn't show up. I remember checking my watch and looking for him. Helen was working the party. There were a lot of rich and influential people there and . . ."

Something. A glimmer of a thought.

Ezekiel sat quietly.

"I thought I saw Andrew. At the edge of the gathering. Just for a second. But that couldn't be. He called to say he was tied up with a client and would miss the party."

"And? Why would this make you remember Begay?"

"Mother told me to mingle, meet people. I introduced myself and we were shaking hands. I thought I saw Andrew, maybe I even said his name, and John turned to look in the same direction. I don't know if he saw anything. He did politely ask me who Andrew was and I told him. Our conversation was a bit longer because of that. And, of course, Andrew committed suicide shortly thereafter." She covered her mouth to keep from talking about the funeral. And the pregnant woman.

"What is it, Tavish?" Ezekiel asked softly. "Tell me."

The old man's eyes did look so much like her grandmother's. The room blurred for a moment and a lump grew in her throat. "Andrew. Andy. I found him. After." She closed her eyes.

She'd been driving to the art store when Andy's text message came. She'd pulled over to read it, opening the window to let in the cool air. "Meet me." He gave directions, then wrote, "I have a surprise for you."

She grinned, waited for a break in traffic, and pulled a U-turn. He liked surprises and having her guess what he was thinking.

She found the parking lot he described. The sun lit up the Sandia Mountains, casting a crimson glow. His car, covered in dust, was the only one in the lot, parked under some large trees. She pulled up behind his car and got out.

A buzzing came from the car.

Her quick steps slowed.

The foul odor came next. Like an outhouse.

She pushed forward, her feet like bricks.

The car door was open. He was slumped sideways, the shotgun beside him.

With a trembling hand, she touched his arm . . .

"Tavish? Tavish, are you okay?" Ezekiel was patting her face. "I thought you were going to faint." He handed her the glass of water.

"I'm sorry. I was just remembering . . . finding Andy." She took a big gulp. "I touched him . . . His arm was . . . stiff . . ."

Ezekiel's forehead wrinkled as he took the water from her hand and placed it beside her. "I'm sorry this triggered those memories. Is there anything else you need to tell me or leave with me?"

"The sniper who killed Dusty Rhodes was probably following a tracking device that Sawyer found in my car."

"But you didn't see the shooter?"

"No. I just ran."

"Why did you go there?"

"Patricia Caron mentioned him. I thought he might have some answers."

"And she's the one who owned the house Begay rented?"

"Yes."

"Hmm. How long has Softmode Testing been in business?"

Tavish blinked at the apparent change of subject. "I believe my mother started the company about eight years ago."

Ezekiel leaned back and stared at the ceiling. "Yes. I suppose that could be," he muttered.

"What could be?"

"I'm trying to connect some dots. It's possible Dr. Begay became aware of your mother when his department was arranging some testing through her company. It was not unusual for some departments to seek corroborating test results from an objective third party. I assume Softmode Testing had staffing cleared for top-secret work?"

"Yes. Helen wanted me to work there and made me go through the background checks, drug testing, polygraph exam, fingerprints, and all the other hoops. I just wasn't sure I wanted to spend my time doing statistical analysis."

"I don't blame you there. It's possible Begay arranged to be at her soiree, maybe looking for a job at Softmode Testing."

"Could be, but if he was looking to be hired, wouldn't his fake name and identity be uncovered?" She took a sip of water.

Ezekiel smiled grimly. "Oh, I'm sure his fake credentials were prepared by the best. But he may not have been looking at a scientific position. He could have been looking at something more inconspicuous. Here's the brilliance of that move. He had the expertise to recognize, steal, and sell new products already developed and in the testing stage. It would fit his profile."

"His profile? How well did you know Dr. Begay?"

"I never met the man. I was aware of him because of . . . Well, I just knew the comings and goings of people, shall we say."

Tavish grinned at him. "You must have been head of security!"

The old man glanced around him theatrically, then put his finger to his lips. "Now, I didn't say that."

"I know. I did. Then you *do* know why he was fired."

Ezekiel pursed his lips and finally said, "I shouldn't speak ill of the dead, but it's important that we get to the bottom of this. Begay was lazy. Took shortcuts. And had a bit of a gambling problem. The ponies. He was always short on money. He was a risk to the company."

"Gambling? Could his death be something the Mafia would do? Like he owed money?"

"Maybe. The risk to the company was if he got in too deep, he might look for a quick way to raise funds. As for the Mafia, well, they have been known for making an example of others."

"That still doesn't explain his interest in me, or those numbers connected to Marley."

He looked directly at her. "I think Marley was his backup plan, and you were his insurance policy. If anything happened to him, he wanted you to find out."

"Why me?"

Ezekiel shrugged and gestured to the sketches spread out across his table, then gave her a knowing look. "You know."

"Trust?"

"Indeed. John Begay must have trusted you."

"Do you think he wanted me to know about my mother's involvement?"

"In what?"

"In . . . whatever is at the bottom of all this."

"I'm sure I can't say. But who better than you?"

Tavish slowly nodded. "It *is* possible that he actually landed a job at Softmode. If he did, the numbers might be the combination to a locker or a passcode for the computer. We talked about Softmode while I was finishing up his drawing, although more in passing rather than anything specific. I could go over there and check it out."

"You have to proceed very carefully. Whatever Dr. Begay knew, or took, or saw, or did, it got him killed."

"Don't worry. I'll be careful."

"What about calling in the police? Maybe—"

"No. The police won't believe me. Sawyer will. I'll let him know you have my sketches. Tonight I'll find a place to sleep. Tomorrow I'll go to the bank and get money, a new cell phone. I'll swing by Softmode and check out employee records. If he worked there, I'll check that out, then head out of town. Put some distance between me and whoever is after me. Everything else I can do by phone. For now, that's a plan, but my brain's on overload."

"You could stay here, at least for tonight. I have a guest room."

"Thank you, Ezekiel. That's very kind of you, but as you said, I need to be very careful. I don't want to put you in any more danger."

"Well then, I will keep you in my prayers."

Tavish's eyes burned. "Thank . . . thank you again. And thanks for the Bible."

"It's not a talisman. It won't protect you from physical evil. But you might find some, shall we say, eternal wisdom in there."

"I will. Would you consider keeping Marley, at least for a few days until I can get settled?"

"Tavish, in case you hadn't noticed, Marley scarcely leaves your side. She's your dog now. And she'll be a good friend and protector for you."

She stood. "I'll call you once I get a phone."

Ezekiel walked her to the door. "If you need anything else, you know where to find me."

She swallowed around the lump in her throat and trotted to her car, Marley hot on her heels. Another storm was brewing and the air smelled of rain. Ezekiel was still watching as she got in. She waved and pulled out.

"Where shall we go tonight, Marley?"

The dog gave a sharp bark.

"We could have hidden out at Kevin's place, but I think it was blown to smithereens. Parking lots are too open. A motel would be cautious of me paying in cash. I'm afraid I'm not very good at this undercover stuff."

Marley barked again.

"Parking garage? That's a thought. The airport is used to parked cars and trucks. We can get a few hours' sleep, hit the bank as soon as it opens, and be on the road before anyone knows we left town. The back seat is small, but we have tinted windows, so we should be out of sight of any security guards."

Her stomach grumbled.

"Okay, parking garage by way of a grocery store. We'll get enough food to last the night and into tomorrow." She pulled the portable GPS from the glove box, pulled over, and plugged it in. It took a few moments to acquire the satellite, then she clicked on the request for a store. She had three to choose from between where she was parked and the airport.

Below the map were the coordinates of her current location. She stared at the numbers. Four sets. Separated by a space. A chill ran through her. "Marley, could the numbers in your microchip be coordinates? Thirty-five degrees, zero-three minutes, seventeen point seventy-nine seconds north? But that would only be half a location." The only other number she had from John long enough for a coordinate was the gate code. Which she couldn't remember.

She closed her eyes and pictured the gate keypad. She reached and punched in the numbers. Her fingers moved from habit. One-zero-six-three-four-zero-three-three-two. "One hundred and six degrees, thirty-four minutes, zero-three point thirty-two seconds west." She opened her eyes.

Marley was watching her.

"You don't need to ask. Of course we'll drive to these coordinates. It's not all that far from here."

Placing the GPS in her lap, she turned the truck around. The direction she drove sent her through an area of town where drunks, prostitutes, and homeless gathered. She made sure all the doors were locked, and sighed when she had to stop at a red light. Sure enough, a homeless man with a cardboard sign shuffled hopefully to her door. She sped off as soon as the light changed, not making eye contact with him.

They soon arrived at a series of steel industrial buildings on the edge of town. The parking lots held only crumpled paper twirling around on the dusty puffs of wind. A solitary streetlight flickered sickly yellow light. A peeling sign offered space for rent. Three buildings circled the lot. She parked the truck, slipped out, and listened.

The wind carried distant street noises and a barking dog, along with the stench of a dumpster in need of emptying.

The first two buildings had doors secured by keyed padlocks. The third had a combination lock that required lining up four numbers. "Okay," she whispered. "He didn't leave a key. The only other numbers he gave me were his phone number. I never called him, so . . ." She checked the vacant lot again. The breeze rattled a bush nearby, and a jackrabbit stared at her from under the branches.

He wouldn't have used the area code or first three digits. That would have been too obvious. The last four numbers were seven-two-seven-three. She tried it.

The lock opened.

She licked her lips, removed the lock, and opened the door.

The space beyond was inky-black.

Feeling inside the door for a light switch, all she touched was a gauzy spiderweb. She snatched her hand back. *Flashlight.* She trotted to the pickup and removed a flashlight from under the seat.

Marley pawed at her hand.

"No, sweet girl, I need you to stand guard. Watch for any approaching bad guys, aliens, or zombies. Okay?"

Marley licked her hand.

Patting the dog on the head, she returned to the storage building. The flashlight needed new batteries and offered only a feeble beam.

She shoved the door wider with her foot and stepped inside.

A single small duffel bag rested in the center of the room.

After playing the light around the interior to be sure nothing else needed to be investigated, she approached the bag. It was unzipped.

She squatted and opened it.

Inside was an envelope with her name on it. Underneath was a stack of cash.

With a shaking hand, she opened the envelope and took out the single sheet of paper.

Tavish,

I knew you'd figure out my numbers.

If you are reading this, I've paid the ultimate price for my actions. All I can do is try to make it right. Please take this money to Mrs. Montez. I am so sorry.

Please take good care of Marley.

—John

She stood and picked up the bag. She had no idea who Mrs. Montez was, but John had entrusted her with what looked like his life's savings. Slowly she left the building, locking the door behind her, and walked to her truck. *Should I turn this over to Sawyer? Maybe it's stolen money . . . Wait . . . Ezekiel said John gambled on horse racing. Could this be his winnings?* She reached the truck and reached for the door.

Marley was lying on the front seat. Motionless.

"Marley? Are you—" Something smashed into her skull.

The blackness was immediate.

CHAPTER 19

When Sawyer returned to Tavish's home the next morning, nothing had changed. His card still rested on the table where he'd left it. Her car was still parked in the garage.

After returning to the small cubicle he'd been assigned at the FBI office in downtown Albuquerque, he placed a round of phone calls to local hospitals and law-enforcement departments. No sign of Tavish. He let Detective Hammen know he'd found her car and asked that he be notified if she showed up. He got an earful on her not showing up for an interview.

Well, that was good, right? He'd told her to stay low. She'd contact him soon.

The prickle of unease wouldn't go away.

Though he'd thought his undercover investigation was over, this morning a memo had come in clearing him to follow up on the pottery recovered from the Four Corners sting. Dr. Caron had identified the pieces as possibly coming from her dig, and the thief who'd died in the shootout had been identified as Vince

Trainor. Sawyer cross-referenced the name. Trainor wasn't on the list of students active at the dig for the past eight months. Sawyer continued to search, finally finding his name on a roster of short-term students who'd worked at the Kéyah dig a year earlier.

Trainor's rap sheet showed petty theft, a drunk and disorderly arrest, and numerous speeding tickets. He also had served time for drugs. Sawyer highlighted *drugs* and beside it jotted *connection to gallery?*

The sheriff's department involved in the shooting at Four Corners believed there was an accomplice who had escaped. Sawyer marked that fact, along with the notation that Trainor's autopsy report didn't reveal anything useful—except he'd been high at the time of the shooting.

Sawyer typed *John Coyote* into the FBI database. A fair number of names came up, but none matched the drawing Tavish had done.

He entered *Tavish* next. Her name didn't show up as a separate entry, but her mother did.

Helen Rose Gordon McTavish Richmond. Intellectual property broker. CEO and owner of several corporations. Art collector. Married Ronald McTavish. Divorced after five years. One daughter, Evelyn Yvonne. Married Lawrence Richmond. Divorced after two years. Owns Daltice Corporation and Softmode Testing, both of Albuquerque, as well as . . .

The list of her corporations followed, along with her education, accomplishments, and other pieces of information. Several links were listed, including one to Tavish's grandmother.

Grace Eileen Sparks Gordon, heir to Gordon Industries.
Married Merle Gordon, founder and CEO of Gordon
Industries until his death . . . Grace became CEO until her
death . . .

He sat up with the next bit of information.

Grace Gordon left her entire estate, estimated value close
to a billion dollars, to her only granddaughter, Evelyn
McTavish. Her daughter, Helen Rose Gordon McTavish
Richmond, is executor of the estate until Evelyn turns thirty.

How did Tavish's inheritance fit into the murder of Coyote,
art theft, microchips, sniper attack, or any of the other odd
events?

Money is a powerful motivator.

Even though the police believed the fringe group Antifa
was responsible for the shooting at Dusty Rhodes's trailer, could
Tavish actually have been the target? If she died, would the estate
go to her mother? Tavish mentioned she wasn't close to Helen.
Considering Helen's mother left her money to Tavish rather than
her own daughter, it looked like Helen hadn't been close to her
mother either.

He pulled out a yellow legal pad and created three columns,
which he labeled *Possible victim*, *Motivation*, and *Suspect*. In the
first row he wrote, *Tavish*, *money*, and *Helen*. On the next line
he wrote *Dusty Rhodes*, *something he said on the radio show*, and
Antifa. He added his own name on the third line, then *revenge*,
and finally *possible accomplice in the theft of Native artifacts*.

Of the three of them, Tavish emerged as the most likely candidate. He looked up Helen Richmond's unlisted number and dialed. A woman answered. "Richmond house."

"Is Helen Richmond home?"

"May I take a message?"

"No." He disconnected. Maybe he should pay a visit to Helen in person. If she knew the FBI was keeping an eye on her, she'd be far less likely to pull something.

Someone was pounding on Tavish's head with a hammer. *Boom, boom, boom, boom!* Like a heartbeat. She moaned.

The pounding continued. The pain was too much. Blackness returned.

Her head hurt. The bed was hard, gritty, grinding into her cheek. Water struck her, cold, dripping down her face, her neck, her body. Her bed was in a shower? *No. Make the pain go away.*

The water increased. Big, fat splats struck her aching head. She opened her eyes, but they wouldn't focus. Everything was gray, except for the spot of black. She blinked. The gray remained, as did the black. *Black what?*

Reaching up, she touched the aching area in the back of her head. The pain increased. She moaned and looked at her hand, now stained crimson.

Nothing made sense. This wasn't her bed. It was . . . outside. The ground. Hard-packed, sandpaper-gritty earth. The wet was rain. She was lying on her stomach in the rain and the black spot was . . . She squinted. Hair. Fur.

Marley.

She pushed up from the ground, but the world spun out of control. Staying on her stomach, she used her hands to pull herself to the dog's side. *Please don't be dead. Please, please . . .*

She slid up to the prone dog, reached out, then brought her hand back. What if Marley was dead?

"Please, God," she whispered. "If you're up there, if you can hear me, please let Marley be alive." She slid her hand over and rested it on the dog's side.

She was breathing.

"Thank you." Tavish raised herself on one elbow, then waited for the spinning to stop. The rain remained steady, chilling her to the bone but helping to push away the nausea. When she was finally able to sit, she ran her fingers over the dog, assessing her injuries. Like herself, the dog had sustained a blow to the head. Her legs appeared unbroken, as did her ribs and spine, but she was in desperate need of a veterinarian.

Where were they?

Still fighting dizziness, Tavish looked around. Her last memory was . . . Ezekiel? No. After that. Driving. Driving. That's all she remembered. *How did I get here? And where is here?* It was daylight, but she had no idea of the time. Her brain was a fog.

Her sight had cleared enough to see she was in a narrow canyon with high walls. That was important, wasn't it? And the rain. Maybe she should drink the rain. Cupping her hands, she collected some rainwater and sipped it.

She vomited. Dry heaves left her weak and with an aching stomach.

She spoke, wanting to hear a voice, any voice. "Pull yourself together. Your name is . . . Tavish. You have a head injury. Marley is hurt as well. You were in a . . . car accident . . . but your car is . . . Okay. It doesn't matter. You need to get help."

She shoved to her feet, ignoring the spinning world, and lifted Marley. The dog was a limp deadweight in her arms. She wouldn't be able to go far like this.

She lowered herself to the ground and took off her soggy jacket. The waist had a drawstring. She pulled the drawstring tight and tied a knot, then placed Marley in the top part. Leaving the dog's head out, she zipped up the front, then tied the cuffs to each other, forming a loop. She could carry the dog like a purse—

The ground trembled.

That was important. Why? "Arroyo. Rain."

Flash flood.

Her stomach hardened to a rock. She'd learned about this. From Sawyer.

She pushed off the ground, using the canyon wall to steady her. *Get out of here.* Grabbing the jacket, she shoved it over her shoulder.

A low rumble came from her right.

Turning, she staggered away from the sound. Her legs were lead, moving in slow motion.

The trembling increased, the sandy silt bouncing on the ground.

She pumped her legs harder. Everything became crystal clear around her. She looked for a way out, a ledge, anything but smooth walls.

We're not going to make it.

A blast of air shoved her forward.

A roaring came from behind her.

Slipping the jacket sleeves around her neck to free her hands, she grabbed at the wall, seeking anything to hold on to. The stone was smooth, scoured by hundreds of years of floods. The rocks scraped her groping hands.

Her fingers found a small crevice. She clung to it.

The wall of water hit, sweeping her feet from under her.

She clutched the chunk of rock, rotating so Marley would be on top. The water flung her around and Marley's head went under. She let go with one hand and tugged the dog up higher.

The pull of the water was horrific, the temperature numbingly cold.

Her grip on the rock slipped. In a second she was swept down the narrow canyon in the roaring flood.

She tried to scream. Her mouth filled with water.

Debris pelted her. The flood swept her from canyon wall to canyon wall. The weight of the dog pushed her under.

She flailed upward, her face breaking free for a moment before the water again forced her down.

Something scraped her arm and she grabbed for it and pulled. Her head again broke the surface. She'd snagged a large tree limb. Wrapping one arm around it, she lifted Marley's head next to hers. The floodwater boiled around them, sloshing around the steep corners.

Something beneath the roaring water snagged the limb. It twisted sideways and jammed between the narrow canyon walls. Instantly the water rushed over her head. She let go of the limb and pulled herself up, clutching Marley. Her head popped out of the water. She took a deep breath of air and again lifted the limp dog's head.

Ahead was a small shelf in the wall. She steered toward it. One chance to snag it. She grasped for the slippery surface, slipped, grabbed again. The water surged, ripping her fingers loose. Once again she plunged forward.

The water was an opaque tawny brown, hiding any objects that could hook her and hold her under. She floated on her back, feet downstream, and shoved Marley onto her chest. The dog's weight pushed her down, and she used both hands to stay afloat.

Her leg smashed into the rock wall.

She screamed in pain. She wanted to grab her injured leg, but she had to keep the dog clear of the flood.

The canyon walls widened. Her foot hit something and twirled her around. She grabbed for Marley before the dog went under.

The canyon walls opened to the high desert. The water slowed, but still sent her hurtling forward. More debris rolled around her, threatening to drag her under.

She had no idea how deep the water was.

Ahead, a boulder split the flood. If she struck it sideways with her body, she'd be pressed against it and would drown. She tried to swim to the side. The water shoved her back. At the last second she brought her feet up. They connected with the rock with a teeth-jarring crash. Instantly she was tossed to the side and swept around it. Her head was now downstream from her feet. She couldn't see where she was heading.

The canyon walls receded. The flood began to lose its fury.

She twisted around until she again could watch for obstacles.

More rocks, a small row of them looking like black teeth, jutted from the water. She was too big to fit through the narrow channels between them. Again she tried swimming, but the inexorable water sent her toward the boulders.

She slammed against one. Instinctively she grabbed it and pulled, freeing her upper body from the torrent. Her legs were pinned, but at least she'd stopped moving.

Small branches pelted her as they floated by. She shifted Marley so the dog lay partly on the rock, then gently brushed the fur from her eyes. They were closed, but the tough little dog was still breathing.

Pain pounded Tavish's leg, and she shivered in the frigid, muddy water. How long could she last on this rock?

Inch by inch, she worked to free her legs. The water seemed to be dropping, as if the rage of the flood was passing.

A branch floated by.

She grabbed for it.

The branch writhed, trying to wrap around her arm.

Snake!

She screamed and splashed at it. It slithered away.

Another branch, this time with a few leaves, drifted past and she seized it. The limb was roughly four feet long. She poked the area around the rock to gauge the depth. The ground was two feet below her. She would be able to walk from here. Assuming her leg would bear weight.

Gingerly she lowered her good leg until she made contact with the earth. The rush of floodwater could take her down at any minute. What was it Sawyer had said? *"Just six inches of water can sweep you off your feet."* She'd have to take her chances. Marley needed help, and she'd die of hypothermia sitting here.

Marley's soaked corded coat added even more weight to

the dog. She would not be able to use her jacket-sling to carry the Puli, nor use both her arms if she hoped to stay upright and use the stick to check for deep areas of water. She finally eased Marley from the jacket around her neck, using one hand to hold the canine's legs to her chest, like a neck scarf. She stood.

The floodwater pushed against her, attempting to shove her down. *Don't fall. Don't fall.* She jabbed at the ground looking for holes, stumbled forward a few steps, then waited to get her balance. Jab, jab. Forward. Pause. Jab, jab. Forward. Pause. This would take forever. How far would she have to go? *Don't think about it. Just two steps forward.*

It seemed like hours but was probably not more than one before she noticed the water was no longer around her knees. It now lapped mid-shin. The canyon walls seemed farther away as well. Jab, jab. Forward. Pause. Jab, jab. Forward. Pause.

The water continued to recede as the canyon opened up.

She wanted to stop and check Marley, sit, rest, take stock of her injuries. She pushed on. She could feel the slight lifting and falling of the dog's chest. *At least she's alive.*

The water reached Tavish's ankles and spread out across the desert on all sides. She had no idea where she was or how she got there. Or how she'd get home.

Could she go home? Something tickled her memory. She couldn't figure out why that was important.

The day was gray and overcast with clouds, making it difficult to work out the time. Her last memory was of . . . night? She couldn't be sure. At least the temperature was rising.

A low, nasal whine came from overhead. A pair of turkey vultures soared in the charcoal sky, circling something to her right.

A light breeze shifted and the stench came next. She clapped her hand over her nose and breathed through her mouth. Apparently a critter had been caught in the canyon with her . . . but it shouldn't stink this soon if it had been killed by the flash flood.

She didn't want to, but she moved toward the smell.

Something was wrapped around a small juniper. The object bobbed slightly in the shallow water. Something . . . make that someone wearing jeans and a torn Wisconsin Badgers T-shirt. She didn't have to see his face to recognize the decomposing body of the man who'd loaned her his pickup. Kevin.

CHAPTER 20

Tavish wanted to run. To scream. To faint. To give in to the panic attack that welled up inside her. *Not now! If you pass out and fall, you'll drown in the ankle-deep water—the same water drifting around the rotting corpse in front of you. And Marley will die.*

She lifted her finger to gnaw on a nail, then dropped her hand to her side. *Deal with it.*

Reluctantly she moved closer to see if he'd died like John Coyote—stabbed in the chest. She could see no sign of a knife. Moving closer still, she spotted a likely answer. The side of his skull looked misshapen. He'd been bashed in the head. *Like me.*

That was it. The illusive memory. She'd been struck from behind as she was about to get into her truck. They must have bashed poor Marley as well and driven both of them to this site—knowing that the rain in that narrow arroyo would form a flash flood and finish her off. She'd been very lucky that the flood hadn't occurred during the night when she was still unconscious. That had probably been the plan, and no one would think she'd been murdered. They'd believe she died in a terrible accident.

Whoever was behind this was diabolically smart. The massive shooting that killed Dusty Rhodes would be blamed on Antifa. Both Kevin and she would have been found after the flood with head injuries consistent with being hurtled down a canyon by raging waters.

More memories returned. The note from John. The money.

She stepped away from the dead man. *Wait.* Wouldn't police figure out Kevin died from the blow to the head instead of drowning? Of course, he could have smashed his head almost immediately when the wall of water struck him, but to be really thorough, he should have water in his lungs—

Missing shower curtain.

She'd assumed they used the shower curtain in his home, and maybe they did, but what if they had bashed him on the head in the living room, then taken him to the bathroom and held his head underwater?

She gagged, her stomach threatening to dry heave. "What am I doing?" she whispered. "I'm standing here worried about the forensic evidence on Kevin, and if I don't start walking, I'll be just as dead as he is."

But he deserves to be investigated.

Looking around, she tried to formulate a plan. If she had pencil and paper, she could leave a note. She'd have to create something that would be clear of the water. Moving upstream, she picked up a floating twig. Then another. And another. Some hearty tufts of grass swirled in the slight current. She pulled a few of them up.

Balancing the dog on her shoulder, she used the grass as twine and tied the sticks together. Breathing through her mouth, she moved to the bush above Kevin's body. She'd use the branches in the shrub to form letters.

She tried not to look at what was left of Kevin. Even breathing through her mouth, the stench was palpable.

She finished and stepped away. Hopefully someone would read it. *It's the best I can do. For now.*

Slogging sideways away from the dead man—she didn't want to walk directly downstream from his body—she continued to move. Jab, jab. Forward. Pause. Jab, jab. Forward. Pause. She kept her eyes on the flow of water. Marley's wet cords dripped uncomfortably down her back. Her drying clothes were stiff where her blood had congealed.

The pain in her leg and head, the gouges on her stomach from the rusty metal in Dusty Rhodes's trailer, plus Marley's weight were getting unbearable. She stopped and took stock of the landscape. Behind her was the arroyo. Stretching ahead were rock outcroppings, sagebrush, tufts of grasses, and junipers.

A log protruded from the water nearby, looking like a good place to sit down and rest. It did seem to move a bit with the water swirling around it. No, not swirling. Undulating.

She drew nearer.

It was covered in scorpions.

Adrenaline shot through her system. She gave up on the stick and limped away as fast as she could, wanting to beat at her clothing to be sure none had crawled up her leg.

What if I don't get help? What if I die out here? People died in the desert all the time. And New Mexico had vast unpopulated areas.

Don't think like that. People have survived far worse than this. She could still walk, albeit slowly. And think. And reason. The worst was behind her.

Eventually she ran out of adrenaline and slowed down. Her head hurt. Her leg pounded. Her shoulders and neck ached where Marley rested. She pushed on. Without knowing where she was, all she could do was follow the water away from the canyon, away from the body, away from the scorpions.

The water was scarcely an inch deep, though still opaque. Without her stick to feel for holes, she looked for ground emerging from the water.

The earth finally leveled and became hard packed. She'd walked about a mile before she realized the hard surface was a road. A paved road under the mud. She could actually see the asphalt in places.

A paved road meant people.

The sun briefly peeked through the clouds directly overhead. The heat felt good for a moment, but soon raging thirst took over. She moved her tongue around in her mouth, trying to work up some spit.

The floodwater was completely off the road, but a few puddles had formed nearby. Water. The same water that had probably washed over Kevin's rotting corpse.

She kept walking. The sun disappeared in the east, but she had no idea where the flood had driven her. She could be on some secondary road leading to Bucksnort, Arizona.

Her steps grew shorter. She concentrated on the road, placing one foot, then the other, in front of her. Her eyelids were sandpaper scraping at her eyes. *If I sit down, I'll never get up. I will die.* That thought didn't bother her. Dying was easy. A black nothingness. The pain would be over and she'd be free—

Marley will die.

One foot, then the other. *Keep walking.*

A different sound from the rustling sage and yucca shoved into her brain. She looked up. Off in the distance, headlights appeared. *Thank you, God.* Was that how you prayed? The Bible Ezekiel gave her was missing, as was her crystal. *No matter.* She would replace them. For now she was going to be rescued.

But what if it was the same people who'd knocked her out and stuck her in the arroyo? They could be returning to see their handiwork.

She stopped walking and stared at the growing headlights.

Hide? Flag them down?

Maybe hope for the best and prepare for the worst. She turned in a slow circle, looking for a stick or rock. A likely looking candidate for defense was nearby.

Approaching gingerly, she checked for snakes or resting scorpions. She finally nudged the rock with her shoe. Nothing slithered or crept out.

The lights were very near. She lifted the rock and held it behind her back, still holding Marley's legs with her other hand. She moved to the driver's side of the road.

A late-eighties burgundy Jeep Grand Wagoneer, complete with wood side panels, stopped. The window lowered and a man in his sixties leaned out. "Well, ma'am, we came out to exercise

Maggie here"—he patted the steering wheel—"and check on the flood. It looks as if you had firsthand experience with it." He spoke with a deep Southern drawl.

Tavish let the rock drop. She tried to keep her cooked-pasta legs from collapsing. "Do you think you could give us a ride?"

"Us?" He glanced behind her.

"My dog and me."

The man looked at whoever was sitting beside him. "Whatcha say, son? Good deed for the day?"

"Unless you're fixin' to leave this lady and her hound out here on their own," a voice with an equally deep accent answered.

The driver jumped from the car.

Tavish jerked backward.

"Oh, now, I'm sorry about that." He opened the rear passenger door. "Didn't mean to startle you none. I'm George. This here's my son, Chad."

"I'm . . ." *Don't say your name. You're supposed to be dead. People talk.* "Um, Taylor. And this is my dog, ah, Puli . . . Puli Ann." *That was remarkably stupid.* She slid into the seat and carefully lowered her dog into her lap. Marley looked even worse.

Chad leaned over the seat. "Your dog looks kinda dead." Chad looked like his father, handsome in a strong-jawed way, but Chad's hair was thick and black, unlike his father's Billy Graham–like snowy locks.

"She needs a vet. We got caught by the storm in that canyon over there."

"Is she in shock?" George asked.

"I don't know. How do you check?"

George leaned into the car so he could see her. "Pull her lip up and let me see her gums."

Tavish carefully lifted Marley's lip. Her gums were pale pink.

"Yep. We need to get her some help." George stepped into the car and started the engine. "Where's your vehicle?"

I'm terrible at lying. "My . . . friends must have driven off with it."

"Not much for friends." George reached over and gave a little tap on his son's shoulder.

"Sure they weren't relatives?" His son tapped him back, then looked at Tavish. "Where ya fixin' to get to?"

"Albuquerque, but really, anyplace that has a phone." *And just who am I going to call?*

"Albuquerque?" George asked. "Now that's what I'm talkin' about." Another tap.

"Sure," Chad said to Tavish. "If you don't mind a couple of Tar Heels and this here old Wagoneer, we'll get ya to Albuquerque."

Tavish wanted to cry, then hug both of them.

They turned around carefully and headed east. Without asking, Chad handed her a plastic bottle of water. She tried not to bolt it down. Once it was empty, she asked, "You're Tar Heels? That means you're from North Carolina?" She didn't want them to question her any further. "Tell me, what brings you to New Mexico?"

"I moved out here to drive truck. Found it to be sweet cherry pie. Far away from them leafers. And that's what I'm talking about. Hey, Chad?" Tap.

Tavish stared at the older man. "Excuse me?"

Chad turned so she could see his grin. "Translation: Dad

moved out to get a job as a long-haul truck driver. He liked what he found, because this place doesn't have all the out-of-state tourists who drive around during peak leaf season. The road would be jammed on the Blue Ridge Parkway. Right, Dad?" Tap.

The two men chuckled at their exchange, then continued to talk about New Mexico, the weather, car repairs, and flash flooding, punctuating every couple of sentences with a light tap on each other's shoulders. They didn't seem to mind when Tavish didn't join in.

"Where in Albuquerque were you heading?" Chad asked her.

Where indeed? Not home. Ezekiel had offered her refuge, but she didn't want to involve him. Kevin helped her and he was now lying under a bush feeding the vultures. She'd put poor Marley and Sawyer in danger too. For a moment she'd allowed herself to think she and Sawyer might have something special between them.

Shoulda, coulda, woulda. No use thinking about it.

Marley lay motionless in her lap. Tavish stroked the fur away from the Puli's eyes, then gently scratched behind the dog's ears. "Stay with me, Marley," she whispered.

What was the name of the veterinary hospital that had put Marley's microchip in? Something with Mountain in it. Mountainside? Sandia Mountain? *Mountain View.* They would recognize the dog. And no one knew John was dead. Marley would be treated and Tavish could lie—tell them the owner would be coming for the dog. That would buy her time to figure out what to do next. "Mountain View Veterinary Hospital."

"Address?" Chad asked.

"I . . . don't remember."

"Not to worry. I'll look it up on my phone." Chad's thumbs flew as he typed the name. "Okay, got it. It's not in a great part of town."

"Right. Yeah. That's the one."

After another half hour, they pulled up in front of a white-painted building with a fiberglass horse on the roof. The sign on the door noted the practice was closed but had an emergency number posted.

"Should I call that number?" Chad asked.

"Please."

He dialed. "Hi, yeah, we're parked outside y'all's pet hospital. We have an emergency . . . Don't know, let me get the dog's mama." He handed his cell to Tavish.

"This is Dr. Anne. What's your dog's emergency?"

"She . . . hit her head. We got caught in a flash flood. She's unconscious."

"What kind of dog and how old?"

"I'm not sure on her age. You put her microchip in so you should have her records."

"Your name and the dog's name?"

Oh great. What name did John bring her in under? Coyote? Begay? "She's actually owned by . . . John Coyote. Marley."

"Oh no, poor Marley!" Dr. Anne clicked her tongue. "I'll be right there. I do need to tell you that there is an additional after-hours fee."

"Don't worry." Tavish stroked the prone dog. "It will be paid." One way or another.

She disconnected and handed the cell back.

"I thought you said the dog's name was Puli Ann," Chad said.

Tavish didn't know what to say.

"Well, girl," George said, "I don't rightly know exactly what your story is, but you need to be careful. You're looking mighty banged up, and I somehow don't think it was your friends who drove off and left you."

"Thank you. I will."

Dr. Anne—Anne Barrett, DVM, according to the name painted on the door—proved to be a tiny woman with a small-town, fresh-scrubbed face and serious eyes. She'd apparently entered the hospital from the rear and was now motioning Tavish to come in through the front door.

"Looks like the doctor-lady's here." George got out of the car and opened the back door. "I hope your little dog gets fixed up. And you find your way home safely."

Tavish got out, holding the limp Marley in her arms. "Thank you, George, Chad. I think you saved our lives." She started to move past him, but he put a hand on her arm.

"Miz Taylor, and I know that's not your name, you take care of yourself. Whoever did this to you and your dog meant business. You need to stay out of sight and talk to the police. Promise you'll do that?"

Tavish swallowed. "I promise I'll stay out of sight. I can't promise anything else."

"Good 'nuff. God bless you." He kissed her forehead as if giving a benediction, then released her arm.

She hurried to the waiting vet, but paused at the door to wave good-bye to the two men. The street was empty.

Dr. Anne took Marley and hustled her through the lobby, past the exam room, and into a treatment area. A thirtysomething, wiry woman in jeans and a smock strolled in just as Dr. Anne rolled out a small blanket and placed it on a wire rack over a tub. "Good. You're just in time. Get an IV line in and let's get an X-ray." Tavish stepped back as the two women smoothly worked around the dog.

"Is Marley going to live?" The lump in Tavish's throat made it hard to speak.

Lifting one ear tip from the stethoscope she had pressed to Marley's chest, Dr. Anne said, "Hopefully. The next twenty-four hours will tell." She looked closely at Tavish's face. "Restroom's through there."

Tavish tried not to run. She made it just in time to the toilet, where she was violently sick. Once the nausea passed, she ran cold water and rinsed her face. There would be no peace until she discovered who did this. And no justice. The police wouldn't help. Her mother could be one of the guilty ones. It was up to her. Alone.

She could barely recognize her image in the mirror. Dirt smeared down her face. Mud had dried in her hair, matting down sections. Her T-shirt was filthy and torn. She looked like a deranged homeless person.

Homeless.

The perfect disguise.

She stepped from the bathroom.

Dr. Anne and the technician were at the X-ray machine, with Marley sprawled on the table underneath. They'd started an IV drip on the dog.

"May I ask, when you put the microchip into the dog, what happens?"

The technician answered, "A number is embedded in a chip the size of a thin grain of rice. It's injected SubQ. This number can be read with a scanner made by the same company. The owner registers the number and contact information with the company."

"Shall we call you if there are any changes with Marley?" the vet asked.

"Call? Um, I was hoping I could just wait . . ."

Dr. Anne faced her. "You can't wait here. Go home, take a hot shower, and get some rest. We'll do all we can for your little friend. She's a tough dog, but she's badly hurt and in shock. And quite frankly, you look rode-hard-put-away-dead yourself."

"But . . ." Her voice came out a squeak. She tried again, but couldn't speak around the massive lump in her throat.

Dr. Anne walked to the door and opened it. "Go home. We'll call."

"I'll call you," she managed to say. Dr. Anne closed and locked the door behind her.

A wrenching sob escaped before Tavish could clamp her jaw shut. She felt as if someone had filled her insides with lead. Her legs gave way and she sank to the sidewalk. Putting her hands over her mouth, she tried to still the moans. *Stop it! Stop it! Oh, Marley, why does this hurt so much?* Tears scalded her cheeks and hands.

Her groans eventually subsided. She wrapped her arms around herself and rocked.

She had no idea how long she sat there, feeling raw. Gradually the burning, aching hurt was replaced with a single thought.

Revenge.

Someone had hurt—maybe even killed—Marley. They'd tried to kill her. Twice. Kevin, Dusty, and John were dead. How many others? She was tired of running, hiding, cowering. Whoever was behind all this was about to regret they'd ever heard of Evelyn Yvonne McTavish.

CHAPTER 21

Sawyer finished up his notes, left his office, and headed for Helen Richmond's home. He swung by Tavish's place, but it was unchanged. He deliberately didn't call Helen first so she would have no time to prepare—or to hide out.

At the main house, he jabbed the doorbell. The double doors were hand carved like Tavish's, but on a much grander scale.

Shortly a woman dressed in a black, long-sleeved dress opened the door. "Yes?"

"Mrs. Richmond, I'm—"

"I am her personal secretary." The woman stepped away from his proffered hand. "Do you have an appointment?"

"I'm afraid not."

"She is not available. You will need to call for an appointment." She started to shut the door.

Sawyer stuck his foot in the opening. "I need to speak to her about her stolen artwork."

The secretary paused. "What about it?"

From behind her, a voice asked, "What is going on?" The secretary reluctantly stepped away and a second woman came into view. It was easy to see where Tavish got her beauty. Helen Richmond wore a gray silk cropped jumpsuit, black ankle-strap high-heeled sandals, a rose gold Patek Philippe watch, and a massive diamond ring. She was lean to the point of bony. "Are you an insurance investigator? The last one who was supposed to come never showed up."

"May I come in?"

"Not without identifying yourself." Helen had a voice that expected to be obeyed.

Sawyer pulled out his FBI credentials and showed them to her.

"FBI? Now what?" Helen shook her head and opened the door wider. "Come in." Without waiting to see if he followed, she strolled across the two-story entrance hall and through a doorway into an office, then sat behind a mahogany partners desk.

Sawyer followed and sat in a leather chair opposite her. The room smelled of lemon oil and fresh-cut grass. The large windows behind her were open to a pleasant courtyard with yet another fountain, this one with elaborate blue ceramic tiles and a bronze child staring into its depths. *Her water bill must be astronomical.*

"Why is the FBI investigating my art? The paintings were stolen and recovered. A man was murdered. Right out there." She nodded at the courtyard. "The art was recovered by the police, who got in a shootout with the killer. Killer died. End of story."

"Ummm . . ." Sawyer rubbed his chin. "Why did you ask if I was with the insurance company?"

Helen glanced down and plucked an imaginary piece of lint off the immaculate desk surface. "Why are you asking?"

"Why are you stalling?"

When she looked back at him, her eyes glittered with fury. "The works were insured for a great deal of money. Millions, if it's any of your business. I hadn't installed the security system I have now. The insurance company felt I . . . may have been somehow involved in the theft. Absolutely rubbish. Libel. I've told my attorneys to deal with it. But the insurance investigators are still snooping around. There now." She stood. "If that's what you came here for—"

"What about your daughter?"

"What does the FBI want with my daughter? What's she done now?"

"What's she done before?"

She waved a perfectly manicured hand in the air as if brushing away his question. "Seeing things that aren't there. Believing things that aren't true."

"Like what?"

"She tends to see murder everywhere, first her fiancé, then some man she claims was murdered at his home. You'd think she was some kind of mystery writer."

"Do you know where she is?"

"Probably at my guesthouse."

"She isn't. But her car is in your garage."

"Oh." Helen's jaw tightened slightly. "Well, I suppose she's around someplace."

"When was the last time you saw her?"

"Yesterday. At a party I held."

Sawyer kept his face expressionless. "What kind of party was it?"

Helen's lips briefly formed a thin line. "Not that it's any of your concern, but it was a soiree for potential clients, business associates, and a few friends. She didn't even dress the way I requested her to. I'm afraid she's . . . shall we say a bit prone to nerves and hysteria. I'll ask you again, what's she done?"

He leaned back into the chair and tapped his lip. *Tavish is almost mowed down by gunfire and blown to smithereens, somehow escapes, and drives home. She probably dressed to cover up her bruises and cuts—and her mother doesn't even notice or care that she's now missing.* "What do *you* think she's done?"

"Mr.—"

"Agent Price."

"Agent Price, my daughter has been deeply disturbed ever since her . . . fiancé"—she sniffed and cleared her throat—"committed suicide. It was a totally irresponsible act on his part. I didn't approve of her marrying him, of course."

"Of course. Did you ever meet him?"

"No. I hired a private detective to find out about him. My daughter's a very wealthy woman, you know."

"So I've heard," he said dryly. "What did the detective find out?"

"Oh, he hadn't started before the man killed himself."

"Why do you think he did that?"

"I *know* why he committed suicide." She glanced at her watch. "I found his phone number in my daughter's things. I called him and left a message that I would be hiring a private detective to look into his background and he'd better be squeaky clean."

"You believe he had something to hide?"

"I'm sure he was after her money. I saw a photograph of him. A man that handsome would never be attracted to my daughter. For heaven's sake, she wears a size 14!"

What does that mean? "And that's a bad thing?"

Helen stared at him as if he'd just loudly belched at her dinner party. "That man could have even been with the Mafia or some other unsavory group. For a while my daughter believed he was murdered. Maybe he was—to keep him silent." She glanced at her watch again. "Agent Price, I really must conclude this interview. And you still haven't answered my question."

Sawyer stayed put. "Did Tavish know you'd hired a detective and called her fiancé about it?"

"No. It was for her own good."

Sawyer struggled not to throttle the woman. "When she said he was murdered, did you tell her you might believe her?"

"Well, he wasn't, was he? The police didn't see it that way, and I wasn't going to encourage her wild imagination."

"If something happened to Tavish, who would inherit her estate?"

Helen's face paled and her jaw tightened for a moment. She stood and stalked to the door. "Unless you are charging Evelyn with some crime, I would appreciate it if you wouldn't contact me again. I will do what is necessary to protect myself and my daughter. Do I make myself clear?" She'd reached the front door and opened it.

"You do. Now let me be clear. I'm running a criminal investigation and have the authority to do so with or without your permission. If I need to return for more questions, I will."

"Then you'll deal with my attorney."

"And you'll deal with my handcuffs."

CHAPTER 22

Night had fallen, and the streetlights cast a jaundiced glow onto the sidewalk outside the animal hospital. Tavish stood in the shadow of the entrance, trying to figure out exactly where she was in the city. The surrounding buildings were tired, old, and empty. A breeze carried the odor of ripe garbage and hustled plastic shopping bags down the street like urban tumbleweeds.

She turned toward the smell.

Several cars with two or more flat tires were parked at the curb. A woman sat next to one on a shredded lawn chair. Her car overflowed with bags, containers, clothing, boxes, and garbage. Even the driver's seat was full. Around her were more boxes, an old cooler, and a mixed-breed dog on a rope. The old woman stopped crooning to the dog and watched Tavish carefully, never making eye contact, to be sure she didn't take off with one of her treasures.

A man in dirty, torn clothing slept on the ground next to a fence. An empty bottle told of his evening's occupation.

Another woman came toward her pushing an overflowing

grocery cart filled with clothing. She was arguing with an unseen companion, and the disagreement had become quite heated. Tavish crossed into the street.

A few cars cruised by. She found a good location next to a homeless shelter where she could watch the traffic. As expected, the drivers deliberately ignored the street people.

She doubted Softmode would be doing middle-of-the night testing. She'd need to find lodging until morning. Food would be nice as well. A sign posted on a telephone pole noted a bus would pick up at noon for a free lunch. One meal taken care of.

The sign on the shelter noted the doors opened at 6:30 p.m. to receive overnight "guests," but a handwritten sign beneath said "Full."

So where am I spending the night? Without a purse, identification, credit card, or money, a motel was out of the question. Although her clothing had dried, the temperature dropped as the evening progressed. Sitting in a cold doorway huddled up didn't sound appealing. Her head still pounded and her leg burned in pain. With an insurance card, she could go to the emergency room . . . *Wait.* Didn't the emergency room have to treat people regardless of insurance?

It was worth a try. The nearest hospital with an emergency room was a long walk, but at least she'd keep warm.

Sawyer didn't want to admit Helen had gotten under his skin. It must have been all those months spent out at the Kéyah site. He'd lost his interrogation edge.

Regardless, he had a persistent feeling that Tavish was in even greater danger. He needed to find her.

He headed out of Helen's driveway toward Tavish's home. After parking, he strolled up and knocked. No answer, nor did Marley bark. Tavish still wasn't here. And she'd not been seen since Helen's party.

≫≪

Tavish finally spotted the emergency room sign ahead. She focused on it like it was a beacon and pushed ahead. She'd never been so tired and sleepy. She tried to think of a chant for renewed energy, but all that reverberated in her brain was *Please God, please God, please God.*

She reached the glass door into the emergency waiting area. All she had to do was shove the door open. Beyond was a security guard and a metal detector. *Come on, all I have to do . . . Please God . . .*

≫≪

Tavish opened her eyes. Everything was white. She was dead.

Slowly, carefully, she turned her head. She didn't think she'd hurt in heaven. Her head, stomach, and leg pounded with every heartbeat. *Heartbeat?* Heaven was full of surprises. Above her, an angel stared down from a dark rectangle. An angel wearing a hard hat. And a tool belt. The angel smiled and waved. "Almost done."

Heaven needed an electrician?

The angel disappeared and a much nearer face replaced him. "So you're awake."

"I'm dead," Tavish mumbled.

"I'm afraid not." The woman picked up her wrist and looked at her watch. "You had a pretty good conk on the noggin, and your leg's got a nasty gash, but you'll live." She let go of Tavish's wrist and adjusted something behind her, then left.

Tavish closed her eyes. She didn't care what that new angel said. She was dead.

═══

She was flying. She had to be careful of electrical lines and the tops of trees. She didn't have wings. She'd grab the air and pull herself through the sky as if she were swimming through the air. Below her people were walking about, oblivious. A young boy spotted her and pointed. Soon others saw her. A man pulled out a rifle, aimed, and fired.

Tavish yelled.

A man and woman appeared above her. "What is it? Where does it hurt?" The man took out a tiny penlight and flashed it in her eyes.

"Dream." Tavish's mouth was parched. "Thirsty," she croaked.

The man disappeared and reappeared moments later with a glass of water and a straw.

Tavish struggled to sit up. The room tilted and swirled.

The woman gently pushed her back into the pillow. "Whoa there. Take it slow."

The man—an LPN according to his badge—placed the

straw into the side of her mouth. Tavish sucked down the liquid. Nothing had ever tasted so good.

The woman, Dr. Kerry Woods according to her badge, patted Tavish's hand. "Looks like you're doing better. You had a concussion, and we had to throw some stitches into the laceration on your leg, but nothing that rest won't take care of. We'll need to get your name and some information for our records, but I'd say you're ready for release." She wrote something on a clipboard, patted Tavish on the hand again, and strolled away.

The man grinned at her. "How about I bring you a sandwich and we'll get that paperwork started?" He sauntered away.

Tavish looked around. She was on a bed, or more likely a gurney, on the side of a wide hallway. Nurses, doctors, and a few patients navigated around her. Several other occupied gurneys were shoved against the wall. She had a headache and her leg throbbed, but her mind was clear. The ceiling was still open above her. That's what she'd originally thought was an angel—the electrician working on the lights above the hall. Shortly the electrician reappeared and slid the panel into place.

She moved her legs. No shoes or socks. No pants. No undies. Her T-shirt had been replaced by a hospital gown. An IV line snaked into her arm. So much for a fast escape. Oh, she might stun a few innocent bystanders for a moment as they viewed her disappearing naked behind, but the doctors and nurses were used to such sights and would soon run her down.

The nurse returned with a plastic container holding a sandwich, a small packet of mayonnaise, a bottle of water, and a clipboard. He lined up the food and water on the gurney next to her, then raised the head of the bed so she was sitting almost upright. The hallway twirled around her for a few moments.

"You okay?"

She nodded. "Can I ask you something?"

"Sure." He wrote something on the clipboard.

"Why did you need to take off all my clothes when I've only hurt my head and leg?"

He didn't look up. "We were searching for illegal contraband? The fashion police said your outfit had to go? We like to see naked people?" He finally glanced at her. "You're serious. Sorry. Long shift, no sleep. We have to be sure you have no other injuries. You were unconscious and we couldn't ask."

"Okay."

He gestured toward her stomach. "And we did find one."

Right. She gingerly touched her side. It was sore but no longer on fire.

"While you eat, I write. Capisce?"

"Sure." The plastic-wrapped sandwich turned out to be turkey on stale white bread.

"Name?"

"Marley Coyote." *Maybe I can pick up Marley today.* She refused to even think about any other outcome.

"Address."

Using her teeth, she opened the packet of mayonnaise. "None. I'm currently homeless." *That, at least, is true.*

He glanced at her, then returned to the clipboard. "Then I suppose phone number, employer, and insurance carrier are all to be marked 'not applicable'?"

"Right." She squirted the mayo on the meat. "So where are my clothes?"

"Gone. We had to cut them off you. Your shoes are in a bag under this bed. Social Security number?"

"525–98— Wait a minute! What am I supposed to do about clothes? I can't exactly run around in this backless outfit."

"I'll ask one of the volunteers from a local church to bring you something to wear. They should be here any moment. Social Security number?"

"I don't remember the last four numbers. Concussion, remember?"

The nurse looked skeptical but handed the clipboard to her. "Sign here"—he pointed—"here, and here."

She started to sign *Evelyn*, but quickly changed it to Marley Coyote. Being treated for free was theft. She'd make sure she returned and paid the bill. With her money, she could add a wing. She'd name it after Marley. The thought made her smile.

"You have a nice smile," the nurse said.

"Ummnh." She'd stuffed the sandwich into her mouth. It proved to be not just stale, but dry and bland. She wolfed it down. She couldn't remember the last time she'd eaten.

After taking the clipboard, he signaled to someone behind her. Two women with Missionary Bible Church badges stepped up. Both were older. One bore a striking resemblance to Aunt Bee from the *Andy Griffith Show*. The second was a clone of Judi Dench.

"How can we be of service to you?" Aunt Bee asked.

"I seem to be missing my clothes." Tavish smiled. "Do you have a spare pair of jeans and a T-shirt? Maybe a jacket?"

"What size?" Judi asked.

"I think a 14. I haven't been shopping for a while." *Not since Grandma passed away.*

The women returned shortly with a small pile of clean clothing and a packet of toiletries. On the top was a small Bible. "Thank you. And thanks for the Bible. I seem to have lost mine." *Not a lie.*

The women beamed at her. "So you're a believer!" Judi said.

"I guess I am." *I do believe in crystals, the signs of the zodiac, and mantras. Technically not a lie either.*

"I have to ask. What's your favorite story?" Aunt Bee asked.

"I've always liked anything with a dog—"

"Oh no, I meant favorite biblical story."

Tavish blinked rapidly. "Um, well, that's a hard one. There are so many good stories, you know."

"What about verse?" They both continued to look at her expectantly.

Oh boy. What did Ezekiel call it? "Um, well, I do love Pro thirty-five."

Aunt Bee pursed her lips, and Judi Dench chewed her lip for a moment, then grinned. "Must be how you . . . what do you call it on the phone?" She wiggled her thumbs at an imaginary cell.

"Text?" Bee offered.

"Yes. Like LOL means laugh out loud. Prov thirty-five is Proverbs 3:5: 'Trust in the Lord with all your heart; do not depend on your own understanding.'"

"Is that what that means? I mean, yes, that's what it means." Tavish bobbed her head, then winced at the pain.

Bee stuck a small card into the Bible. "Come and worship

with us sometime. We meet in an old store, but the worship is good and our door is always open. God bless." Both of them gave her a final pat, then headed for the next gurney.

Tavish emptied the bottle of water. She needed to go to the bathroom, get dressed, and get out of this hospital, in that order.

The nurse, this time with a small cart, returned. "Let's get that IV out of your arm."

While he tended to the IV, Tavish went over her next steps. She'd retrieve Marley and maybe try to contact Sawyer. He'd tell her to stay clear and stay safe. But clear and safe wouldn't lead her to the people who'd tried to kill her. And Marley. And had killed Dusty, Kevin, and John.

Motivation. That's what the police always looked for. What was the motivation for all that happened? How did it connect?

Money. That made the most sense.

She had money. Or would have in a few years.

But all these events happened very recently. Just in the past month. So what was different or new?

Both Dusty and Ezekiel had pointed her toward Softmode Testing. Certainly John Coyote's expertise in engineering, shady background, and presence at her mother's party fit. Hiring her to do a commission also fit, if he had been looking to pump her for inside information about her mother. Maybe he'd sold some of Softmode's testing data—hence the money.

But who was Mrs. Montez?

She had to start somewhere, and what her mother said when she first approached Tavish about working for Softmode gave her an idea.

"We've just about made a decision on that job opening. You've

shown no indication you want to return to your own company, and this might be a good fit. You won't get another chance at it if you don't decide now. We're starting a major testing with the homeless and could use your math background."

What kind of test would they do on the homeless? Dusty said the current state of microchips wouldn't allow for any long-distance tracking, but what if that's what they were testing? A microchip or nanochip with long-range abilities.

But it would be more than that. Getting the chip into someone without their knowledge would be a challenge. The homeless would be the perfect test subjects. Most people didn't care what happened to them. She knew that firsthand. She'd looked away from the beggar she'd passed on the street.

No one would recognize her now. She'd never even been dirty.

She knew her way around Softmode. If she could get inside the building, she could access the mainframe computer and see if any of the testing had to do with microchips or nanotechnology, and if so, if there was anything going on that John Coyote wanted her to know about.

She could also look up the name he'd given her—Mrs. Montez.

She had a plan of action. That felt good.

CHAPTER 23

Sawyer hung up the phone. He'd pulled the records on the house Tavish had described as belonging to Kevin's mother. He had her name now, and Kevin turned out to be Kevin Chase from Sunnyside, Washington. He'd put out a BOLO—be on the lookout—for Kevin and gave his description according to Tavish. A second BOLO went out for John Coyote.

He'd put in a request to flag Tavish's credit cards and bank account. Unfortunately it wasn't illegal to disappear, and his request would probably be denied without probable cause. He'd nudged Lieutenant Hammen to do the same, as she was a material witness to the murder of Dusty Rhodes. Hammen said he'd follow up, but Hammen's investigation didn't necessarily include keeping Sawyer in the loop. Sawyer didn't want to sit around twiddling his thumbs and waiting to see if she'd show up.

There was a chance she'd sought treatment for injuries from the sniper. He'd do the rounds of clinics and hospitals. At least he would be doing something. Albuquerque only had a couple of hospitals. Fast legwork.

≡≡

With help, Tavish made it to the restroom. Her leg was impressively bruised and a line of stitches marched up the front. She'd have a scar. No matter. It wasn't as if a homeless woman would warrant a plastic surgeon. Without the gown, her body looked like someone had taken a baseball bat to it. "You should see the other guy." She grinned at her reflection in the mirror. "I've always wanted to say that." A street person grinned back. Purple bruises circled her eyes. Her lips were cracked and dry. Someone had attempted to clean her face, but her nostrils were still rimmed with dirt. Her hair had so much muck in it that it appeared brown. Except for her white, years of orthodontically straightened teeth, her face was practically unrecognizable.

She blinked. She'd read somewhere that the homeless were often veterans, children and women who were victims of domestic abuse, and the mentally ill.

Invisible people. The negative space that no one ever notices.

Gingerly she pulled on the provided jeans, T-shirt, and jacket. The jeans were huge, the gray T-shirt baggy, and the jacket was an unhealthy shade of mustard yellow.

She stepped from the restroom.

"That's better." The nurse beamed at her. "You're ready to go. You'll need to get some pain meds—"

The loudspeaker gave a tiny squeal. "Code blue in room 227. Code blue in room 227." The nurse took off. The hallway erupted with medical staff racing to her left. She turned right and headed for the door.

≫≪

Sawyer tramped through the hospital lobby to the information desk and pulled out his credentials. The woman behind the counter examined them. "Yes, Agent Price, what can I do for you?"

"I need to know what room Tavish, make that Evelyn McTavish, is in."

The woman typed for a moment, then shook her head. "I'm sorry."

He drummed his fingers lightly on the counter. "Could you have a Jane Doe?" *And hopefully not in the morgue.*

She typed again, then pointed to a sign on the wall. "You might try the emergency room."

≫≪

Once outside, Tavish aimed toward the animal hospital. She hadn't gone far before a car pulled up beside her and a man rolled down the window. "How much?"

She stopped. "I beg your pardon?"

"Listen, you look like you need money. I'll give you a twenty." The man had a five-o'clock shadow, bad teeth, and was balding on top. His neck broadened into his shoulders like a weightlifter's, and his hands were rough and scarred.

"That's very kind of you, but—"

"Not kind. You'll earn it. Get in." His eyes had narrowed and his hands now gripped the wheel as if to squeeze it to death.

He thinks I'm a prostitute. She straightened and glanced around. The street was empty and she was in front of a vacant condemned building. If she screamed, no one would hear. *Help me, God, if you're up there.* One word popped into her brain. *Bible.* She reached into the pocket of the jacket and pulled out the Bible and stuck it in the air. "I'm glad you stopped by, brother." She put on her best televangelist voice. "I'm Sister . . . Mary Clarence of the order of the . . . Missionary Bible Church. I want to share . . . um . . . Proverbs 3:5 with you today—"

The man called her a rude name, rolled up the window, and drove away.

Tavish kissed the Bible and put it back in her pocket. By the time she'd reached the animal hospital, her leg was throbbing and her headache was worse. It was stupid of her to leave the emergency room without pain medication, but that would have just complicated things. Maybe the vet would take pity on her.

In daylight, the building looked far more cheerful and the parking lot overflowed. The lobby had a dog side and cat side. She ignored the waiting owners and dogs and went straight to the reception desk. "I brought Marley Coyote in here last night, or maybe early this morning. I'm here to see her."

The receptionist nodded and pushed a button on the phone. "Marley's person is here."

A man carrying a thin brown dog approached the counter. He smelled of garbage, and his clothing was little more than rags. "Is Dr. Anne here?"

A stern-looking woman entered from the back room. Her lips tightened at the homeless man. "Go. And tell your beggar-friends to stop bringing their mutts here. We don't treat for free." Her gaze shifted to Tavish. She jerked her head toward a door marked with the number 3.

Tavish stepped into a small exam room that smelled of cleaning solution. It held a sink, a counter with glass containers full of ear swabs and cotton balls, and a stainless steel table. The wall had a chart of fleas and ticks.

The woman entered behind her. "You are here about Marley?"

"I am. Where's Dr. Anne?"

"Busy. I'm the office manager. We tried calling Marley's owner, John Coyote. His phone is no longer in service. We need to know if you"—her gaze took in Tavish's filthy hair, baggy T-shirt, oversize jeans, and muddy running shoes—"are going to be responsible for Marley's hospital bill?"

"Is Marley . . . still . . . still alive?" Tavish's lips felt numb.

"Yes."

"May I see her?"

"We need to get this bill taken care of first."

"You needn't worry about that. I have a great deal of money."

"Harrumph. I'm sure you do. Dr. Barrett is a good vet, a great vet, but she has a soft heart. She treats the pets of homeless people for free. She says they 'need' their dogs more than most." The woman made quotation marks in the air. "But *free* doesn't pay the bills around here." She handed Tavish a piece of paper. The vet bill came to $1,478.56.

"I'll write you a check—"

"Cash. Or a credit card."

Her purse was with her mother's truck, and who knew what happened to the truck. She sucked in a deep breath and reached for the crystal around her neck. It was gone. Her breathing became ragged. What was she going to do? Oh, God, what was she going to do?

Break into my own house. Call the bank from my home phone and say I want to pick up some cash. Get cleaned up and retrieve the money from the bank. Get Marley.

She relaxed slightly. "Not a problem. Will Marley be taken care of while I get the funds?"

The woman's lips formed a straight line. "Of course. Dr. Anne wanted to keep her a few more days. There will be a boarding and medication charge—"

"Of course. I'll be back."

Sawyer followed the indicated sign marking the way to the emergency room. A loudspeaker announced, "Code blue in room 227. Code blue in room 227." A number of nurses, two of whom were pushing a crash cart, ran toward him, then into a room on his right. He stepped aside, then ambled on.

The harried receptionist barely looked at his credentials. "Jane Doe you said? No. Everyone here is identified."

"May I see the list?"

"Absolutely not."

He clenched his jaw, turned, and left.

CHAPTER 24

Tavish's home was several miles away. She started walking.

Her route would take her within a block of the Hogarth and Montgomery Art Gallery. It would be nice to see the empty hook where her drawing had hung. The drawing Sawyer had purchased. But Lambert would take one look at her and show her the door.

She smiled at the thought.

A woman swerved and stepped off the curb to avoid getting near her.

What if I yell "boo" at her? Her grin turned into a chuckle.

Several blocks later a police cruiser roared past her. Then another. She ducked her head and shuffled on. Both turned down the street toward the gallery. Breaking into a limping trot, she crossed the street and turned the corner. She smelled the smoke before she saw it.

A red-and-white hazmat truck was parked in front of the gallery. Firemen had trained their hoses on the smoke.

Her stomach tightened. She stopped dead. Her artwork, the drawings she'd labored over for months, would be ruined by water. A deep weariness settled over her shoulders. Had a year of her life been washed away in a few moments? Weariness pushed into her exhaustion. She couldn't stand. Leaning against the building next to her, she slid down the wall until she was on the pavement. Her vision sharpened and focused on the acrid smoke.

Marley barked.

Tavish whipped her head back and forth, looking for the small dog. It took her a moment to realize the shrill sound had only been in her mind.

Marley's right. I've got to move.

She shoved off the ground. This was not a time to be weak, to give in. *To be the same neurotic woman I've been.*

"Right," she said out loud. *Reason this out.* What were the chances that a fire accidentally broke out at the gallery while she was having a show?

The gallery door opened and Lambert emerged, hands cuffed behind his back. He tried to duck and keep his face turned from the gathering crowd.

A man hurrying to the scene paused long enough next to her to hand her a dollar bill. He moved on without making eye contact.

The currency fluttered in her hand. A dollar. Last week she would have tossed it in a jar she kept by the washing machine for petty cash. When the jar was full, she would have given it to one of her mother's overpaid staff.

Until now she'd never paid attention to real need. She tucked the money in her pocket.

A small crowd gathered at a distance from the gallery, with a policeman standing guard. Tavish angled into the throng. "What's going on?" she asked loud enough for the cop to hear.

As she expected, he didn't look at her. "Drug bust. Lotta dope upstairs." He turned around.

Tavish melted into the crowd.

"Okay, folks, move on, nothing to see." The officer put out his arms and waved to the crowd. She started limping toward home, thinking. The break-in at her house. The empty safe at Patricia Caron's house. Had someone been looking for the money and note from John Coyote that she'd found in the abandoned building? Her smack on the head and attempted murder in the arroyo would be the villain cleaning up loose ends. Just like the "gas leak" that destroyed all those homes in Patricia's neighborhood.

Was Lambert's drug dealing another loose end getting cleaned up? Or the coincidental result of an independent investigation? Or something else? "I'm getting as paranoid as a regular street person."

≥≤

Sawyer picked up the ringing phone. "Agent Price."

"Yeah, this is Deputy Sanderson, Catron County Sheriff's Department."

"Yeah, what ya got?"

"A body."

≥≤

Street people were rare in this part of Albuquerque. Most of the homes were on several acres and all were gated. This was the neighborhood of not just Mercedes and BMWs, but Lamborghinis and Rolls-Royces—with lots of private security guards.

Through the fence surrounding a portion of her mother's estate near the guesthouse, Tavish scouted the landscape. Two gardeners plucked dead leaves and flowers out of the potted plants near the front entrance. A pool cleaner skimmed debris from the fountain. Another worker had a leaf blower and was systematically clearing the cobblestone pavers.

She didn't recognize any of them. She'd paid no attention to her mother's staff. For all she knew, they'd worked there for years.

Maria, her housekeeper, stepped from the house and approached the pool cleaner.

One of the gardeners waved to her. "Señora Montez?"

The woman turned and walked toward him.

Maria is Mrs. Montez?

A security patrol car turned the corner and headed in Tavish's direction. She bent down and pretended to tie her shoe.

It stopped beside her.

Rats! She stood, but kept her head down as she'd noted some of the street people did.

"Kinda in the wrong part of town, aren't you?" a male voice asked.

She knew that voice.

"Well?" he asked.

Risking a quick glance, she grew faint.

The fake cop. The one who'd moved John Coyote's body. The one who'd shot at her.

"Got lost," she muttered.

"Yeah, that's a good idea. Get lost. You'd better be gone when I return."

"Yes, sir." She kept her head down and stared at the sidewalk until the sound of his car grew faint. Then she broke into a limping run.

CHAPTER 25

Sawyer shifted the phone to his other ear. "A body." He worked to control his breathing. "How can I help you, Deputy?" He closed his eyes and said a quick prayer that they hadn't found Tavish.

"We think it's your Kevin Chase. Anyway, it's a bit of a puzzle. They said you were here on a special assignment and were an expert on artifacts, that kind of thing."

"I have a background in archaeology."

"Close enough."

Several agents sauntered by his cubicle, leaving the scent of freshly made coffee in their wake.

"What is it?"

"I'd like to send you the photographs of the scene."

"Now I'm intrigued. Sure." He gave the deputy his email address. "Tell me the circumstances. Are we talking murder?"

"That's what we don't know. A couple of folks backpacking found him. It seemed like a routine case—a hiker caught in an arroyo, a slot canyon during a flash flood."

"That's routine?"

"You're not from around here, are you? Drowning is the second leading cause of accidental death in New Mexico. His body got snagged on a bush, and the turkey vultures had been working on him."

"Sounds nasty. Cause of death?"

"We're waiting on an autopsy. The flood banged him up quite a bit. No ID on him, but the description and clothing fit your BOLO. Caucasian male, early thirties or so, blue eyes, brown hair. Jeans. Wisconsin Badgers T-shirt."

"So what made this unusual?"

"Take a look at the photos. You should have them by now."

Sawyer opened his email, found the attachment, and downloaded three photos. The first was the body as it was found—as the deputy had described—wrapped around a bush. The second was a series of sticks apparently wrapped together in a pattern. They'd been attached to the bush. He studied the small twigs but could make nothing of it, except it had been deliberate.

The third photo was of the man's face.

Sawyer rubbed his thumb over his lips, thinking. Although swollen and distorted, the man looked like the sketch Tavish had drawn of the man who helped her. "The face looks familiar, and the clothes are right. He's from Sunnyside, Washington. I'll get you the address."

"That would be a great help. We can see if we can get his dental record. Do you know of any next of kin?"

"I don't know. His mother is deceased. He was here working on her house."

"Okay. What about the twigs in the bush?"

Twigs in the bush. A memory teased him. His conversation with Tavish the last evening at the Kéyah site. *"My hand is a positive shape. The negative space is the shape between my fingers. If I focus on the negative space, I will always draw the positive shape correctly."* She had pointed at a nearby shrub.

He brought up the twig photo. This time he studied the twigs combined with the shape of the shrub behind it.

The single word jumped out at him. *Murder.*

⇛⇐

Tavish didn't stop running until she was totally out of breath. She'd dashed down a side street to get out of sight, but now she wasn't sure exactly where she was. Sandia Mountain was on her left, which meant she faced south. That was the direction of the homeless shelter. She only hoped they'd serve a meal.

Marley would have to wait, for now. At least she was being cared for. Marley's revenge, however, couldn't wait.

She shuffled forward, trying to fit the new pieces of the puzzle together. If Maria Montez was the woman John Coyote wanted to give the money to and apologize to, who was she and what relationship did she have to him? Why was the fake cop driving around her mother's house? Who was the Dali-mustache guy? All of them seemed to have some connection with her mother.

She didn't want to think about it, but her mind circled back to the comment Dusty Rhodes had made about how her mother liked to spend money. She had recently bought that Frida Kahlo painting. That would have set her back several million.

Was there a chance that her mother had dipped into Tavish's inheritance?

But my mother is rich in her own right. She doesn't need my money.

What if her businesses weren't as profitable as they once were?

"No. That just doesn't make any sense."

A couple walking toward her crossed the street and stared at her.

She'd been talking to herself. "Well, why not?"

The couple hurried away, glancing over their shoulders.

"I've been talking to a dog now for several days," she called after them. "Quite stimulating conversations." Next would be a shopping cart for all her belongings—which at this point amounted to the few toiletries and Bible from the missionary ladies.

Finally arriving at a cross street she recognized, she shifted direction, angling toward the shelter. She passed a thrift store and paused at the window. They did have a mismatched selection of shopping carts. Was this where the disenfranchised found their portable home-on-wheels, or in the parking lots of grocery stores? A clock inside noted it was almost noon.

Noon. Free meal. But she needed to catch a bus.

A man stood at the door to the shop.

"Excuse me."

He glanced at her.

"How far to the shelter?"

"Two blocks. That way." He pointed.

"Thanks," she called over her shoulder. Rushing as fast as a gimpy leg would let her, she raced up the street.

The rear end of an older bus was barely visible parked on the corner of the block.

She hobbled to the end of the street.

Two women, one wearing a torn black sweatshirt with a cardboard sign under her arm, the second carrying a paper sack, were about to get on the bus. The driver spotted Tavish and waved her over. "Come on now. We're about to leave."

She approached. "Is this the free meal?"

He glanced at his watch. "Yep."

Moving closer, she could read the patch on his uniform. Softmode Testing.

"Perfect." She climbed into the bus.

It took a bit of convincing for the deputy to see the word in the shrub. "I would have missed that completely."

"I would have too, but I have an artist friend who told me about negative space just a few days ago. I take it neither of the hikers who found the body made the word or were artists?"

"I didn't ask about art, but I will. Our initial thought was someone else found him and didn't want to become involved. Of course, we can't discount a joke—although why someone would think it funny is beyond me. Who knows, maybe the murderer did this. Like I said, a puzzle. Thanks for the heads-up on art. And the identification."

Sawyer disconnected with the deputy. His next call was to the SAC—Special Agent in Charge. "Sawyer Price here. Did you get my report?"

"Sure did."

"Could I speak to you in person?"

"Yeah, come on over."

As Sawyer entered his office, SAC Healy looked up, stood, and offered his hand. "Good to finally get to meet you beyond just reading your reports. How's the desert?"

"Dusty."

Healy grinned. "It is that. Anything new since you sent that in?" They both sat.

Sawyer leaned forward. "Yes, sir." He updated the SAC.

"What do you need?"

"I want to see if the various agencies would be willing to compare notes."

"Sounds like a good idea." He picked up his phone and pushed a button. "Is the conference room open?" He listened a moment. "I'm not sure. For the next few days at least . . . Thanks." He disconnected. "The room is yours. Just keep me in the loop."

Sawyer stood and left, heading back to his cubicle. Once there he opened the desk drawer and took out a business card. *Detective Mike Mullins.* He'd start with the detective who'd shown up at the dig and told him about the supposed "gas leak" that may have conveniently destroyed evidence. Before he could dial, the phone rang.

"Patricia here." Her voice was shaking.

"Is everything okay?"

"I don't know. I think I found out one way the looted artifacts were transported. And . . . something else. Can you come back to the Kéyah site?"

"On my way."

The close confines of the bus brought out a fact that Tavish had never thought about—living on the street meant few, if any, baths, and no deodorant. The acrid stench of urine burned her nose and made her eyes water. She found an empty seat and sat sideways so no one would join her. Three rows ahead on the other side a woman was chattering away—with no one.

A woman of indeterminate age with unbrushed shoulder-length brown hair and a dirty green sweatshirt sat in front of her. A second woman, older, wearing a hoodie, took the seat opposite. "He beat you up?"

It took a moment for Tavish to realize the woman was addressing her. "Um, not really."

"Still defending him, are ya?" the hoodie woman asked.

"No."

Green sweatshirt asked, "Where'd ya find the shoes? Them look like gen-u-ine leather."

Tavish nodded. "I . . . um—"

"I bet I know where," Hoodie said. "The St. Vincent de Paul over on Menaul. Lotta rich people leave stuff out after hours. Am I right, or am I right?"

"Of course." Tavish looked back and forth between them. "Have you done this before? Gone over to Softmode Testing?"

"Is that where we're going?" Hoodie said. "Hey, it's a free meal. And they don't bother ya none, know what I mean? Hey, Angie"—she addressed the other woman—"you got any money? Or better yet, a cigarette?"

"Nah."

Tavish reached into her pocket, pulled out the dollar, and handed it to the woman. "It's all I have right now, but—"

"The widow's mite." Hoodie took the bill and poked it into her bra.

"I'm sure there aren't any mites or other parasites on it," Tavish said.

"Oh, you're funny," Hoodie said.

"I don't think she was trying to be," Angie said to Hoodie.

"Widow's mite," Hoodie said to Tavish. "From the Bible?"

"I'm afraid I'm not familiar with that . . . story? I've never gone to church."

"Me neither," Hoodie said. "Bible study. In jail. 'Bout the only thing they let us do. I do trust in the Lord, as the Bible says. Trust in him every day."

"Amen, sister," Angie said. "We're like the lilies of the field."

"Lilies?"

"And the birds of the air." Hoodie pointed out the window.

"Free?" Tavish asked.

"Cared for," Hoodie said.

"Loved," Angie said.

The bus turned into the large parking lot of Softmode Testing, drove past the imposing tinted-glass and stone facade, and pulled up to a side door. A security guard held the door open as the bus emptied.

Tavish stood, then bent over and peered out the window to be sure the security guard wasn't someone she knew.

Hoodie touched her arm. "Don't worry about it, honey. To the world, we're invisible. They look through us, not at us." She smiled a gap-toothed grin and joined the line leaving the bus.

She'd make this fast. Get in. Watch to see if anything strange was done to the homeless—like a "vitamin" shot or other injection. Next, get to a terminal and check employment records for John Begay or John Coyote. If he'd never worked there, get out as fast as possible.

CHAPTER 26

Sawyer connected with Detective Mullins on the drive to the Kéyah site.

"Why didn't you identify yourself as FBI when I first showed up?" The annoyance was clear in Mullins's voice. "I thought you were an archaeologist."

"You didn't ask. Undercover operation. We're mopping it up now."

"I see. So tell me again, what interest does the FBI have in a gas leak?"

"Are you *sure* it was an accident?"

"If you have information about the explosion that I should know, Agent Price, I'd appreciate it if you'd share it, for a change."

Sawyer gripped the steering wheel tighter. "What's that supposed to mean?"

"The FBI's notorious for running roughshod over local agencies and conducting operations without seeking cooperation. For example, your little undercover gig at the Kéyah site—"

"No one knew about it except the single person in charge at each location. We were seeking looters."

"Just once, it would be nice for you to let us know. That's all I'm saying."

"Request noted. I do need your help on something." Sawyer signaled his exit from the freeway.

"Go ahead."

"There was a young woman at the site, Evelyn McTavish. She's missing. Two days now. She was present at the shooting in Bernalillo." Mullins was silent so long Sawyer thought the connection had been lost. "Hello?"

"Yeah. I'm here. Listen, she reported a murder—"

"I know all about it. She told me as well. But one of the people she mentioned, the one who hid her from the guy she calls Fake Cop, has turned up dead."

"I think it's time for us to compare notes."

"That's exactly why I called."

Tavish was unfamiliar with this part of Softmode's building. They were in a small auditorium that looked like it doubled as a basketball court, with scattered tables and a long banquet table along one side. About a hundred people of various ages, including a number of children, were already seated and eating, apparently from other buses that had arrived earlier.

She'd planned to remain aloof and observe whether the people were getting an injection, a pill, or anything else that might indicate a microchip was being placed in the body, but the smell of fried chicken changed her mind. *I can observe and eat.* Keeping watch for any sign that she'd been recognized, she grabbed a tray and silverware. When she reached the fried chicken, she was given three choices in the way they were prepared. She went for extra-crispy.

Her tray was soon loaded with mashed potatoes, green beans, a sizable chicken breast, and a bottle of water. She'd revisit the entire vegan thing again once regular meals were a part of her life.

She found a table near the closest door leading to the interior of the building and sat so she could monitor it. Various staff came and left, using ID cards on lanyards. Casually glancing around the room, she spotted three security cameras.

Unless the microchip or nanochip was in the food, she could see no sign of any individual testing. The staff, in fact, acted like they might get cooties from the diners, avoiding touching, talking, or looking directly at them.

A sign with the male/female outline and the word *Restrooms* pointed to the near corner. Placing her silverware on her almost empty plate, she started to rise.

Her mother entered the room.

She froze.

Two male employees approached Helen and started talking.

Tavish lowered herself and hunched over her food.

Helen nodded to the men, then slowly walked around, one hand cupped over her nose and mouth. The men trailed closely behind, still talking.

They wandered close enough for Tavish to hear a part of the conversation.

"... over twenty-three percent chose the regular chicken, but the test program estimated ..."

Chicken? They were testing a probability program for taste in chicken? Hardly the ominous Big Brother scenario she'd imagined.

How did her mother and John Coyote figure into all this?

Other staff members watched her mother's every movement and were still paying no attention to the homeless diners. *Good.* When Helen reached the far end of the room, Tavish stood and raced to the restroom.

As soon as she entered, three women she'd seen on the bus abruptly stopped speaking, then resumed as they saw her. The room was hazy from their cigarette fumes. Tavish nodded at them and entered a stall.

The women finished their smokes and left. Tavish checked around her, then the rest of the room. No windows. No other doors. A floor vent was too small to crawl into. *How is this such a good idea?* Maybe her mother wasn't involved and Tavish could just walk up to her and ask whatever she needed.

What if I'm wrong? She knew for sure that the Dali-mustache guy had been at her party, along with John Coyote. That several people were already dead. Softmode may be a dead end, but that didn't mean her mother wasn't involved. Even though Tavish hated the idea, her mother could have spent too much money on her art and be in need of more cash. As in Tavish's trust fund.

One of the cigarettes the women had discarded still smoldered.

The towel dispenser was motion activated. She waved her hand under the machine and gathered a pile of towels. Crumpling the paper, she added it to the garbage can until it was almost full.

She gingerly picked up the cigarette and placed it on the top paper towel, then gently blew on it.

The paper erupted in flame. Soon the trash bin was engulfed in fire.

She listened for the fire alarm. Nothing.

The plastic bin started to melt.

She turned on the faucet, scooped a handful of water, and tossed it on the blaze. It puffed smoke and continued to burn.

A female employee entered, took one look at the fire, and left. A moment later a fire alarm sounded.

Tavish raced from the restroom into the auditorium. An eardrum-shattering klaxon had sent a panicked throng screaming and shoving toward the exit doors. Others tripped on overturned chairs, crawled under tables, or stood frozen in place. Overhead, the sprinkler system showered the room with cold water.

Helen was nowhere in sight. Tavish hovered by the door leading to the rest of the building, waiting for an employee to unlock it. She didn't have to wait long. A woman charged up, used her access card, and dashed through. Tavish followed. A steady stream of men and women were emptying from offices on either side of the hall and scurrying for the nearest exit. The alarm blared, but the sprinkler system hadn't been activated in this section.

Tavish dodged into the nearest office, decorated in beige and white with numerous photos of children on the desk, and found a computer already running. She quickly checked the company directory. No John Coyote or John Begay. Next she attempted to access human resources to see if he'd worked for Softmode in the past. A pop-up box appeared asking for her name and password.

She typed in H-e-l-e-n. For the password she tried her mother's phone number.

The pop-up box turned red with the words *Denied. You have one more attempt before this terminal will be locked down.*

The fire alarm ceased. She heard the wail of a fire engine in the distance. She was out of time. She backed out of the HR system. Employees would be returning any second. She looked around the desk, then opened the top drawers. A set of car keys was on the right-hand side. Snatching them, she checked to be sure she was alone.

The reflection of a man standing behind her appeared on her screen.

Tavish jumped, then spun around.

"Why didn't you leave when you heard the fire alarm?" The fireman stood in the door. "It's dangerous not to evacuate when the alarm goes off."

Tavish moved her hands, then tapped her ear.

"Oh, so you're deaf?" He spoke louder. "Come with me." He motioned.

She stood and followed the man to the exit. Outside the parking lot was full of employees and the homeless diners. A bus driver was attempting to load one of the buses.

Moving purposefully through the crowd, she headed for the employee parking area. If she could find the right car, she might have until the end of the workday before her theft was discovered. She pulled out the keys to see if they gave any indication of what kind of vehicle she should be looking for.

The key ring bore the Softmode Testing logo and a number.

She stopped, then turned toward the company vehicles in a fenced-in lot, complete with a security guard.

≡≡≡

By the time Sawyer arrived at the Kéyah site, he'd arranged for Detective Mullins of Bernalillo County, Deputy Sanderson of the Catron County Sheriff's Department, and Lieutenant Hammen of the Sandoval County Sheriff's Department to meet him at the FBI building in Albuquerque in the morning.

He left word with Helen Richmond's secretary to contact him immediately if Tavish showed up. He wasn't sure Helen would comply, but a thinly veiled threat about consequences should she stonewall pried an agreement to cooperate.

Professor Caron greeted him with a frown. "It's good to see you."

"You don't look so happy. What's wrong?" He stepped from the car with his briefcase.

"I need to show you what I found. We'll start with the easy answers."

He followed her to the dining tent. A blue plastic water container lay open on a table. "This was in my tent. The looters used this water storage to haul individual artifacts out. It would appear to be empty and they'd place the items into this padded middle section. Water filled the bladder at this end, so it really did function as a water container. Weights, probably rocks, would be added to the other end to make it feel full when returned. It would just empty of water quickly."

Sawyer examined the container. "Quite clever. How'd you figure it out?"

"I'd love to tell you I was brilliant, but basically it came down to luck. I dropped the container and it broke open."

"Great job." Sawyer opened his briefcase. "That certainly explains why all my surreptitious searches of vehicles, outgoing garbage, and shipments netted nothing."

"Garbage? I had no idea." They both sat at the table.

"All part of my glamorous FBI career. Now we need to know who did it."

He pulled out a file, opened it, and placed a photograph in front of the professor. "This was the man who died in the shoot-out at the Four Corners. Recognize him? His name was Vince Trainor. He worked here briefly over a year ago. He is most likely the thief—"

The professor put her hand over her mouth and let out a soft groan.

"Patricia?"

"I was afraid of that." She stood, moved to the side of the tent, and returned with a piece of paper. "I found this in the garbage." She smoothed it out on the surface of the table.

Sawyer recognized it immediately. It was Tavish's crumpled-up drawing of her fiancé.

"This is Tavish's drawing." Patricia sat down. "This looks exactly like my son, Howard."

CHAPTER 27

Tavish hesitated. The guard was watching the chaos outside the building and hadn't yet noticed her. She'd never stolen anything in her life.

It's not really stealing when it's your mother's company and her car. But if her mother was somehow involved in all this, she could make a pretty good case that Tavish was a carjacker. She reached for the crystal. Oh right. It was gone. And Marley was out of reach.

What should I do? She couldn't go far, only as far as the gas in the tank would take her. She didn't even have the dollar the man gave her.

Trust in the Lord. The words of the homeless woman and her grandmother's wisdom echoed in her mind. "Okay, Lord. I trust you. Now what?" she whispered.

Nothing happened. The world didn't shift. A big voice didn't shout an answer from the sky. An angel didn't hand her a solution.

She was still homeless, broke, missing her dog, and with people sincerely wanting her dead.

The security guard's interest in the chaotic parking lot was waning and he started to look around. Tavish crouched behind the car.

Her mother strolled through the milling crowd, parting them like royalty through a throng of beggars. She did have a commanding presence, something Tavish had longed for. That, and maybe just a little attention.

Tavish hugged herself. She'd had a loving grandmother. A grandmother who'd left her a fortune. Was that motive for attempted murder?

A man approached Helen and spoke to her. Tavish couldn't see his face, but whatever he said made her mother shake her head. He reached in his jacket and pulled out something, showed it to her, and put it away. Her mother stiffened. He turned toward Tavish and pointed to a beige Toyota Camry parked nearby.

It was Dali-mustache man.

Tavish stood. Before she could move, her mother had crawled into the car. The man jumped in beside her and the car pulled out of the visitors' parking. Shortly a white sedan followed. The driver was the fake cop. He appeared to be following the Camry.

Tavish dashed toward the security station by the gate to the company cars.

The guard picked up a pen and clipboard, then stopped. "Whoa, what happened to you?"

"When the alarm sounded, the sprinkler system went off. I got caught in the downpour." She smiled in what she hoped was a convincing grin. "Helen Richmond told me I could go home and change."

"She said you could take a company car?"

Tavish held up the keys.

The guard took the keys and checked the number. Tavish shifted from one foot to the other, trying to watch the rapidly disappearing Camry without drawing attention.

"Sign here, print your name here." He handed her the clipboard. "It's the white sedan over there." He pointed.

She swiftly signed and printed an illegible name, grabbed the keys, and trotted to the car. She just hoped she'd be able to catch up with her mother—and the men with her.

$$\Longrightarrow\Longleftarrow$$

Sawyer stared at the professor, unable to think of what to say.

"Howard was a friend of Vince's. And now this all makes so much sense." She waved her hand at the water container, file, and drawing.

"Um, could you explain?"

"It's not an admirable thing to dislike your son, but I did. When his father died in Afghanistan, Howard was a teen. He . . . went wild. I couldn't control him. I finally kicked him out when I found him having a party with drugs and girls while I was out of town. We barely saw each other for several years. I went back to my maiden name, but Howard knew where I lived. Then one day he showed up here."

"When was that?"

"Um . . . maybe five or six months ago? He offered to help. Guess how?"

"Transporting water containers?"

"Bingo." She didn't speak for a few moments. "I let it slip that you were coming and were with the FBI." She shook her head. "He always was a con man."

A con man with a record. Not a coincidence. There are connections.

"So tell me," Patricia asked, "why did Tavish draw him?"

"They were engaged."

"Were? They're not anymore?"

She didn't know her son was dead. He said a quick prayer. "Patricia, I have some bad news." He explained her son's suicide.

Patricia didn't move, her gaze never leaving his face, her skin turning parchment white. Only when he'd finished did she do anything. She stood, straightened her back, and headed to her tent.

Sawyer stayed for several hours, but it was clear Patricia wanted to grieve alone. He collected the file and Tavish's sketch.

The setting sun was casting a crimson and orange glow on the Sandia Mountains by the time Sawyer returned to Albuquerque. For the duration of his undercover work, when he wasn't at the dig he'd been booked into a decent hotel with an open, airy atrium in the center. He had a bedroom suite, allowing him to use the living area as an extended office.

With the deputies and detectives from the different agencies meeting in the morning, he needed to update his research to be prepared.

Once in his room, he ordered a dinner of salmon and tossed

salad from room service, then laid out the files and computer on the caramel-colored wood desk. He could access the police files from his laptop. He stared at the drawing Tavish had done of Howard. A con man. After her money. Scum.

Sawyer pulled out his yellow legal pad. He'd work on a timeline.

January 1	Paintings stolen.
January–March	Thefts occurred at archaeological sites. Howard shows up.
March	FBI called in to investigate theft. Stealing stops.
March–April	Howard "falls in love" with Tavish. John Coyote seeks out Tavish for commission.
April 30	Shootout at Four Corners. Vince killed. Paintings and artifacts recovered. Suspect 2nd person. Howard?
May 2	Howard commits suicide.
May 6	Paintings returned.
May 28	Tavish goes to Pat Caron's house, thinking it belonged to John Coyote.
May 30	Marley shows up. Tavish finds John's body.

He stood and moved to the window. He had a clear view of the lights of downtown Albuquerque. "You stole some paintings, Andrew, or Howard, or whatever you called yourself, you and your friend Vince. You killed a man in the process. But you find out you can't exactly get rid of them, at least not as easily as you thought. Bet that was a surprise. So you moved on to something more portable, ancient Native American artifacts. More portable, more salable, but hard and dirty work. And not nearly so profitable. Move on to Plan C: woo a millionaire heiress. Tavish."

He tried not to think about where Tavish might be at the moment. "I'm not sure how John fits in just yet, but I'd guess you had some connections, and I'd just bet that Fake Cop was one of them." He paced. "But why would a beautiful woman fall for you?"

A soft knock on the door indicated his dinner had arrived. He signed for it but left it untouched. He'd lost his appetite thinking about Tavish.

Returning to his desk, he did a quick internet image search on Evelyn McTavish.

The page of photos loaded.

He stared at the images. *This can't be right.* The photos showed a much heavier woman with mousy brown hair, baggy sweats, and no makeup. She bore little resemblance to the woman he met at the gallery and dig. The images were at least a year or two old.

She'd mentioned all the life changes she'd made after her grandmother's death. Could she still see herself as looking like this?

No wonder she fell hard for the con man Howard. *And was terrified of any feelings for me.*

"That's hardly the type of thing I need to present tomorrow at the meeting." He stood and paced. "Get organized. What don't you know? What events might connect? And how big is this thing?"

Picking up his yellow legal pad, he sat on the bed and began to write.

⇒⇐

Tavish drove as swiftly as she dared, looking for the Camry or the sedan driven by the fake cop. For once, luck and a red light were in her favor. She spotted them at the second intersection. Keeping a few vehicles between them, she followed. She knew the route well. They were driving toward her mother's estate.

As they approached the neighborhood, Tavish slowed, then turned down a side street. The sedan had parked where Fake Cop could see into her mother's driveway. She didn't want to drive past him. There was a break in the landscaping on this side of the estate where she could see what was going on. She parked, got out of the car, and trotted over to the fence.

Her mother had left the car, as had Dali-mustache man. Helen's body language spelled fury. She pointed at the man, then toward the driveway exit. She couldn't hear exactly what her mother was saying, but her last words were clear. "Don't you dare threaten me!"

He got into the car and started to turn around.

A falling-out among thieves? If they'd been working together in the past, it would seem the partnership was at an end.

Tavish could confront her mother now point-blank, ask her about Softmode, John Coyote, Dali-mustache man, Fake Cop, and Mrs. Montez and the money . . . but her mother could simply lie about everything. Lie, then call someone to take care of her once and for all.

A heavy weight pressed on her shoulders. Her mother had never really loved her, but Tavish always thought her mother at least cared. After Andrew died, Helen had gotten her help, instructed her staff to buy clothes and food and . . . Her staff. Not her.

Shouldn't I have seen the writing on the wall?

But not loving a child wasn't the same as having her murdered. Tavish couldn't, wouldn't believe it.

I'm after revenge for Marley. I have to see this through, no matter where it may lead.

She couldn't see Fake Cop from this angle, but if she wanted to know more, she'd have to move. She raced back to her sedan, then did a U-turn and aimed for the road she knew they'd have to be on.

Sure enough, both the Camry and Fake Cop's security car drove past. Not slowing down for the stop sign, she swerved into the street behind them. An angry driver laid on his horn.

"Sorry," she muttered. The two vehicles were ahead with a truck between. She fell into line.

They drove steadily out of town. She kept several cars or trucks blocking their view in case someone looked out the rear window. The final set of turns had her slowing almost to a crawl. Both vehicles had turned off the main road and onto Loco Drive, which led to Patricia Caron's home. A warning sign beside the pavement noted Road Closed, Local Traffic Only.

The road was a dead-end trap. She'd be an obvious target if she turned to follow them.

A row of middle-class, neatly tended homes lined the street across from the turnoff to Loco Drive. Tavish pulled over and stopped in front of one of the houses. She could see anyone coming from the closed-off road. After shutting down the engine, she slid down in the seat. There was nothing left of the Caron house, according to Detective Mullins. What did anyone expect to find?

Wait. The garage was separate from the house. Could that have been spared? So many questions banged around in her skull she was getting a headache—or make that building on the dull headache she already had. She'd never seen anything in the garage except John Coyote's car, but she'd never looked for something suspicious either.

Those two men could have been responsible for Coyote's, Kevin's, and Dusty's deaths, as well as the attempts on her life.

Just turn around. She could use this opportunity to confront her mother, with the two of them accounted for.

The warm sun soon heated the inside of the car to an uncomfortable temperature.

A curtain in the nearest house twitched. *Great.* She'd waited too long in one spot. She gulped air, started the engine, and checked the rearview mirror.

When she looked forward again, her jaw dropped.

Fake Cop had returned, slowed at the stop sign, then sped off in the opposite direction, away from town.

She waited a few moments for Dali-mustache man to follow. The few minutes turned into twenty. The car was running low on gas. She pulled out and turned onto the road. She'd drive past the remains of Patricia Caron's house and park somewhere on the road beyond.

The devastation was immense, having leveled an area roughly the size of a large city block. A crater showed where the pipe carrying the gas had been. After she reached the first destroyed home, now cordoned off with yellow and black warning tape, it took her a moment to realize it was the remains of Kevin's place. The blackened shell looked like a dinosaur's rib cage. The next house was the same. Mustache man had parked the Camry between the road and the crater. She kept her face forward in case he was watching. *I wonder if he knows this isn't Caron's house.*

Of course he knows. He confronted me here the first time we met.

She continued up the road until the end, then turned around and parked out of sight. If she climbed the hillside behind the houses, she would be able to see what was going on, but the cover would be thin—and there would be the problem of rattlesnakes and scorpions.

Her skin crawled. Maybe just a cautious approach down the street. Most of the houses at this end of the road had plantings in front for privacy.

This is a stupid idea.

What choice did she have? She'd already gone to the police several times and they'd concluded she was mental. Her mother would confirm it. At least she wasn't identifiable in her present state to anyone who knew her. She hoped.

The road sloped gently downhill, and enough trees shaded the street to keep it relatively cool. The air smelled of burned timbers and scorched earth. At the open gate to Caron's house, she paused. The garage seemed to be in one piece with no evidence that anyone had been ransacking it. Cautiously she approached, making sure she made as little noise as possible.

Looking through the window, she saw an empty building. A

black metal storage cabinet stood open and empty. Circling the structure, she discovered a stained rag and an empty metal coffee container with a faint odor she couldn't identify.

A trail behind the burned-out house appeared to lead to the next lot, where Dali-mustache man had parked the Camry. She ended up at the back of that property.

Mustache-man was sitting in the driver's seat.

The blood rushed from her face. She ducked behind a shrub.

Mustache didn't move.

Despite the heat, Tavish felt chilled. Something about his complete stillness was wrong. Very wrong.

She stood and moved forward, sliding down the burned ditch, sending rocks rattling to the bottom.

No reaction.

She crawled up the other side and approached the car.

He was staring straight ahead.

Her steps grew shorter, her legs heavier.

The gun glinted from the ground beside the driver's side door. She bent over and stared at it. Did she need a weapon? Some way to defend herself? *No.* She'd never fired a gun before, and this one had already killed one person. A fly buzzed through the open window, landing on his sightless eye.

Hands trembling, Tavish reached through the window and pulled open his jacket.

A crimson patch stained his shirt over his heart.

She couldn't breathe. A buzzing started in her head, and the world faded except for the crimson stain.

"Oh, Lord, help me, not now, stay with me, don't faint, don't faint," she gasped out.

The buzzing faded. She tore her gaze from his chest to his jacket. With great effort she released her grip. Her hand was smeared with blood. She wiped it off on her T-shirt, then reached for the pocket. His wallet. After yanking it out, she opened it. His driver's license said he was Jack Cave. A second card identified him as a licensed insurance investigator.

The wallet dropped from her suddenly numb fingers. He *was* the investigator after all.

Sweat beaded on her forehead, and the numbness took over her body.

Obviously Fake Cop had killed him. Were her mother and Fake Cop working together? If they were, that could mean Helen had arranged to have her own paintings stolen in order to collect the insurance money. And maybe she'd never paid it back.

CHAPTER 28

Sirens in the distance were growing closer. Tavish shook off the numbness. *I can't be caught with another body.* She sprinted for the trail.

Behind her, the sirens screamed to a halt, followed by slamming doors and shouts.

She ran faster, leaving the trail and climbing the hill.

Footsteps pounded behind her. "Stop! Police!"

A shot of adrenaline coursed through her body. She jerked to a stop.

"Show me your hands!"

Tavish put both hands in the air.

"Get on the ground! Don't move."

She wanted to turn around and face the police. She dropped to her knees and a sharp pain shot up her leg.

"Get on your stomach. Arms spread wide."

Don't let there be scorpions.

Footsteps approached. A calloused hand grabbed her wrist

and twisted it behind her. *Snap!* A handcuff ratcheted into place.

She bit her lip to keep from crying out.

The officer captured her other wrist and clipped the cuff in place, then hauled her upright by her arm.

She tried to keep upright on the uneven ground, but her injured leg gave way. The sharp sting turned to a pulsing burn.

The officer, a thick-necked, ruddy-faced man in his forties, yanked her upright.

She stumbled and went down again.

He cursed, jerked her up, and shook her like a rag doll. "Stop resisting arrest."

She wanted to cry out, to protest, to plead with him to stop hurting her. But she couldn't form the words.

A second officer joined the first, and together they dragged her down the hillside and across the crater, then propped her up against the patrol car.

"Do you have anything that will cut, stick, or otherwise injure me?" one of them asked.

She shook her head and closed her eyes.

The back of a hand ran under her bra line, down her front, slipped into her pockets, then down her legs. The searcher grunted when he found the Bible. He pulled her away from the squad car far enough to open the back door, then shoved her into the hard seat. The car smelled of old vomit and sweat.

She kept her head down. Blood smeared the front of her T-shirt. Her leg throbbed, and her shoe felt wet.

Next to the open door, a uniformed deputy pulled out a card and began to read it. "'You have the right to remain silent.'"

Concentrate. The police won't listen to me. I have to figure this out.

"'Anything you say can and will be used against you in a court of law.'"

Why would he murder the investigator, then leave? He hid the last murder. Actually, counting Kevin, he hid the last two murders.

"'You have the right to an attorney. If you cannot afford an attorney, one will be provided for you.'"

Of course! He was going to get rid of the body. He had the problem of two vehicles. He killed, then left to get help. So there are more of them out there.

"Do you understand the rights I have just read to you?"

She nodded. *If Helen was so desperate for money that she had to resort to insurance fraud, what would she do to get her hands on my trust fund?*

"With these rights in mind, do you wish to speak to me? Do you want to tell me why you killed him?"

She could hire the most expensive attorney—make that legal team—in the world. She just needed to get to a phone and call . . . whom?

"Okay, fellows, take her away and book her."

She had to make a plan.

Her door slammed shut.

She winced but kept her head down. They'd uncover her identity soon enough when they compared fingerprints. Her mother had her printed for the application to Softmode. Was that all part of a grander scheme?

≡≡

The patrol car stopped in front of a garage door at the police department. It rose with a loud, grinding roar. Pulling forward, they entered a cinderblock and cement-floored room and parked next to another squad car. The door ground shut. The officer opened her door and hauled her out, strolling toward a steel door with a glass window. A series of small lockers lined the wall next to the door. He pushed her against the door. "Don't move." Removing his pistol, he locked it into one of the lockers, then buzzed to have the door opened.

What am I even doing here? If she escaped, she'd be a fugitive, but maybe she could get someone to help her. Ezekiel? Sawyer? They both knew she was innocent.

The door finished its slow, squealing journey open and the officer pulled her forward. The door closed as sluggishly, clanking shut with a *bang!* that hurt her ears and shot through her like a physical wave.

The officer checked his watch.

The door in front of them repeated the grinding open. Beyond was a bleak cinderblock room filled with people. A line of inmates in orange two-piece uniforms were across the room, and a second line of men in street clothes loitered against the far wall. The stench of a landfill in the dead of summer hammered her nose. Someone was screaming, "I want to die! I want to die!" A number of inmates yelled suggestions to the screamer. Nearby, a woman bellowed out an off-key rendition of "Amazing Grace."

The deputy had to shout to be heard. "Stand here." He made Tavish face the wall, leaving a scant two inches between it and her nose. "Don't move from this box."

The box was a painted square on the floor.

She wasn't sure she could stand. Her leg was on fire and her hands were still cuffed behind her. She could place her forehead against the painted cinderblock surface, but a grease stain showed where others had done just that.

Her stomach clenched. *I'm okay. This will pass. Breathe in calm, breathe out fear.* The chant didn't work. She wasn't okay. She was in jail. And breathing was a chore.

People moved past her with a brief rush of air, followed by the smell. Feet. Armpits. Worse. She learned to hold her breath when she felt the slight puff.

Talk? Remain silent? Ask for a lawyer? Call my mother? Tell them I'm innocent?

A woman's voice behind her said, "Do you have anything in your pockets that's gonna hurt me or stick me?"

Again she shook her head.

The pat-down was repeated, then the female officer, a bored woman in her forties, took Tavish's arm and led her to a long metal counter. Wolf calls and jeering whistles followed their movement. A computer terminal and keyboard sat on the counter. The deputy behind the counter looked at her. "Name?"

Tavish bit her lip and stared at the floor. If she said her name and someone recognized she was rich, she'd likely end up a punching bag if she went into any kind of holding area with the general population. Violence, anger, frustration, and depression swirled around her with almost palpable dimensions. All those emotions sought a common target.

The woman sighed. "Address? Birth date? Social Security number? Single, married, divorced, separated? Height? Weight? Have you been in custody before? Were you in protective custody for any reason? Are you on any medication? Are you feeling suicidal today?" After each non-answer, the deputy would type something. "Okay, Jane Doe, on to the fun stuff."

Once again taking her arm, the woman led Tavish to what looked like a shower with honeycombed rubber mats on the floor and shower fixtures on the wall. In the distance toilets flushed regularly. A second female deputy joined them.

"Strip," the new one ordered.

"I beg your pardon—"

"You heard me. Everything off. Put them into this bin." She thumped a blue plastic tub on a nearby bench. Next to it she placed an orange uniform, underwear, and beige plastic sandals.

Tavish grew light-headed. *Don't faint. Not now.* With shaking fingers she unzipped and pulled down her jeans.

Her stitched leg had come open. Blood dripped to the floor.

"Okay, we gotta problem," the new one said. "We need a nurse."

"Good luck on that," the first officer said. "Let's just send her over to—"

"Can't. Let's call a medical code and get her over to the hospital."

The new one left, leaving the bored woman. "Put your jeans back on for now. We'll finish processing you later. Sit on that bench. You're not gonna faint or anything, right?"

"No." Her light-headed feeling wasn't because of blood loss.

Shortly a man and woman wearing one-piece coveralls arrived with a gurney. Wordlessly they pointed. She crawled onto the padded surface. The female transport guard—her stitched name said Randall—placed a handcuff on her wrist, then snapped it to the gurney, repeating the process on the other arm. Both her legs were shackled. They threw a blanket over her and started snapping the restraints across her body. One restraint went directly over her wound.

"Owwwwww!" Tavish screamed.

Randall gave the restraint a second tug.

"Aaaaaahhhh!"

"Shut up." Her tormentor wouldn't look at her.

Tavish closed her eyes. Tears burned down her cheeks. Her nose ran. The relentless pain from her leg battered her mind. *I've got to get away.*

≈≡

Sawyer's cell phone rang. The screen said *Private Caller. Who knows this number?* He answered. "Sawyer Price."

"Mr. Price, I'm sorry for the late hour. You don't know me, but I believe Tavish is a friend of yours."

"How did you get this number?"

"From a lovely woman, Dr. Patricia Caron. Oh dear, I should explain myself. My name is Ezekiel Lewis. I'm retired from Sandia National Laboratories. Recently I became friends with Tavish, er, Evelyn McTavish. I have become very worried about her. She told me the last time I saw her—"

"When was that?"

"Let's see, today is Wednesday, so it had to be Monday evening."

"Go on."

"She left some sketches with me, and some notes. I got Dr.

Caron's name from the notes, and when I called her, she gave me your cell. Tavish said she'd call me when she was safe, but I haven't heard a word. She told me you were the only person she trusted."

Sawyer sucked in a quick breath. *Poor Tavish.* "You don't know where she is?"

"I just know she was going to get out of town as soon as possible. But I did expect her to call."

"Yes. I'm . . . concerned as well."

"Ah, so you feel something for her." He chuckled. "My dear Ruth and I were married for over forty years."

Sawyer's cheeks burned. He was glad the phone wouldn't show his blush. "I have a meeting in the morning. I wonder if you might bring the drawings to me?"

"Certainly. I'll leave a note on the door here in case she returns without calling first. When she left, she didn't have a cell."

Sawyer rubbed his chin. "That doesn't sound very safe—announcing you're not at home. How about I come by after my meeting?"

"That would work, and I'll call you if she gets ahold of me in the meantime." He gave his address and disconnected.

Sawyer moved to the window and looked out at the city lights. *Please, Lord, watch over Tavish, and if it's your will, bring her back to me.*

≥≡

The pounding burn in Tavish's leg was relentless. Every bump and turn of the ambulance sent a sharp jab up her body. She tried to think of something else, to focus on the ceiling or the cruel face of the guard, but the tears blurred the world around her. There was only the Pain. She had no idea of the passage of time or how far they drove.

Finally, finally they stopped, the door opened, and someone yanked out the gurney. Far overhead fluorescent lights cast a yellowish glow on the orderlies.

She recognized the doctor who'd treated her a lifetime ago, Dr. Kerry Woods, bending over her. "I know her," the doctor said. "What's going on here? Get her inside."

The gurney rattled and thumped across the pavement and into the hospital.

Tavish moaned and squeezed her eyes shut.

The thumping ache in her leg lessened as the strap was removed.

"You idiot." The doctor's voice, directed at Randall, dripped fury. "You deliberately strapped her down across her injury."

Randall muttered something.

"Get these cuffs off her. The leg shackles as well. There's no way she's going anywhere."

"I'll have to put it in my report—"

"If you don't get these handcuffs off her right now, I'll tell you what you can put in that report!"

If Tavish hadn't already been crying, she would have burst into tears when the restraints came off. She was lifted onto an exam table as the doctor swiftly checked her over.

"She's lost a lot of blood. Get her started on an IV . . ." The orders continued, but Tavish wasn't listening. She was staring at the square of suspended ceiling above her.

CHAPTER 29

"Are you done?" Randall asked.

Tavish was floating in a sea of pain-free comfort. Her clothes had once again been cut off, but after they worked on her leg, they covered her with a warmed blanket.

"Almost," Dr. Woods said.

"I need to cuff her again." Randall rattled the metal handcuffs.

Dr. Woods glanced over at Randall, then muttered to the nurse, "Get an IV line into her other arm. Don't hook it up." She leaned over Tavish. "I don't know what you did, Marley, but no one should be treated like that."

Marley? That's right, she'd given them the name of Marley Coyote when she'd come in the other night. Hopefully that might slow down her identification.

"I'm admitting her for observation for the night," Dr. Woods said to the guard.

"Once she's transported to the bed—"

"Then she's going to sleep."

"Look," Randall said. "She's a prisoner. She's in custody—"

"She's a person, an injured woman"—Dr. Woods's voice rose—"that you further traumatized by your cruel treatment. You're a contract transportation company. What would your bosses think if they lost that juicy prison contract because of you? You'd be lucky if you weren't arrested for assault! You can sit in the room with her if you need to, but you're not chaining her up again. At least not tonight."

Randall was silent after that, but Tavish was under no illusion that the woman had surrendered. Randall would get even with her the first chance she got.

An orderly transported her to a private room on the second floor with a window. Randall pulled the chair out of the corner and placed it where she could see Tavish and the door.

Tavish pretended to sleep. She had no idea if her plan would work, but going back to the detention center wasn't an option.

Nurses entered and left the room at regular intervals roughly every hour. Tavish monitored the time and actions through barely open eyes. Randall would rouse herself and watch while the nurse took her temp or checked her IV line.

The night dragged on, with the clock barely moving. Tavish was exhausted and weak, but keeping the image of Marley in her mind helped. It wasn't until a hint of gray nudged the hospital blinds that Randall failed to wake up when the nurse entered. *This is it.* If Randall continued to sleep, she'd have about an hour to carry out her plan.

Once the nurse left, Tavish slowed the drip until it was almost stopped, then unhooked the line under the covers and pulled back the sheet.

Randall shifted.

Tavish froze and watched for the steady breathing of sleep. After an eternity, she dared to move again.

Once again she was in a backless hospital gown. The pain was gone because of the drugs given earlier, but she knew the hurt would return once the drugs wore off.

She'd plotted her escape for hours. Get on the window ledge. Push the ceiling panel aside. Keep moving. Get clothes. Leave hospital. Become invisible.

Silently she slipped from the bed and padded to the window. Crawling onto the ledge took more work than she'd figured. From the window ledge, the panel was still almost out of her reach. Using her fingertips, she lifted, then nudged the panel over until the opening was large enough to fit through. She then crawled off the ledge and tiptoed across the room. Her heart thumped so loud she was sure Randall would wake.

Randall snorted once.

She stopped, then crept to the door. The hallway was clear. After slipping through the opening, she padded up the hall until she came to a door marked Maternity. The nurse's station—a large, curved counter—was empty for the moment. Movement, someone talking, and a crying baby came from some of the rooms. Quickly she passed by the rooms with sound coming out of them and peeked into the silent ones. She found what she was looking for—a still-packed suitcase on a chair. The woman in the bed was sleeping.

Tavish swiftly opened the case, snatched out the neatly folded clothing, and turned to go. She peeked around the door.

A nurse was coming down the hall in her direction.

She slipped into the bathroom and hid behind the open door.

The nurse entered and woke the sleeping woman. "Do you need anything? It's almost time for your baby to visit."

Tavish held her breath. *Please don't have to use the restroom.*

"More water," the woman said.

The nurse picked up a dark pink pitcher and turned toward the bathroom.

Tavish pressed against the cold wall.

The nurse flipped on the light and filled the pitcher from the sink, then turned the light off as she left.

Tavish leaned her head against the cool white tile on the wall. *Thank you.*

The moment the nurse was gone, Tavish yanked on the clothes she'd taken. Jeans, a black-and-white T-shirt, sandals— the clothes were roomy, except the sandals, but they would have to do.

The nurse entered the room again, this time pushing a baby in a portable bassinet. "Here you go . . ."

Tavish didn't wait to hear the rest. She slipped from the bathroom and out the door while the nurse and mother were concentrating on the baby.

She spotted a side exit and headed for it. Just as she hit the release bar, the loudspeaker announced, "Code silver. Code silver. Lockdown."

The lock clicked, but she was already outside.

≈≈

Sawyer rose early to work out in the fitness gym, then showered and headed to the FBI building to prepare for the meeting, taking only a short detour to Dunkin' Donuts. The conference room had a spacious oval walnut table, padded chairs, and an impressive AV setup. One wall had a built-in flat-screen television, another had a whiteboard, and the third a set of cabinets, a counter, and an oversize coffee dispenser. The fourth was a wall of glass overlooking a hallway. Sawyer flipped a switch and security blinds lowered, blocking the view of the room from casual observers. He started a pot of coffee brewing.

By the time he had posted the photos and known facts on the whiteboard, Lieutenant Hammen and Deputy Sanderson arrived. Sanderson proved to be a thick-necked, husky officer with massive hands. Detective Mike Mullins arrived for the meeting a few minutes later.

"Gentlemen, thank you for coming." Sawyer nodded toward the coffee and donuts. "Help yourself before we get started."

The men did so, then stood in front of the whiteboard and read the posted information.

Deputy Sanderson, munching on a donut, pointed a powdered-sugar finger at Howard's name. "You note this scumbag 'fell in love' with Tavish. Who is this Tavish?"

"Oh, sorry, Evelyn McTavish." Sawyer took a sip of coffee. "She is our common denominator. Daughter of millionaire Helen Richmond and extremely wealthy in her own right."

Lieutenant Hammen nodded. "I wouldn't be surprised if Howie here got a look at Tavish's photos or saw her when he cased the home."

Sawyer nodded. "Makes sense."

"We should have the autopsy on Kevin Chase sometime

today," Sanderson said. "Dental records are on the way, along with a current driver's license photo. Now we just need to know if we have another murder on our hands, or an accident."

Lieutenant Hammen pulled out a file. "We fingerprinted the note found on the bush near Dusty Rhodes's trailer attributing the attack to Antifa—"

"I hate to seem stupid here, but what's Antifa?" Sanderson asked.

"An extremely militant, far-left movement," Sawyer said. "It includes anarchists, socialists, communists, punk fans, revolutionaries, and other assorted malcontents. They were responsible for some of the more violent protests recently."

Hammen nodded as Sawyer spoke. "We have a few in our county. Unfortunately for us, they were busy that night with a protest at the University of New Mexico."

"So *not* involved in a sniper attack. An attempt to throw us off," Sanderson said.

Mullins reached into his briefcase and pulled out a printed sketch. "This is the composite Tavish sent to the department of the man she calls Fake Cop."

Sawyer stood and taped the sketch to the whiteboard. "She drew Fake Cop for me, as well as sketched Kevin Chase and John Coyote. And her fiancé, the late Howard, whom she knew as Andrew." He taped the crumpled sketch on the whiteboard, then circled John Coyote. "This is a missing piece of the puzzle. And the one she calls Fake Cop."

"Coyote's the one Miss McTavish reported to me." Detective Mullins glanced at the men. "And she did sound and look like a nutcase." He pulled out a notepad. "Said he looked like he'd been burned with a cigarette, tortured, tied up, then stabbed when he tried to escape. What do you think happened to his body?"

The men were silent. Finally Sawyer said, "A lot of desert out there."

"What about associates of the probable thieves?" Mullins said. "Vince and Howard?"

"Here're the printouts on both." Sawyer placed the papers on the table.

Sanderson picked them up and began to read.

"Late last night I got a call from an Ezekiel Lewis," Sawyer said. "He said Tavish left her drawings with him along with some notes. I'm meeting with him later to pick up everything."

"Did Ezekiel know her whereabouts?" Mullins asked.

"Unfortunately, no."

"What do you know about Coyote?" Sanderson asked.

"He looked native, maybe Navajo. I have a call in with Sandia Way Management, the company that rented out Dr. Patricia Caron's house." Sawyer tried to keep his voice level. He could almost feel the minutes slipping through his fingers. Tavish was out there somewhere in grave danger, or worse. "I've asked them to email or fax me the rental agreements from past renters. Long shot. With the destruction of the house, fingerprints and other evidence have been destroyed."

"Here's something." Sanderson looked up from his reading. "There's a John Begay listed as an associate of Vince. Begay is a common Navajo name."

"Let's get a look at him." Sawyer tapped on the computer. A photograph loaded. Sawyer gave a short jerk of his head. "Got him. Yes, looks like the picture Tavish drew. Disgraced scientist from Sandia National Laboratories. Spent a month in the slammer with ol' Vinny here. Became a small-time crook."

"Scientist? So, a brain." Mullins jerked a thumb at the board. "Howard and Vinny wouldn't have the brains between them to pull off an art heist, but a scientist?" He looked around the table. "I'd bet there was a fourth. The muscle. Fake Cop. Remember a guy got shot at the robbery, a gardener or something? Thieves usually don't resort to violence. That killing probably shook them up. They went their separate ways, at least until the heat died down a bit."

"But Vinny, or Vinny and Howard, decided to make a run with the art," Sawyer said.

"And someone reported them," Sanderson said. "Someone not crazy about them taking off with the paintings."

"That wouldn't be Fake Cop," Mullins said. "He would just as soon shoot them himself."

The men were silent while they pondered the information. Soft murmurs carried through the walls from the people in the hall. Hammen stacked some papers in front of him.

Sawyer stood and faced the whiteboard. "Begay wanted out. He wanted to connect with Tavish, maybe to warn her. He commissioned her to do some work for him, to get close to her. He put her name into the microchip of the dog and turned Marley loose when he saw trouble coming."

Hammen finally spoke up. "Tavish drove to the Kéyah site, then almost died at the firestorm at Dusty Rhodes's place. So we know Fake Cop is after her. Probably panicked when she went to a radio station, thinking she was going public. Now she's missing."

Sawyer turned, jaw tight.

"Gentlemen," Hammen said. "I hate to be the one to say it, but everyone connected to this heist is dead. Everyone but Fake Cop and—"

"Then don't say it," Sawyer said. "I'll find her."

CHAPTER 30

Tavish was soaked with sweat despite the cool of the morning. She expected someone to yell *Halt!* at any moment. Sirens screeching toward the hospital told her they would be actively seeking a solo female wandering the streets the minute they figured out she wasn't in the ceiling's crawl space. She needed to be invisible. Becoming one of the homeless wasn't going to work this time. Who else faded into the background? The workers taking care of her mother's estate?

What if she became part of the positive shapes? Not invisible, but blending in.

A jogger?

More like a limper. But she could bicycle. She could get into her mother's garage where Helen had her bicycles. The exercise room was off the garage. Helen kept her workout clothes in there. She could change and use the bike to get around. Maybe even slip into her own house and pick up a checkbook and identification. Cash a check. Get Marley from the vet.

I need to stop running. The words crashed into her brain.

The police were looking for Marley Coyote, or a homeless Jane Doe, not her.

My fingerprints will lead them straight to me.

No! She hadn't been processed. No photo or prints. They drove her straight to the hospital. She just might have a little time before someone came knocking at her door.

But what if her mother was home?

I have to stop running. Living in the shadows. Being afraid. Fractured by fear.

It was time she confronted Helen and asked her directly if she was behind everything. *What do I have to lose at this point?*

She grimaced. *Just my freedom. Or my life.*

Silence again spread around the table. No one would look him in the eye.

Sawyer turned and looked again at the display. "Negative space," he finally muttered.

"What's that?" Sanderson asked.

"It's an art term." Sawyer continued to look at the whiteboard. "We're looking at the thieves and their connection to all these events. They're the positive shape—the thing we are focusing on. We need to focus on the negative shape, the shapes of the surroundings." He turned and looked at the men.

All were staring at him as if he'd grown horns.

"The art. Why steal art? What do these bozos know about original paintings?"

"Probably nothing. But even I know the name of Georgia O'Keeffe." Mullins shrugged. "But they were recovered."

Sawyer tapped Helen's name on the whiteboard. "Why steal them in the first place?"

"So where do we go from here?" Sanderson asked.

"I have an idea." Hammen turned to Sawyer. "You said Begay was a scientist. What kind?"

"Design engineer," Sawyer said. "Why?"

Hammen nodded toward Sawyer's timeline. "You have a four-month span between the art heist and the recovery. Doesn't that strike you as a rather . . . large negative space?"

"Maybe they were looking for buyers," Sanderson said.

"I suspect they'd already have buyers." Mullins scratched his chin. "Don't design engineers draw?"

"Of course!" As soon as Mullins said it, Sawyer saw the possibility. "Design engineer. Artist. Forgery."

"That's a pretty big jump in logic," Hammen said.

"One way to find out." Sawyer looked up a number, then dialed. "Yeah, Special Agent Sawyer Price, FBI. I need to talk to human resources."

"Hold, please."

Mullins poured another cup of coffee, then examined the box of donuts.

"Nancy Lee, Human Resources."

"Ms. Lee? I'm Special Agent Sawyer Price with the FBI, and I need some information on a former—"

"I don't give out information on the phone." The woman's voice sounded like it belonged to a starched schoolteacher.

"I understand. I'm conducting an investi—"

"How do I know you're with the FBI? You could be anyone."

Sawyer clenched his teeth. "Ms. Lee, I'm going to hang up. You will call the FBI Albuquerque number. You will ask for Special Agent Sawyer Price. Then we will complete this conversation. If you don't call immediately, I will come over there. You will have delayed my investigation, which is critical. At this point you do not want to meet me in person. Do I make myself clear?"

"Yes."

Sawyer hung up.

Mullins raised his eyebrows and took a bite of a cheese Danish.

A few minutes later the phone on the counter rang. Sawyer picked up the handset. "Agent Price."

"How can I help you, Agent Price?" Ms. Lee's voice had gone from starched to icy.

"John Begay. He was a scientist with you, was fired a few years ago."

"Yes."

Sawyer pursed his lips and glanced at the men in the room. "You know him? Knew him?"

"Yes."

"Well then, why was he fired?"

"He was a security risk. Money problems. Work-related issues. Many reasons. He was repeatedly warned. Why?"

"Was he an artist?"

Ms. Lee was silent so long he thought the connection had broken. "Ms. Lee?"

"Sorry. I had to look that up. No. His application says nothing about art. His work was . . . less than artistic. Why?"

"Thank you." Sawyer hung up and looked at the men. "It looks like Begay may not be our forger. We'll have to keep looking. But I still think I need to pay a visit to Helen's place and look at those paintings."

Mullins's phone rang. "Detective Mullins . . . Yeah. When? Who's on it? . . . Where? . . . So what happened?" He listened for a few moments. "Yeah, thanks. I'll get back to you." He hung up. "It looks like things just got a whole lot more interesting. We have another homicide near the Caron place. Caught the killer red-handed. But she escaped when they transported her to the hospital for treatment of an injury. SWAT team has the hospital on lockdown while they do a sweep."

"And . . . ?" Hammen opened his hands in a get-on-with-it motion.

"And the murdered man was Jack Cave, a private insurance investigator. Specializing in art."

The room was deadly silent.

"The escaped woman was identified by a doctor as a homeless woman treated the day before. Called herself Marley Coyote."

Sawyer dropped into a chair. Tavish.

Tavish kept to back alleys and side streets, working her way to her mother's estate. She passed by a pickup with an open trailer holding lawn mowers, rakes, shovels, and other equipment with the name of a company on the side. Workers were busy mowing and raking an already flawless lawn. She filched a straw hat and a pair of work gloves without slowing down and kept walking.

Gathering her dirty hair, she stuffed it under the hat and pulled on the gloves. Shortly a patrol car appeared in the distance. She stepped off the sidewalk onto a well-tended verge and began picking up dead leaves. Her hands trembled.

The patrol car didn't slow down.

She wanted to run, to make it to her mother's house before another cruiser spotted her—but there was a vast difference between jogging in a pricey outfit and running down the street. Make that limping.

Once in the wealthy neighborhood, twice more she pretended to be a gardener. The sandals had rubbed blisters on both feet, the painkiller had worn off, and her mouth was as parched as the landscape. Only the thought of what would happen if she failed kept her moving.

For once no one was tending Helen's grounds. She let herself into the garage with a keypad by the door. Helen's car was missing, which was usual during the day. She spent a lot of time at her various businesses.

The bicycles were a bit dusty, but the tires were inflated should she change her mind and make a run for it. Her mother had purchased the best bike and had every bell and whistle mounted on the frame. She'd probably never even ridden on it.

A second keypad let her into Helen's exercise room, filled with a state-of-the-art stepper-climber, treadmill, weights, rowing machine, and every other workout machine imaginable, most still unused. Hanging on the wall were two of Tavish's drawings from the gallery. Neither showed signs of smoke or water damage. She felt her face burn. Her mother must have purchased them before the gallery fire.

She'd assumed everything she did was a disappointment to her mother, but her mother had taken that first step toward her. Maybe they had more to discuss than she thought.

A refrigerator in the corner contained a selection of chilled organic energy drinks. She downed two.

Directly off from the exercise room was a spacious bathroom with an oversize shower, a bowl of fragrant soaps, and fresh, fluffy towels. She looked at them longingly. Shower later. She needed to find out the truth.

Not much had changed since she'd last been inside Helen's home. The mahogany floors gleamed where they showed under the handwoven Navajo rugs. The pale taupe walls were hung with Helen's painting collection, each with its own light, and interspaced with sculpture stands and pottery displays.

"*Oh! Me sobresaltaste, Señorita Evelyn!*" Maria, her housekeeper, had her hand to her heart.

"I'm sorry. Do you know where my mother is?"

"*Mi inglés no es muy bueno, pero lo entiendo. Tu madre se fue con dos hombres. Uno de ellos manejo su auto. El otro siguió. No sé cuándo volverá. Ella se veía enojada.*"

Why hadn't her mother hired Spanish tutors? French wasn't all that useful in the Southwest. "I'm going to shower here," Tavish said slowly, then pretended to scrub her armpits.

The woman frowned. "*Sí, señorita. ¿Necesitas algo?*"

"I'm not sure what you just asked, but if my mother, um . . ."

"*Madre?*"

"Yes. *Sí*. My *madre* returns." She pretended to drive a car. "Come and get me. Call." She cupped her hands as if yelling.

"*Sí, Señorita Evelyn.*" She turned to leave.

"Maria. Maria Montez?"

"*Sí.*"

"Why were you crying at my place?"

"*Mi esposo fue asesinado.* My husband." She pointed to the courtyard. "Killed. I miss him."

She gasped. "Your husband was the gardener. The one—" The one murdered when thieves broke into the house.

John's note. *All I can do is try to make it right. Please take this money to Mrs. Montez. I am so sorry.* That was what John wanted Tavish to do. Try to make things right.

The woman made a slight curtsy and scurried off before Tavish could say anything more.

I will make things right. Not for John. For Maria.

Tavish glanced at the artwork one more time. Maria's husband died defending these paintings. She hoped her mother appreciated their true value.

Because I finally know their true cost.

The new Frida Kahlo self-portrait hung by itself on the wall on her left. The first three paintings on the right were the Georgia O'Keeffe originals—two florals and a rare self-portrait that had been part of a private collection since the 1950s. On a bookstand between the two florals stood a thick tome cataloging all the O'Keeffe works. Her mother had been so proud of the book, with the description underneath each photograph. "'White Flower with Blue,' 1933, oil on canvas, from the collection of Helen Richmond."

She turned the pages, finding each of the works Helen owned marked with a thin silk bookmark. Even if the artwork disappeared again, her mother's name would remain as the last owner.

The self-portrait was the most unusual. Tavish had no idea of its worth. One of the florals had sold at auction for more than $44 million. The book identified the piece as "Self-Portrait in Red."

The hand was wrong.

Tavish stared at the painting, then the photograph in the book. The difference was infinitesimal, a tiny shift in the negative space between the fingers.

She found the photo of the first floral, a morning glory. In the lower right corner, the negative shape of the blue was off.

The final recovered painting was of a vivid orange-red set of three poppies. This time it was a shadow on the top poppy that was off.

All the recovered paintings were forgeries.

CHAPTER 31

Sawyer pulled up in front of Ezekiel's house, double-checking the address. An older man opened the door before he even had a chance to get out of the car.

"I'm so glad you're here." The man opened the door wider. "I'm Ezekiel Lewis. Come in. Come in."

Sawyer left the car and walked up to the man. "Thanks for calling me about Tavish." He held out his hand. "How did you happen to come to know her?"

They shook hands. Ezekiel stepped aside. "Through my wife, Ruth." As the two men entered the house, he explained the meeting in the cemetery. "I think I was the only person she felt she could trust, outside of you. Anyway, I've laid out everything she left with me." He nodded toward the dining room, then followed Sawyer to the oak table.

Sawyer pulled up a chair and began to read Tavish's notes. The early-morning donuts and coffee sat in a lump in his stomach. *Or maybe that's worry about Tavish.*

Ezekiel left for a moment, then returned with two frosty glasses of iced tea and placed one on a coaster in front of Sawyer. "What kind of trouble is she in?" Ezekiel asked. "The last I saw her, she was going to find a place for the night, cash a check in the morning, do a bit of investigating, then head out of town."

Sawyer took a sip of tea. "That's good. What kind of investigating?"

"One of the companies her mother owns, Softmode Testing, might have something to do with the events of the past few days. Microchips, nanotechnology, human testing, that type of thing. She was also looking into John Begay's connection to her mother—"

"So you know about John Begay?"

"Oh my. I identified this person"—Ezekiel picked up the drawing of John Coyote—"as Begay." He explained the connection, but his voice became muffled to Sawyer's ears.

The room spun. "I don't feel so good . . ."

"Oh dear." Ezekiel picked up a phone. "I'll call an ambulance."

⇒⇐

Forgery. Does my mother know? Did she do it? Or maybe when they were stolen, they were copied? Did the insurance investigator spot the discrepancy the other night at the party? Or was the insurance company suspicious for another reason? Could he have been killed because he was going to reveal the forgery? Tavish's thoughts whirled through her brain.

She trotted down the hall to her mother's office. The door was locked.

The housekeeper wouldn't have a key.

What now? Wait? She paced, each time coming back to stare at the door.

This isn't getting me any answers.

She ran back to the exercise room. There she found a pair of long pants and a short-sleeved bicycling jersey in the closet next to the shower. The gloves and helmet were on a shelf under the bike, as were the lightweight shoes. After tucking her hair under the helmet, she took down the bike and headed out. Pedaling the bike hurt like the dickens but was easier than running. She just had to be sure she didn't pull out the stitches. Again. Only when she was out of sight of her mother's home did she allow herself to think.

Maybe Helen *did* know the artwork was fake. Maybe *she* was the brain behind it all. Hire Begay to steal the art and paint the forgeries. Sell the originals. Get the insurance money.

No. That didn't work. There would be no need for forgeries if she wanted to get the insurance money for stolen art.

Maybe she wanted to sell the art on the black market more than once . . .

What if she came at this from a different angle? The insurance investigator must have been looking at the possibility that Helen was involved in the theft. She didn't want him to stay away from the art. She wanted him to stay away from her. To not sully her reputation.

Tavish was riding around in circles trying to get a handle on the thoughts that seemed to ping around like bingo balls. *Where should I go? Who should I call?* Maybe she just needed to talk through it out loud. *Grandma.*

Her grandma had been the secure constant in her unstable life. She'd always seemed to know what to say to make things better and smooth out the bumps. She'd been Tavish's inspiration.

She arrived at the cemetery, got off the bike, and pushed it to the bench by her grandmother's grave. No one would bother her here.

"Grandma," she whispered. "Help me put it together."

The lettering on the tombstone stared at her. *Prov. 3:5.*

"I know what that means now, Grandma. 'Trust in the Lord with all your heart; do not depend on your own understanding.'" She folded her hands. "I'll try that. Lord, if you're up there, help me." The pines rustled above her, the breeze bringing the scent of roses. She closed her eyes. No thunderous voice came from heaven. Gradually, though, her jumbled thoughts started to organize.

John had approached her after the art was stolen. He must have been looking for a way to get the money to Maria. His commissioning art from her was a ruse to get more information, to find a way to assuage his guilt without being caught. He had left Tavish the number clues that led to the location of the money and note.

"But why hide the clues? Why not just get the money to Maria along with the apology?" Because . . . because he was being watched? He couldn't approach Maria directly. How had Ezekiel phrased it? *"I think Marley was his back-up plan, and you were his insurance policy. If anything happened to him, he wanted you to find out."*

Something had happened to him. He was tortured. Was that to find out the location of the money and note?

"*I think Marley was his back-up plan, and you were his insurance policy. If anything happened to him, he wanted you to find out.*"

Trust. John trusted her, gave her the clues to unravel the location of the money. What else had he given her or told her?

He'd talked about negative space and used hands as an illustration. He'd told her where to look on the forgeries to spot the discrepancies.

She opened her eyes and glanced around. No one lingered nearby.

Start over. Start at the beginning.

"Okay, Grandma, I'm going to tell you what I think happened. John stole the paintings to be reproduced, then someone made sure the fakes were recovered. Law enforcement wouldn't keep looking for paintings they'd already found."

So far, so good. It all fits.

"Our last meeting was at Patricia's house—the only time we met there. He made a point of mentioning the Kéyah site . . . directed my attention to it? Patricia hadn't rented the house to him, so he was squatting out there. Was he hiding out? Why?"

He was hiding from Fake Cop, of course. But Fake Cop found him anyway, and tortured him, then killed him.

"You were wrong, John," she murmured. "I'm not smart enough to figure out your clues."

Her gaze drifted to Andrew's grave. She hadn't even looked at the finished headstone she'd ordered. *Look now,* a voice whispered in her brain.

Pushing the bike, she walked the short distance to his grave. No flowers had been left under his name. So much for the woman who'd been pregnant with his child. She wasn't exactly missing him. *Nor am I.*

The whispered thought startled her. She hadn't loved him. She'd only loved the feeling of being loved. No. That wasn't right either. Andrew was using her for her money. *And I knew it. And didn't care.*

John used her too. Used her to get information, to solve his problems. By doing so, he'd placed her squarely in the crosshairs of . . . Fake Cop?

Fake. Fake Cop. Fake art. She stared at Andrew's gravestone. She'd stopped thinking that Andrew was murdered because of the pregnant woman. *Fake lover?*

You'd stop looking for the real art if you thought you had recovered it. You'd stop looking for the real cause of death if you thought you'd discovered it.

She'd seen Andrew's body. Touched his stiff arm . . .

Why would his arm be stiff? She'd just received his text telling her to meet him at that location. Rigor mortis wouldn't have set in so fast. *Fake text.*

So what else had been faked?

The final attempt on her life, when she was knocked on the head and left in the arroyo, came after she'd given all her notes to Ezekiel. Slowly she walked to the grave with the angel on the top. Ezekiel's wife, Ruth.

The gravestone read *LeRoy Little. 1919–1944.*

"Fake friend," she whispered.

"I knew eventually you'd figure it out." Ezekiel leaned against the trunk of a ponderosa pine, his gun aimed directly at her heart.

CHAPTER 32

Yes." Tavish licked her lips. "I only told Andrew about my visits here. But you knew where to find me. And you were so interested in what John might have given me. I should have put it together long before now." She looked around. "Do you have a game camera hidden in the trees?"

"Something like that."

She nodded at the gun. "I don't understand. You have the original artwork. You have all my notes. I led you to John's money and the letter directing me to give it to Maria. You thought you killed me. All the loose ends tied up. Why are you here?"

"Well, first of all, you're *not* dead. Which, as it turns out, is lucky for me."

"And for me," Tavish said dryly.

"Sam tends to be a bit impetuous."

"Sam?"

"Samuel, my brother. You've called him Fake Cop."

She pressed her elbows into her sides and risked a glance around her. They were alone. "So I'm still useful to you."

"Of course. You just have to tell me what I need to know."

"And if I have no idea what it is?"

"Oh, I think you'll remember soon enough if you're properly motivated."

"Shooting me won't help me remember."

"The gun is just for emphasis." Ezekiel glanced at it. "And to show you I am sincere in my desire to recover my art."

"*Your* art?"

"Don't quibble about semantics," he snapped.

Tavish clutched the bicycle to keep upright, her hands clammy on the handlebars. *His art* could only mean one thing. "John hid the originals. And you think I know where he put them."

"I knew you'd know the answer."

She took a half step forward. If she could get within reach of him, she could kick him. Knock the gun from his hand. But she had to keep him talking. "I'll . . . I'll have to show you where he hid them. Once we get close, you can let me go. I'll never tell anyone—"

"That's what your so-called fiancé said, just before Sam shot him."

Tavish's head buzzed. "Andy was involved with all this?" Another half step.

"Vince, Andy, John, and Sam. John was there to identify which art to steal. Vince and Andy didn't have enough brains between them to remember. Sam, well, Sam had the gun."

"So Sam killed Mr. Montez."

"Some people shouldn't try to be heroes."

"But John felt guilty about that, even though he didn't pull the trigger. He did as you told him, right? Painted the forgeries? And you must have checked up on his progress. Gone to where he was working to see the art and forgeries. You *know* where the art is."

"John took photographs of his progress. I couldn't take the chance of being seen or recognized. After the forgeries were finished and dry, I got Andy and Vince to deliver the work to a client. I called the police. They were both supposed to die in that shootout where police so conveniently recovered the art. But Andy escaped, unfortunately. And John got cold feet."

"Killing Andrew was a mistake."

He shrugged. "Not at all. I thought I'd covered all the bases. I'd been suspicious of Andy and thought he might try to pull something, so I hired an actress to get a photo with him. I'd heard he was sniffing around you. I had planned on sending the photo to your mother. Later, with a convenient pillow under her dress, she pretended to be his lover. It certainly kept you from pursuing his demise."

"She'll talk to police when—" She slid a foot ahead.

"Not anymore. Eventually everyone becomes a liability. Tavish, you should know by now that I plan everything out—including how best to motivate you. And not one step closer or I'll put a bullet in that pretty kneecap of yours."

Tavish froze. "You killed John without knowing the location of the art?"

A shadow of annoyance crossed Ezekiel's face. "I didn't kill him. Sam was simply encouraging John to share where he'd placed the art. When Marley got loose, Sam panicked.

"Sam drove off, leaving the body, and told me what he'd done. I nearly killed him on the spot, but blood being thicker than water . . ." He shrugged. "I made him return and clean up the mess he'd made. He ended up taking out the neighbor and setting off a gas explosion."

"What about the sniper attack on Dusty Rhodes? You almost killed me as well. Why did you do that if I held the key to finding the art?" Another step.

"Sam again. He was following the tracking device that he'd put in your car. When he saw you turn into that radio station, he thought you'd worked it out and were going public. He opened fire."

"Why me? Why did John choose me?"

Ezekiel cocked his head. He looked like a quizzical grandfather, except for the gun in his hand. "You worked it out before. Trust."

"But you gave me a Bible—"

"The quote on your grandmother's grave gave me the inspiration to gain *your* trust. But if you'd read it, you'd know all about wolves in sheep's clothing."

She swept the cemetery for anyone in earshot.

"You won't find any help, Tavish. And time is fleeting. Your dear mother, well, maybe not so dear to you, is currently in a sweat lodge. A little purification is good for the soul, don't you think? That and a combination of ayahuasca and peyote will keep her still." He smiled without humor. "Did you know they usually have the temperature at around one hundred and two? Of course, with the plastic tarp we added to hold more heat, and much longer time . . ." He stared at her face. "Unless you tell me the location of the art, she will suffer an unfortunate accident. Like the poor souls who died in that sweat lodge a number of years ago."

Sweat dampened Tavish's back. She clutched the bike. "You couldn't—"

"Oh, don't worry. Your mother's not alone. Your boyfriend, Sawyer Price, is with her."

Her stomach twisted. *Sawyer!* She wanted to vomit. "How..."

"I dangled your sketches and notes in front of him. He came running to save you. A little Rohypnol in his iced tea and he was quite easy to manage. Now, not to put too much emphasis on this, but a sweat lodge will bring on dehydration and a rather painful death. Where. Are. The. Paintings?"

Her brain went blank. "I'll take—"

"No. You'll write down the directions. He tugged a piece of paper from his pocket, added a pen, and laid them on the ground. He stepped backward, the gun still pointed at her heart. "Hurry now. Tick-tock, tick-tock."

She didn't think her legs would move. Still holding on to the bike, she forced herself forward and picked up the paper and pen.

She looked down.

"Time's fleeting, Tavish. Every moment counts. Write down the address and I'll tell you the location of the sweat lodge."

How long had her mother been in his control? A day? And what about Sawyer? She could already be too late.

She scribbled an address and held out the paper. She had no idea if it was a real place.

He pulled out a cell phone, swiped it open, pushed a button, then put it to his ear. "Yeah. Now."

"Now what?"

He disconnected and grabbed the paper.

"Where are Sawyer and my mother being held? You said you'd tell me."

"Correction. I don't have to tell you anything."

The drip of sweat sliding down her back was an exclamation point to the fate of Sawyer and Helen. "Please, Ezekiel, I'll pay you. I'll give you far more money than those paintings are worth."

"Save your breath. You'd never be able to liquidate enough stocks and bonds to make it worth my while in the amount of time your mother has to live."

"But you said—"

"I told you I was a wolf in sheep's clothing. Tut-tut."

Distant police sirens pierced the quiet of the cemetery.

He held up his gun. "I won't shoot you, Tavish. That would make for an unsolved murder that would have the police looking too closely at my work. I need a bit of time, you see, and I'm an expert on misdirection. Sam got the message to call the cops on you. The police—actually, I imagine the entire SWAT team—are racing over here at this very moment to arrest you. By the time anyone will listen to you, it will be too late." He turned, pulled out his keys, and strolled to an SUV parked along the paved cemetery road.

She tackled him.

CHAPTER 33

zekiel fell with Tavish's full weight on him. He let out an *oof!* The pistol flew from his hand. *Out of reach.* She'd have to get off of him to grab it.

She pushed up, then knelt on his back, grinding her knees into his spine.

He put his hands on the ground and pushed, lifting her a surprising distance.

She grabbed his shirt and held on.

The sirens grew closer.

He flipped over, knocking her sideways, and swung at her face. She ducked, but not enough. His fist glanced off her jaw, bringing stinging tears to her eyes.

On hands and knees, he scrabbled for the gun.

She shoved away from him, leaped to her feet, then brought her good leg up in a powerful kick to his head. The shock of the blow ran up her leg. Her foot hurt like she'd broken a bone.

He dropped to the ground and remained still.

Opening his hand, she pried out the keys. She grabbed the phone he had used to call Sam.

The sirens seemed to fill the air. She identified his SUV with the key fob, ran to it, and jammed the key into the lock of the rear compartment. Leaving the door open, she flew to the pistol and stuck it in her waistband, then dashed to Ezekiel and grabbed him by the ankles.

The police had to be surrounding the cemetery. The sirens were everywhere. She dragged the unconscious man to the rear of the SUV, took a huge breath, and lifted him inside. She threw the pistol and phone into the front seat. A blue plastic tarp was in the corner of the cargo area. She opened it and tossed it over him.

The first patrol car raced around the corner.

She wanted to check if the gun was out of sight, but there wasn't time. Casually she returned to the bike and walked it to the SUV, her hands holding the handlebars with a white-knuckled grip.

The cruiser stopped next to the open rear compartment and a cop jumped out. All he had to do was turn his head and he'd see the lump of Ezekiel's body. And probably that pistol.

Tavish could barely breathe. If Ezekiel moved or moaned, the officer would hear him. "Good heavens, Officer," she managed to say through frozen lips. "What's going on?"

"Have you seen a woman dressed like a homeless person around here? Or anyone acting strange?"

"No, but I just finished my ride."

He looked closely at her.

Oh, Lord, did they have my picture in the news?

He finally asked, "What happened to your face?"

"Dog ran in front of me and I took a spill. Shortened my

workout. Now I just need a shower." She tried to frown as she moved the bike closer to the SUV.

"Let me help you with that." The officer lifted her bike and placed it on the tarp.

Tavish couldn't breathe.

"You need to invest in a bike rack."

"It's on order." She lowered the door.

He waited to move on until after she'd climbed in the SUV and started it. The pistol she'd tossed to the front seat had mercifully landed on the floor. More law-enforcement vehicles surrounded the area.

Tavish bit her lip and carefully maneuvered around them. She cranked the air-conditioning to high, but sweat still poured off her.

Where was that sweat lodge? New Mexico had dozens of them. Some were used for the traditional Native American sacred purification ceremony, but many were run by commercial resorts and retreats.

Think. The lodge would be someplace remote. But Ezekiel would have visited it, or had his lackey, Sam, check it out. And it would need to be in or near Albuquerque. It probably would have taken both of them to transport both the disabled Sawyer and Helen into a sweat lodge. Otherwise he wouldn't have had time to do all that and still be around when she showed up.

Ezekiel's phone was on the seat beside her. She swiped it open, but it took a password to engage it.

Now what? Ezekiel would regain consciousness any moment.

She retrieved the gun from the floor. The pistol was surprisingly heavy. Pushing the release on the grip, she dropped the magazine to the seat. One by one she ejected the bullets, then snapped the empty magazine back into the grip. Rolling down the window, she dropped the bullets out at regular intervals. She placed the empty gun on the floor.

The digital readout on the dashboard clicked down the minutes. How long before Helen and Sawyer couldn't be revived? *Think, Tavish!* Resort. Sweat lodge. Spa.

The photograph. The one the pregnant lady had in her purse so long ago at Andrew's funeral. Someone had taken that photo. Ezekiel claimed he had hired an actress to pose as Andy's lover. He would have staged the "proof."

The photo had been in front of the Spirit Lodge and Spa on the edge of town.

She wanted to jerk the SUV around in a U-turn but couldn't risk the police seeing her and pulling her over. She pulled into a grocery store parking lot, reversed direction, and headed to the spa as fast as she was able.

The digital clock reproached her for taking so long to figure out the location. "If they die it will be because I was too stupid to figure out where he hid them."

After what seemed like an eternity, she pulled up in front of the resort's massive stone-and-adobe facade. An attendant in khaki shorts and a light blue golf shirt with the spa's logo rushed to open her door. "Are you checking in?" He did a double take when he saw her bike gear.

"No. Quickly, where are your sweat lodges?"

"They're not operating right now."

"Where are they located? Quickly!"

He pointed beyond the well-landscaped parking area toward

a line of golf carts. "You can walk out there, but it's pretty far. I mean, like over a mile. Most people take the carts—"

"Thanks." She drove over to the nearest cart, slammed the SUV into park, and leaped out.

"Wait!" The attendant raced after her. "Stop! I'll call security!"

She jumped into the cart. "Do that. And while you're at it, call 9-1-1. There are people dying in your sweat lodge." The key was in the ignition. She turned it and floored the accelerator. The cart shot ahead. She steered it up a paved path, past a huge landscaped pool full of splashing children and bronzed bathers, then a series of cabins isolated from each other by rocks and trees. The path split, with a small sign giving directions. She slowed to read it. Golf course, right. Shooting range, left. Sweat lodge, straight ahead. A few more twists and she came to an elaborate wrought-iron gate standing open. Yellow warning tape crisscrossed the entrance, and a sign saying Closed for Repair was posted on a lamppost.

She drove through the tape.

The cultivated landscape opened up to wild, high desert. Only the paved track showed anything was in this direction. Around her, sagebrush, mesquite, and creosote bush dotted the countryside. The trail climbed a small rise. In the distance were three domed huts surrounding a large cabana. One of the three sweat lodges had blue plastic tarps over the top.

Don't let me be too late. The cart wouldn't go any faster. She willed it to speed up, but the huts remained stubbornly distant.

Finally she arrived at the structures. Dashing from the still-moving cart, she ran toward the opening of the hut with the tarp.

Sam stepped out of the cabana holding a gun. "Hold it right there."

She stopped and put up her hands. "The police are on their way. They're right behind me. Take the cart and run. You can still get away."

"Why would I do that?"

Behind her was the soft whirr of another electric cart.

"Behind me are witnesses. The security guard from the resort. You can't shoot everybody—"

"He doesn't have to," Ezekiel said from behind her.

She spun.

Ezekiel, crusted blood leaking from one ear, was standing next to the cart. He held on to the seat with one hand. The other held a gun.

Tavish cleared her throat. Her voice came out high and breathless. "The police will be here any minute—"

"No, they won't. I told them you were a novelist testing out an idea for a book. I said I was your uncle, that I was along to clear up any misunderstandings because you have quite a dramatic streak, and that we didn't want any trouble with the resort or to disturb the guests. I gave him a very fat tip for his trouble."

Ezekiel held the gun she'd emptied on the way over, but Sam's pistol was loaded. Tavish clenched her teeth to keep them from chattering.

"Sam, get the drugs."

A hand grabbed her arm. Sam. He'd silently moved closer while she'd been focused on Ezekiel.

She twisted but couldn't break his grip.

He squeezed so hard she thought he would break the bone. "Hold still!" His breath was rank. He jammed a small syringe into her arm, then released her so fast she fell.

"What did you do to me?"

Sam replaced the cap on the syringe, stashed it in his pocket, and pulled out his holstered pistol. "Just gave you a little something to calm you down. Soon I'll be able to really send you on a trip. Nothing like a little IV mescaline."

"But the attendant saw you." Her lips were growing numb. "He'll know—"

"Nothing." Ezekiel moved closer. "Like I said, I tipped him very well." He reached into his pocket and tugged out the slip of paper. "Let's take a look at the address you wrote down."

Lean not on your own understanding. Trust . . . The words rose in her brain. *Break the tiny amount of trust between the two.* "You now know where the art is stashed," she said to Ezekiel. "Why didn't you simply drive away? Why did you come over here? Sam would take the fall for killing Sawyer and Helen." She glanced at Sam.

Sam straightened. The gun was now pointed closer to Ezekiel. *Sam's impetuous.* "Didn't you say that eventually everyone becomes a liability?" She continued to focus on Ezekiel. She felt the minutes ticking away, the effects of the drug intensifying.

"Shut up." He stared at the paper, pulled out his cell and typed something, looked at her, then raised the pistol.

"You called Sam a fool." The ground wavered beneath her. "I seriously doubt you were ever going to share the money those paintings will bring on the black market. Over seventy million."

"Seventy million?" Sam's hand shifted the pistol farther toward Ezekiel. "You said twenty thousand!"

"I lied. And sometimes blood *isn't* thicker than water." Ezekiel pulled the trigger.

Bang!

The sound rammed her eardrums. She'd forgotten about the bullet in the chamber. She rolled away from the two men, then pushed to her feet. Her legs moved slowly and refused to hold her weight. She sank back to earth. No one would investigate the sound of gunfire. Not with a rifle range in the same general area.

Sam lay on the ground, motionless, a short distance away.

Ezekiel turned the pistol on her. "Now you will stop lying and tell me where the art is hidden."

"I did."

"This address is an empty lot. If I have to ask again, I'll shoot you in the foot. Then the leg. And keep going."

She stared at him. *Please, Lord, let the gun still be empty.* Her vision narrowed until all she saw was his hand on the pistol.

His finger tightened on the trigger.

She couldn't look away.

Click. Click. Click.

She shook her head. "I didn't lie. You may be a wolf in sheep's clothing, but every so often the sheep win."

Bang!

She jumped. Her heartbeat rammed in her ears.

Ezekiel dropped the gun and grabbed his chest.

Bang, bang!

He spun and collapsed to the ground.

She slowly turned her head toward Sam. The man had propped himself on one elbow. The pistol he pointed at her wavered.

Trust in the Lord. Help me. The drug had spread throughout her body. She wouldn't be able to walk, run, or even scream for help. *Help me, Lord. Trust.* She closed her eyes. *What does he trust? What makes him tick?*

Money.

"Sam." It came out a whisper. She tried again. "Sam, listen to me. I have money. Lots of money. I've never hurt you. Let me save my mom and my friend and I promise, I *promise* I'll make you wealthy."

He stared at her, then lowered his head until it rested on his arm. The hand holding the gun relaxed.

She couldn't move.

He kept staring, but now his eyes gazed at infinity.

CHAPTER 34

avish tried to stand, but her legs wouldn't hold her weight. She pushed to her hands and knees, then crept toward the sweat lodge. Near the hut was a faucet and hose. Good. Water.

She passed near Sam.

Flies had already discovered him.

She kept crawling. The black asphalt was rough and hot, scraping and burning her hands and knees. She finally made it to the hut.

The wooden door was held shut with a simple latch and a shiny new combination lock.

Tavish grabbed the lock and pulled.

It firmly resisted her tug.

She wanted to cry, to scream and beat on the door, but even if they could hear her, they wouldn't be able to get out. Rolling to her back, she kicked at the door. It wavered a bit, but her legs had no strength in them.

Inching her way over to Sam, she picked up his pistol. Blood made the grip slippery. Again she worked her way to the door, lifted the gun, placed it on the lock, and pulled the trigger.

The blast made her ears ring. The odor of cordite burned her nose.

The lock dangled by one side. She jerked the lock away and pulled open the door.

The heat was a solid wall, the stench enough to make her gag.

Both her mother and Sawyer were just inside the door. Their hands were torn and bloodied from trying to scratch their way out. Both had foam around their mouths.

Neither looked alive.

She wanted to drag their prone bodies free, but she still couldn't stand. She grabbed her mother's wrists and pulled, but her clothing caught on the rough flooring.

Help me, help me, helpmehelpme. She looked around.

The hose and faucet.

Both her legs now refused to work. Using her elbows, she dragged herself to the faucet and turned it on. Without a nozzle, the water spurted out the end and she was quickly soaked. Holding the gushing hose, again she made her way to the sweat lodge and turned the hose on her mother, then Sawyer.

Heat was still pouring from the entrance. Inside the heated stones glowed red.

Leaving the water running over her mother's body, she twisted around until she could reach the edge of the blue tarp thrown over the top. She tugged it and it moved. Another tug and it started to slide. The third yank brought the tarp off the roof.

Gathering the material as best she could, she shoved it between the two bodies. Her arms barely worked. Using both her hands, she wrenched her mother onto the tarp. Slowly she wormed backward, hauling the thin woman from the deadly heat. She used her entire body to heave Helen off the plastic and onto her back.

She snagged the hose and again nudged it so the water splayed over her mother.

Returning to the sweat lodge, she crossed her arms and used them both to pull herself forward.

Sawyer was a big man. She'd barely been able to pull her slender mother from the interior. How would she get him out? "Oh, Lord, I don't know you, but if you help me now, I promise I'll be . . ."

What? She didn't even know what she would need to do to keep her promise.

"I'll be yours." It was all she could think of.

Still dragging the tarp, she crept inside the sweat lodge. The heat was like a burning hand pushing her to the earth. Breathing was difficult.

Stuffing one edge under the motionless man, she grabbed his arm and pulled.

He didn't budge.

"No!" It came out a sob. *Please. Please.* She hauled herself onto his stomach and grasped the other arm. Holding on with what little strength she had, she slid off his stomach, bent his arm at the elbow, and used her momentum to roll him facedown onto the tarp. Carefully she nudged his face sideways so he could breathe. *If he can breathe.*

She scrabbled out of the sweat lodge, pulling herself forward six inches, Sawyer two. Then stopped. She couldn't move him.

Trying a different angle, she pulled with all the strength she had left. He remained motionless.

With the last bit of muscle control she had, she wrenched the hose from her mother and directed the water onto Sawyer.

CHAPTER 35

ONE MONTH LATER

Tavish sat on the bench, staring at her grandmother's grave. *Prov. 3:5. Trust in the Lord with all your heart; do not depend on your own understanding.* "I learned that the hard way, Grandma." The day was cool and held the smell of rain. The cemetery had a few visitors this time.

After the resort attendant thought about her behavior and Ezekiel's strange excuses, he'd called the police after all. She'd spent two days in the jail's infirmary, this time shackled to the bed, before being released to a regular hospital. Another few days and she was home. The whirlwind of interviews with various police and sheriff's departments had continued.

Outside of retrieving Marley, she hadn't been able to get away from home before today.

Marley rested under the bench, one paw touching Tavish's foot. When Tavish had gone to the animal hospital, the bookkeeper had handed Tavish the statement with a look of scornful triumph. The total was considerably higher than the original bill. Tavish paid it in cash, then set up a trust fund to pay the practice when Dr. Barrett wanted to provide free veterinary care for the pets of the homeless.

Marley hadn't left Tavish's side since returning home.

Tavish spotted her mother in a wheelchair, lap full of flowers, coming up the paved walk. Maria Montez was pushing the chair.

"*Hola, Maria, es un herm . . . um . . . oso día.*" Tavish smiled.

"*Sí. ¿Como te sientes hoy?*"

"Um . . . *Tengo agujeros?*"

Now Helen laughed. "She asked you how you felt and you said you have holes. I think you mean *agujetas.*"

"Who knows, Mom, maybe I do have holes." Tavish stood and carefully hugged her mother. Taking the flowers from her lap, she placed them at her grandmother's headstone, then regained her seat.

The heat and dehydration had left Helen with a stroke. With daily physical therapy she was gradually regaining her ability to walk, but doctors warned that she'd probably never fully recover.

At least she was alive.

"Maria, I've tried to get this settled, but it looks like it will still take time." Tavish opened her purse and handed the other woman an envelope.

Maria took it, looked inside, then frowned at Tavish. "What is this?"

"John left money, probably all he'd been paid for the forgeries, and a note to give it all to you. The police recovered the cash and note at Ezekiel's house, but they're still trying to figure out what to do with it. I figured you and your children could use it sooner rather than later."

Maria crossed herself, then burst into tears and hugged Tavish. "*Gracias.*" She stepped away to collect herself.

"That's the sort of thing your grandmother would have done," her mother said quietly. "She obviously inspired you."

Tavish nodded toward the Scripture verse. "Yes, and showed me *her* inspiration."

The three of them quietly stared at the grave for a few moments.

"Are you coming for dinner?" Her mother's question broke into Tavish's thoughts. "The new cook makes the best stuffed sopapilla and calabacitas."

"Sounds great."

A dog barked in the distance and Marley whined.

"No, you can't go and play. Not yet." Tavish stroked her head. Marley jumped into her lap and licked her cheek.

"Uck. Don't *do* that." Tavish swiped at her face with her arm.

A Cooper's hawk, high overhead, called out to his mate with a grating *cak-cak-cak-cak-cak-cak.*

"Have you heard anything yet, Tavish?" her mother asked.

Tavish slowly shook her head. "The last contact with Sawyer was a message on my answering machine that he'd call me once things got sorted out in Washington." She smiled, but it took an effort.

They settled into a comfortable silence again.

"The art appraiser submitted her report. She confirmed the paintings are forgeries. The insurance company already paid me, and I never got around to paying them back, so I guess we're even," her mother finally said. "Nothing turned up in all the searches. It looks like that awful forger hid them too well. Or maybe he destroyed them."

Tavish thought about John Coyote, also known as John Begay. The man had done a lot of bad things, but she didn't think he'd destroy such valuable art. "I think we need to look someplace unexpected."

Her mother smiled. "Ah, yes, at a negative space, as you so often call it."

Ezekiel's chilling voice came back to her. "*I think Marley was his back-up plan, and you were his insurance policy. If anything happened to him, he wanted you to find out.*"

"Are you coming right home?" Helen asked.

"No. The gallery called. Actually, they've been calling me to pick up my work. I should get going." She headed for the Uber parked nearby. They'd never recovered her Audi, and her new Land Rover was on order. With a bike rack. And the ability to do some off-road exploring—or visit a certain kind professor at an archaeological dig.

The Uber driver, a nice college student who had assured her he didn't mind waiting, had been driving her around when she needed to go someplace. He was silent on the drive over to the gallery, for which she was grateful. She gave him an extra tip to wait for her once again after they pulled up to the entrance.

The water damage had already been erased. A new clerk spotted her as she entered. "May I help you?" Her gaze went to Marley. "Therapy dog?"

"Yes. I'm Evelyn McTavish. I'm here to pick up my art."

"Oh, wow, I've wanted to meet you. I've loved your drawings.

Over here." She led Tavish to a small room off the main section of the gallery.

"I think you have a check. I'll be right back." The woman moved to the front of the gallery.

Tavish meandered to the room where she'd had her show . . . How long ago was that? A lifetime. Today its walls featured a group showing of the Women's Art Guild. A lot of bad florals and oddly shaped barns. A tray of cookies and a guest book stood open on a table.

"Found it!" The clerk returned with an envelope and a small package. "This had your name on it as well. Looks like it came some time ago."

Tavish took both, then opened the package. Inside was her folded preliminary sketch for John Coyote. Tracing paper was placed over the sketch with some notes on changes. She checked the date. It had been posted two days before she'd found his body.

She swallowed hard and licked her lips.

"And"—the clerk handed Tavish a framed drawing—"here you go."

"Thank you. Where are the rest of them?"

"They all sold. All but this one."

Tavish's mouth dropped. "You're kidding me! That's . . . I'm . . ." She wanted to dance around the room doing a high-kicking, fist-pumping jig.

"Mrs. Hogarth told me after the first drawing sold at your opening, everyone wanted to get in on the action."

"So my show almost sold out?"

"It did sell out. I'm buying the last piece." The voice came from behind her.

She spun. Sawyer, almost unrecognizable in suit and tie, stood in the middle of the room. She couldn't speak. She could only stare until his image blurred.

"I'm sorry I couldn't get back here any sooner." He smiled.

She gripped the desk to keep upright.

"I had so much to say, but I didn't want to say it on the phone."

Marley, impatiently dancing around her legs, jerked the leash, propelling her toward Sawyer. Once moving, she couldn't stop. *He might be here to tell me good-bye, but—*

His open arms caught her, lifted her off her feet, and spun her in a circle. He gently lowered her, but didn't let go. "I love you," he whispered. "That was one thing I wanted to tell you."

"And I love you," she whispered back.

"Now I think I need to have a conversation with your mother." He released one arm but kept the other around her.

"What about?"

"If I'm going to be courting you, I need to know she won't call a lawyer, or a private investigator, and she needs to know I won't be putting her in handcuffs."

"What are you talking about?"

"Never mind." He pulled out his wallet. "What're the damages?"

While he paid for the drawing, Tavish gingerly picked up her commissioned sketch of John and Marley. She looked closer and caught her breath.

"What is it, Tavish?" He looked from the sketch to her face. "What's that?"

"I think it's John's last message to me. The location of the art."

He took the drawing and tracing paper overlay from her. "I don't see anything written."

"It's in the negative space. Remember? The fingers. The edge of a shadow. The shape of a petal." She traced several pencil lines with her finger. "He drew this on tracing paper to show the changes on the sketch beneath. Do you see?"

"I see, but I still don't understand. John wasn't an artist. He couldn't have forged anything."

A memory came back to Tavish. When they met at Patricia Caron's house that one time, he smelled of turpentine.

Just that once. He'd claimed he was doing woodworking crafts, but she'd never seen any signs of it, nor had his garage shown anything like a craft area. She'd found only the rag and an empty metal coffee can outside his garage. Had that faint odor been linseed oil, used by artists to adjust drying times and smooth out the paints?

The truth struck her hard.

"There never were any forgeries. John simply altered the originals to make them look like fakes. Anyone could have done that. Eventually the new oil paint would have cracked and flaked off and we would have discovered the truth."

"But Ezekiel—"

"Only saw the photos that John sent him. We'll need to hire an art-restoration expert, but the originals are *under* the fakes. Hiding in plain sight."

"Your mother will be happy."

"She's going to have to return the insurance check after all, but yes, she'll be happy. For many reasons." She grabbed his arm. "Especially about you."

They turned to leave.

"Don't forget your money." The clerk held out the envelope. "Or your art."

Tavish took the envelope, peeked at the contents, then closed her eyes. *Suggestions, Lord?* Two faces appeared in her mind. "Could we make one stop before heading home?"

"Sure."

"There's a storefront church run by Aunt Bee and Judi Dench. I think they can use a donation."

"Now what are *you* talking about?"

She touched his cheek. "I made several promises that I have to keep. One was to read the Bible. Grandma wanted me to know Proverbs 3:5. Did you know the next verse? Proverbs 3:6 says, 'Seek his will in all you do, and he will show you which path to take.'"

AUTHOR NOTE

My Dear Readers,

As I write this I am deep into a North Idaho winter and far from the high-desert heat of New Mexico. I hope you enjoyed the adventures of Evelyn Yvonne McTavish. The name of the character was taken from my mother—Evelyn McCandless Stuart. In high school she was just called Mac. I liked Tavish better. Yvonne was my mom's best friend. The impish Puli, Marley, was chosen as a breed that is unusual and interesting (and if you follow my books at all, you'll know there *has* to be a dog somewhere). My husband suggested the Albuquerque location, which allowed me to combine two very different subjects: the work at Sandia Labs and the Native American archaeological sites.

If you have a book club that chooses this book, please let me know. I love personalizing the experience. I also love hearing from you and answer all my emails.

Blessings,

Carrie

ACKNOWLEDGMENTS

Once again, my husband, Rick, suggested the location—this time Albuquerque, New Mexico. Part of his reason was his over thirty-five-year friendship with Garilyn and Johnny Ulibarri. When we approached them about placing the location in their hometown, they immediately sent a care package of books and offered to show us around. Johnny's knowledge of national laboratories, the history of New Mexico, and Native culture was invaluable. Thank you both so much for your kindness and friendship.

I hadn't worked as a technician in a vet hospital for over thirty-five years, so I had to rely on my local veterinary hospital—Silver Valley Veterinary Clinic—when I had some questions. Thank you, Tashua Seaton, Technician, and Patty Barrett, DVM.

The hospital visit—including the sandwich and packet of mayo (!)—came from my favorite nurse, Shelley Griesinger. Thank you and I love ya, girlfriend!

My dear friend Trish Hastings provided me with information

on the homeless. She is the manager of Christ Kitchen, PO Box 3391, Victoria, TX 77903 (in case you feel inclined to make a contribution to their ministry).

All things archaeological I was able to glean from Sharon Moses, PhD, RPA, Associate Professor, Anthropology Department, Archaeology and Forensics, Northern Arizona University, Flagstaff. If I got it wrong, it's my fault. *She* was awesome!

I once again relied on my law-enforcement students for insights on all things in policing and the jail system. A special thank you goes to Officer Anders Tenney, Coeur d'Alene Police Department, Idaho; and Kali Steppe, Clackamas County Sheriff's Department, Oregon, who assured me she was assistant regional manager . . . or assistant to the regional manager . . .

Kathryn Robinson, a talented writer and member of my writers' critique group, helped me with the Spanish translation. Thank you to my beta readers Gayle Noyes, Gary James, Michelle Garlock, Lorrie Jenicek, and Shelley Griesinger.

I am totally grateful to my fantastic agent, Karen Solem, who believes in me even when I doubt. I consider the dream team I have at HarperCollins Christian Publishing as family—the good kind of family! Editors Amanda Bostic and Erin Healy know how to polish my manuscripts until they glow. The rest of the HCCP group, from Jodi Hughes and Paul Fisher to Kerri Potts and Allison Carter, and all the rest of you, bless you, bless you, bless you!

Thank you to Frank Peretti, who started this journey and mentored me through it. And finally, an eternal thank you to my Lord and Savior, Jesus Christ, in whom all things are possible.

DISCUSSION QUESTIONS

1. The theme of this story is trust. Tavish trusted in a lot of things. Discuss how her trust shifted as the book progressed. Have you had times when trust was a problem?

2. Marley the Puli became a true sidekick and friend to Tavish. Have you had pets that responded to your moods like she did?

3. Tavish's self-image in the beginning was totally out of kilter with what she really looked like. How could this be dangerous?

4. Dusty Rhodes was an interesting character. What are some of the more, shall we say, interesting conspiracies you've heard?

5. Tavish had a terrible relationship with her mother in the beginning. What were the original signs, and how do you know if anything changed?

6. The "negative space," the people around Tavish, became real because of what?

7. You are Tavish's best friend and adviser. She has just now

inherited her grandmother's money. How would you advise her on good stewardship of her wealth? (Or will you encourage her to rent a jet and go on a shopping spree?)

8. There was a wolf in sheep's clothing in the book. Have you had any in your life?

An artist hiding from an escaped killer uncovers one of World War II's most dangerous secrets—a secret that desperate men will do anything to keep hidden.

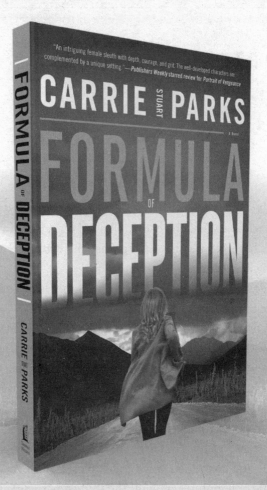

"The sinister tone of this fast-paced story line creates an almost unbearable tension that will keep readers glued to the page."

—*Library Journal* for *Formula of Deception*

CHAPTER 1

Murphy Andersen's mission to Kodiak Island was about to collide with her lies. She hadn't planned on getting in so deep.

But here she was in a dying Russian's bedroom, with a cop standing beside her.

The stench of Vasily Scherbakov's deteriorating flesh engulfed her. She blinked and breathed through her mouth.

"Cancer's a nasty way to die," Detective Elin Olsson whispered.

Boy howdy, you can say that again. "I'm used to such things. You know, messy crime scenes, dead bodies, stuff like that." *Liar.*

The Russian Orthodox priest standing beside the bed inspected Murphy from head to foot.

She'd already ducked her head and turned it sideways. They always stared at the scar first, the angry red one that split her eyebrow and continued down to her cheek. Her oversize glasses hid some of it, but not enough. She studied her scuffed shoe tips, waiting for his scrutiny to continue. Despite her cheerful scarf, he no doubt noted the threadbare navy blazer, stained shell blouse, and too-big khaki slacks.

A quick peek told her the audit was over. Here came part two.

The priest spoke with a slight Russian accent. "But she is a child. A young girl."

Bingo. It never failed. It came from her short stature, thin frame, and childlike face. Whenever she ordered a beer, servers always carded her. To some, looking young would be a compliment. But not to Murphy.

"You said you would bring an experienced artist. A . . . what do you call it? A forensic artist."

The priest didn't look so . . . priestly himself. She'd expected an elderly man wearing fancy embroidered layers of clothing, with a long gray beard reaching his stomach, and a big hat. And he should have an oversize ring, something for people to kiss.

This character appeared to be in his midthirties, with a brown beard, piercing dark eyes, and hair pulled into a hippie-style low ponytail. He wore a black cassock, a big cross, a brimless soft-sided cap, and lime-green tennis shoes.

Detective Olsson tucked a stray lock of white-blond hair behind her ear. "The regular forensic artist from the agency was tied up in a case in Montana, but I assure you, Father Ivanov, she's a trained forensic artist."

Okay, so Detective Olsson didn't know that she had fudged the truth. Murphy *was* an artist, and she had a decent portfolio of pencil portraits, and since her purse had been stolen with every last penny to her name, she needed the work.

When she had asked her landlady yesterday for an extension to pay the rent, Myra, against all of Murphy's protests, called the police to report the theft. And when Detective Olsson saw the portraits spread out on Murphy's kitchen table, her lies began in earnest. *Yes, I have experience in forensic art. Yes, at a police department in West Virginia. No, sorry, my credentials were in my purse. Yes, I'm available tomorrow.* How hard could forensic art be to someone already good at drawing figures? She spent quality time last night watching a YouTube video on the subject. She was practically an expert.

The priest turned to Vasily. *"Eta genshina budet risovat' litso mugzhiny kotorogo vy videli. Ya ne dal ey nikakoy informacii."*

He took the words right out of her mouth. She stared at the floor until she could control her grin. Too little sleep, not enough coffee, and her own nerves only led to the giggles. Once the mirth passed, she pulled up a chair to the bed, sat, and opened her art bag. She removed the packet of mug photos—provided by Detective Olsson—a pad of bristol paper, and a pencil.

"What did you tell him?" Murphy asked the priest.

"You are the art lady."

Detective Olsson smiled. "The priest has offered to translate for the interview."

That didn't sound good. Rather like watching a foreign-language film with subtitles. The actors always said more than what appeared on the screen. "Vasily doesn't speak any English?"

"His English is limited," Father Ivanov said. "He understands it better than he speaks it."

"I just hope you can understand my Virginia accent, y'all." Murphy smiled slightly at Vasily.

"I thought you said West Virginia?" Detective Olsson asked.

"That's where I worked." Murphy nodded quickly.

Detective Olsson looked at the priest. "Where is the woman who called this in? She seemed distraught."

"His caretaker, Irina. Yes, she was very upset. She's one of my parishioners. I wish she would have talked to me before calling you. She'll be in later today to look after Vasily. Do you want to interview her?"

"I do. I just want to be sure I cover all the bases."

The priest nodded.

Murphy's hard and uncomfortable chair was as spartan as Vasily's bedroom. A wooden icon of the Virgin Mary was the sole item on the wall. The furniture consisted of two straight-backed chairs, a nightstand covered with prescription bottles, and a metal cot. A faded piece of cadmium-red calico fabric blocked the closet, and a matching curtain sagged at the window.

Vasily lay on the bed, quilt pulled almost to his chin. His chalk-white skin stretched across his skull, and wisps of fine light-brown hair haloed his head. His skeletal hands clutched the blanket while his sunken eyes watched her.

"Good morning, Vasily," Murphy said. "May I call you by your first name?" She was grateful when he nodded, considering she couldn't pronounce his last name.

"Well, Vasily, my name is Murphy Andersen. I've been asked to draw a portrait from your memory. I have no idea what you saw, other than Detective Olsson said it's a cold case."

"Technically, it's a new case from the past. The Alaska State Troopers have asked us to do the preliminary interviews." Detective Olsson moved to the foot of the bed. "We're taking your report seriously and have several technicians on their way. Maybe you could tell Murphy what you saw."

Vasily straightened slightly, adjusted his blanket, and began speaking in Russian, never taking his eyes from Murphy's face. He spoke for some time before pausing to cough. The priest held a glass of water to Vasily's lips.

The room was overheated. Murphy clamped her jaw shut to stop the yawn that threatened to emerge and peeked at her watch. The sun rose early and stayed up late in Alaska's June, and she'd been awake since 4:00 a.m., too nervous to sleep with the upcoming interview. Her eyelids felt like gravel pits.

Vasily took a sip of water from the priest, closed his eyes, then waved for Ivanov to translate.

She prepared to take notes.

The priest took the chair next to her. "Vasily hunted on various islands, first with his father and uncles, later alone. About ten years ago he was hunting on Ruuwaq Island when he stumbled across five men."

"Five men?" she asked. "No women?"

"No," Vasily answered, then waved Ivanov to continue.

The priest leaned forward. "He remembers one man's face as if it were yesterday."

"I see." She glanced at the blank paper. "And what were the men doing that was so memorable?"

"Doing?" The priest raised his eyebrows. "They weren't doing anything. They were dead."

"Dead. Of course, but are we talking about an accident? Murder?"

Father Ivanov spoke briefly to Vasily in Russian, listened to his reply, then said, "He says it looked like they killed each other with their bare hands."

Murphy's adventure continues in *Formula of Deception* by Carrie Stuart Parks.

LOOKING FOR YOUR NEXT GREAT NOVEL?

"I love Carrie Stuart Parks's skill in writing characters with hysterical humor, unwitting courage, and page-turning mystery. I hope my readers won't abandon me completely when they learn about her!"

—Terri Blackstock, *USA TODAY* bestselling author of the If I Run series

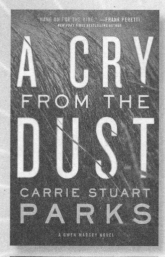
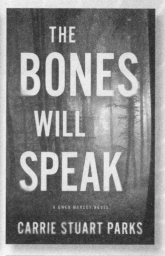
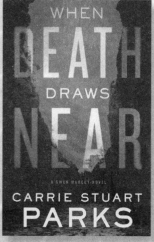
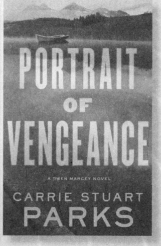

ABOUT THE AUTHOR

Carrie Stuart Parks is a Christy finalist as well as a Carol Award–winning author. She has won numerous awards for her fine art as well. An internationally known forensic artist, she travels with her husband, Rick, across the US and Canada teaching courses in forensic art to law-enforcement professionals. The author/illustrator of numerous books on drawing and painting, Carrie continues to create dramatic watercolors from her studio in the mountains of Idaho.

⟩⟩⟩══

CarrieStuartParks.com
Facebook: CarrieStuartParksAuthor
Twitter: @CarrieParks